Hellhound III

False Flag

Suzanne Brodine

For Ava and Nora. Thanks for reading over my
shoulder. Now go do your homework.

Do not give what is holy to the dogs...lest they...turn and tear you in pieces.

Matthew 7:6

CHAPTER 1: FLOAT LIKE A BUTTERFLY

Navi. Proper Noun. A binary star in the Cassiopeia system. Navi (I & II) has unusually high x-ray emissions in a variable and unpredictable pattern. Comprised of two blue supergiants, its luminosity exceeds others of its type. The combined effects allow for a habitable zone far distant from the star. Three rocky planets orbit Navi.

Hour 2230
May 5, 2156

Maker let the hot water pound against her face. Steam clouded her small bathroom with the clean fragrance of soap. A muffled thump from her quarters reminded her of the time. She sighed. The move to third shift bridge duty was technically a step up from her position as a supervisor in comms, but after the twenty-second straight day of an eight-hour shift that always seemed to run long, she was nostalgic for her old station – even with the mildly insubordinate staff.

"Mind if I use your shower?"

She patted herself dry and wrapped her hair in the same towel before answering. "Sure. Don't use my shampoo." She stepped out of the brightly lit bathroom to see Gormann seated at the foot of her bunk, sheets tangled around his thighs. His hair, a little longer than regulation, was sticking out on one side. The dimmer lighting from a reading lamp cast interesting shadows along the lean muscles of his chest and arm; the snake tattoo that wound up his bicep and onto his shoulder eyed her carefully.

He snorted, which morphed into a yawn. "No problem. I brought my kit."

"Kind of presumptuous, don't you think?" She ignored the temptation to shut his ever-running mouth, imagining all the ways he could use it that wouldn't irritate her, and opened her wardrobe. Lotion and deodorant were followed by plain gray undershorts and a supportive tank top.

Gormann leaned back on his elbows, making no effort to conceal his ogling. He grinned. "I earned it." Maker couldn't argue that, but she wasn't going to admit it either. "Besides, my team's quarters are on deck nine." Maker winced. Sandwiched between green recruits on their mandatory tour and the secondary entrance to engineering, the bunks assigned to the Raiders would be loud, uncomfortably warm, and fraught with eighteen-year-olds scared out of their minds but too stupid to realize it. "One of the common shower units is down for maintenance, too. There is no need for a sponge – you get scrubbed off just walking past everyone else."

"That's disgusting." She slid her uniform pants on and reached for a long-sleeved shirt.

His grin got wider. "If I didn't know I was going to get jumped as soon as we were alone, I might have enjoyed it."

"You are such an asshole."

"You aren't seeing me for my personality, Short Stack."

"I'm not seeing you at all, Gorm. I am taking advantage of your body. Your personality is an unfortunate obstacle to my enjoyment." She pulled on her jacket and fastened it, leaving the top few inches at the collar open until she was on duty. Maker sat down next to him to pull on her boots.

"Yeah," he let out a breath, "that's what I like about you. Practical about sex. Speaking of, we're scheduled to rebase with the *Saladin* at 0600."

"Are you asking for a quickie?" Maker raised both eyebrows, her lips twitching into a smile in spite of herself.

"Do you have time?" At the shake of her head, he continued, "Didn't think so. I wondered if I could crash here for a few hours before I have to suit up."

Maker hesitated for a moment, not sure she wanted to leave Gormann unattended in her personal space. "How about I let you sleep here, but you have to do me a favor?" He leaned closer, smiling licentiously. "Again – I don't have time for that. Can you deliver something on the *Saladin*? To Lieutenant Richter?" She pawed through a drawer under her bunk and pulled out a small vinyl envelope. 'Seamus Richter' was printed on the outside.

"Wow, I knew we were keeping it casual, but using me to send love notes to your boyfriend is a little cruel. That hurts me. In my special heart place."

"If I had a boyfriend, I wouldn't have to put up with your…you…I wouldn't have to put up with you just to get laid. He's my cousin. A belated present for his promotion." She set it on the desk and quickly combed her hair and twisted it into a Coalition-approved knot at the back of her head.

"Okay. Where can I find him?"

"He's the primary shift helmsman, but his quarters are listed on the back there." Gormann whistled, and Maker rolled her eyes. She grabbed her tablet and snapped her bracer onto her wrist. "Throw the bedding in the laundry, please. And Gorm," she paused, the door to her quarters opened automatically to the empty corridor, "try not to get dead out there." He winked and grinned, and she left without another word.

Scrolling through her tablet for messages occupied her on the way to the mess. Communications and Encryption, like every department on every ship, was understaffed. Increased enemy activity meant that the *Khalid* was months overdue for docking and restocking – both crew and supplies. High priority Culler translations were still sent to her for verification, which meant extra hours on top of her shifts on the bridge. She ate her reconstituted eggs and fruit as quickly as possible to avoid the taste and savored her tea. With twenty minutes until her shift, she cleared her table. Rodriguez was coming in as she was leaving, but he pivoted and followed her as if that had been his intent all along.

"You are looking ravishing this morning, LT."

"No."

"Your hair looks extra shiny – have you done something new?"

"Whatever you want, the answer is no." Maker could see him out of the corner of her eye, smiling and nodding as if they were in agreement.

"Of course, of course. Did I mention how delightful you smell? Is that…" He leaned closer and took an appreciative sniff before his smile slipped in confusion.

"It's unscented," she answered shortly.

"You didn't like the products I gave you on your birthday?" He actually looked wounded, and Maker had to struggle to keep her frown in place.

"Sensitive skin," she said, thinking she would explain how some peppermints still suffered from things like mild eczema, then immediately regretted it when his smile turned suggestive. She punched the control for the lift and avoided the lewd comment she was sure was coming. "What do you want Rodriguez?"

"A party," he answered promptly. "To celebrate your graduation. I finished my level one exams last month, and you're slated to graduate the Academy level twos next week. We should drink and play cards and forget about the war for a while."

"We do that every Thursday." The lift doors opened and two soldiers stepped out, leaving only Bretavic inside, lounging against the rear wall. She nodded at him, noting his wrinkled uniform and the irritation clear in his expression. She reached for the door controls.

"Yes," Rodriguez followed her into the lift, ignoring her attempt to leave him behind and end the conversation. "But this would be extra special. I have real liquor. The kind not made in repurposed hydroponics equipment and smelling of rubbing alcohol."

"Are you bad-mouthing my vodka?" Bretavic's usual scowl deepened so that his eyebrows met over his nose. His accent thickened, making his Standard English difficult to understand.

"And we haven't yet toasted to our good friend's promotion," Rodriguez continued. He poked Bretavic in the shoulder, right over his poorly attached sergeant's stripes. "We should-"

"Touch me again and I will knock out your teeth."

"Okay! Okay!" Rodriguez held up his hands and smiled, but it looked strained to Maker. She felt a little guilty for that. If every department was shorthanded, engineering was running on a skeleton crew and had been for over a year. Rodriguez was severely overworked, and with his personality he needed social interaction a hell of a lot more than Maker did.

"I'll think about it," she hedged.

"Yes! That's a yes!" He pumped a fist in the air and threw a gloating look at Bretavic, who scowled back.

"That's an 'I'll think about it'," she countered. A tone sounded and the doors opened to the corridor outside the bridge. She had ten minutes until her shift started. Bretavic followed her, practically dragging his feet. He may have been promoted, but he was certainly not happy with his reassignment from transport detail to the helm of the *Khalid*.

"Great, so we're on. Wear something sexy, LT."

"Not even to your funeral, Rodriguez." The doors closed on his chuckles, and Maker caught up with Bretavic as he entered the break room.

"Why do you put up with that shit?" he asked as he poured himself a cup of coffee.

"He can't help himself," she shrugged. "And a party sounds a lot better than another night watch, right?" From his expression, Maker guessed that Bretavic was weighing the two options and having trouble determining which was worse. The rest of the third shift crew straggled in, and they all reported to their positions.

Maker stood next to the senior comms officer on duty, monitoring lines and sorting information for three hours before a high priority alert came through. M'benga handled it.

"This is *Khalid*…Authorization? Putting you through now."

Maker glanced up from her display, trying not to show her surprise. M'benga caught her eye and shook his head – he was still listening. After only a few minutes he terminated the line and signaled to the acting captain.

"Sir, I advise readying the bridge for Captain Jones, sir."

The lieutenant commander and M'benga had worked together longer than Maker had served on the *Khalid* and didn't seem to need to say anything else. Orders were given for coffee to be put away and status reports readied. An air of tension swept the tired officers on the bridge, but the last uniform was straightened just as Jones' voice came over the comm. She ordered a new heading and requested that the all-ready call be sent out. Maker turned on her boots' magnetic locks and dialed them to the lowest settings. Wherever they were headed, she doubted it would be good. The ship shuddered as they fell out of ISG. Bretavic and the primary helmsman – an ensign so green she left grass stains when she walked – input the new destination and pushed back into ISG before the engines had completely spooled down.

M'benga organized the incoming and outgoing lines for combat readiness, distributing so that he and Maker could share the workload. He didn't speak Culler, barely understood the most basic words, so enemy comms were delegated to her along with any ship-to-surface and ship-to-ship communications. More experienced by several years and many, many battles on the bridge, M'benga kept fighter comms for himself. That would be the most pressing and fast-paced work. He had just finished briefing her on how he wanted emergency traffic handled when over her headset she heard something in the background.

At the Academy, Maker's first instructor had strongly recommended that she keep an open line at all times in case there should be something unexpected – even in deep space. Most of the students had ignored that advice. Listening to the radiation of the cosmos for an entire shift was not particularly appealing. But that instructor had had a look in his eye – the human one, not the implant that had replaced what he lost in the war. When Maker was on the bridge, she always kept an open comm.

She heard it then, not half an hour into their new trajectory. A quiet *whrrew* sound that faded in and out without pattern. The hair on the back of her neck stood up. There was no sound in the vacuum of space, but the frequency waves that carried sound still traveled – just waiting for something to bounce into. Maker selected the band on her display and maximized it, increasing the volume gradually.

Whrrew. Whrrew. Whrrrewwwww.

Whreckwew. WhreckWew.

WHRE-

She dialed it up as far as it would go, and an unmistakable screech of Culler language whispered through the Dark. She double-checked against the computer, but it couldn't identify. M'benga was monitoring an outbound comm for Captain Jones. Maker hesitated for only a moment before pulling one side of her headset off.

"Lt. commander!" Her sharp call, which protocol dictated should have been directed to her supervisor, made M'benga loosen his headset and the acting captain raise an eyebrow. "There is an enemy ship in our gravity wake."

"Sensors," the Lt. Commander snapped.

"I have nothing, sir."

M'benga spoke to her quietly, "Are you sure you-"

"Look again." Maker spoke directly to the ensign manning the sensors station. She kept her eyes on her, but her attention was on what she was hearing. She typed swiftly onto her display. "I'm calculating the Doppler shift...it's closing from behind, Ensign." She sent the information over even as the computer was completing the math. There was a long pause while they waited for confirmation. Maker felt like her skin was shrinking, anticipation and anxiety making her muscles tight and jumpy.

"Got it!" The ensign yelled. Helm was suddenly a flurry of activity as new information was brought up on the main display. The lt. commander took his seat. "Aft, sixteen million kilometers. Their speed exceeds ours, sir. Comms is hearing a fifty-three second delay."

"Time to weapons range?"

"At current speed...three hours, sir."

"Comms, do they know we've spotted them?"

There was no question that the Cullers were intentionally following the *Khalid*. It took precision and skill to enter the ISG wake of another ship. The chances of it happening unintentionally were infinitesimally small. Maker frowned, trying to clear the signal enough to make out words. M'benga dropped to his knees, popping open a panel and leaning in to reach the circuitry.

"One moment, sir," he called out.

The ship-to-surface comms went dead, and volume for the Cullers increased – although still not as loud as intentional communications would have been. Maker could only parse out tone, but it was enough. "I don't think so, sir. I am just hearing general chatter on their ship. There is no sense of urgency."

"Stay with it, Lieutenant. M'benga, get me-"

Captain Jones entered the bridge then, followed closely by Giradot and Soon. The lt. commander vacated the captain's chair and succinctly explained the situation. The CIO stepped over to the auxiliary tactical station while Soon waved the ensign at sensors into the second chair and took over the main console there.

"How long until we reach our destination?" Jones looked as unflappable as ever, sitting straight-backed and legs crossed.

The green ensign was sweating a little. Maker could see even across the bridge that her hand trembled on the control display. It was probably her first time in ISG combat – maybe her first time in combat at the helm. Bretavic surreptitiously slid her the calculations from his own station. The ensign sighed in relief before answering, "Five hours, ma'am."

"Captain," Giradot spoke up, "we are rendezvousing with the fleet, are we not? It would be tactically wise to increase speed and wait until we are within range of assistance before engaging."

"We're already at maximum recommended," Ensign Green blurted. She quickly ducked her head back to her console and focused her attention there.

"We have no way of real-time communication or sensors with anyone within two light-years of the Navi system until we are out of ISG," Soon stated. "X-ray emissions from that star are variable and too intense to allow for subspace transmissions at this speed."

"Captain-" Giradot fell silent as Jones held up one hand.

"How much reserve fuel do we have?" Soon named an amount, and Maker held her breath, still listening to the distant alien ship. "Start a leak, XO. One microgram of dark matter per minute. Helm, be prepared to slow and then drop out of ISG on my mark. Let's hope they think we have maintenance trouble. It should buy us some time to reposition."

"If they begin firing while we are in range of the dark matter-"

"I am aware, Giradot. But I'd rather fight them in the Dark than lead them to the fleet. Without real-time comms we have no way of knowing how the engagement at Navi is progressing. We could be bringing enemy reinforcements to a bad situation. We will clean this up before we rejoin with the other ships in-system."

"Aye, Captain." Soon typed in commands and repeated orders to the helm. "Prepare for slow to one-half maximum." Maker took over a portion of the intraship communications, transferring them to visual readouts so that she could focus her hearing on the enemy. M'benga picked up the rest. Captain Jones placed the ship on silent running on the off chance that the Cullers might be able to get a clearer signal from the Coalition ship.

Bretavic caught her eye just before they left ISG. He sent a message to her console: *You wanted a party.*

Maker didn't have time to reply. Although it would have taken hours for the Culler ship to overtake them in ISG, once the *Khalid* was effectively standing still the distance was quickly closed. With proximity, her comm signal increased. "They see us, Captain!" Maker was correcting the James as quickly as it translated the few signals picked up from the Cullers. There was far more activity than she expected.

"ISG engines are cooling," Soon reported.

"Orange alert. Tactical, seek firing solutions, all weapons. Have medical stand by for-"

Maker came to the same conclusion as Soon, just a few seconds earlier. "There's two of them!"

"Second ship, running in the wake, Captain. I'm tracking a *Titian* and a *Citrine.*"

"M'benga, alert the gunnar to prep squadrons of *Emici* and *Ictus.* And get me Ben-Zvi."

For Maker, the rest of the battle passed in a blur of shouting voices over the comms and cool orders from Jones. M'benga held the comms for two squadrons of *Ictus* and four of *Emici* while Maker handled intraship communications and monitored the Cullers. The main display faced their enemy, and sensors kept pinging and painting targets for the captain. Comms had no time to even glance at the images of the massive battle, too engrossed in the life and death conversations in their ears to even acknowledge the occasional shudder as the *Khalid* took fire.

"Delta-one, you are cleared to make your run. Echo squadron, check your sensors. *Khalid* is picking up a second deployment of Urchins, port quarter of the *Titian*. Tactical," M'benga snapped across the bridge, "Mike and Kilo requesting heavy support. Coordinates-"

"-understood Chief. First Engineer, report to lower ISG bay. Sensors," Maker sent information over to the ensign in the secondary chair as she spoke, "we have reports of impacoral leaks on deck nine. Please confirm. Medical, three *Emici* are down, two limping home. Meet casualties in the carrier hanger." Through it all she could hear the faint comms between the two enemy ships.

Take down the fighters.

Target ventral weapons.

"Tactical! *Citrine* is targeting our lower rail guns!"

"Confirmed!"

"Evasive action, helm." Jones' order was easier said than done, and Maker was briefly glad that she was not expected to turn a two hundred thousand ton hunk of metal and delicate circuitry on a dime. Bretavic and Ensign Green acknowledged the order, and their hands flew across the controls. Artificial gravity made the movement almost surreal; the stars and ships outside the display dipped and soared, but the deck remained firmly under her feet. An explosion rocked the ship, and reports streamed in to Maker even as the captain demanded, "Status!"

"They have switched targets to the ISG ports." Soon worked with glowering efficiency, the ensign beside him floundering in an attempt to keep up.

"Engineering is reporting casualties. Visual inspection underway," Maker reported. She listened to Soon describe the damage as Giradot and the tactical officer continued to update on hits to the enemy ships. M'benga was coordinating an attack between Delta and Echo squadrons against the *Citrine*.

"Comms, prep a report for the fleet, send as soon as the nearest array is clear of interference. Captain to Ben-Zvi-"

Whatever command the captain had been about to give was cut off as another explosion rocked the ship. Alarms sounded from every station, but there was no question as to what had been hit. The same magnetic field that held the ISG in proper containment also regulated the artificial gravity on the *Khalid*. Maker was glad she had thought to turn on her boots. Ensign Green had not considered the possibility and began floating away from her station before the Captain got hold of her and switched on the ensign's mag locks. Green fell to the deck with a thump and a groan.

"Status!" the captain barked.

The battle continued for another two hours, engineering crews working desperately to contain damage and repair the ISG under continued fire. At one point, gravity came back online only to increase to more than twice Earth standard. Only two of the bridge officers managed to remain standing during the ordeal. When the last shot was fired, Maker could feel a tremble in her legs, and her eyes burned from focusing on her screen so intently. Each station reported in turn to the captain. Injuries, damage, repairs, deaths. Thankfully, those were few. M'benga completed a review of mechanical systems and then Jones' gaze turned to Maker.

"How is the fleet?"

Maker coughed, surprised to find that her voice had gone scratchy from too much shouting and not enough liquid. "Still not able to get a signal through the interference from Navi, but we are receiving data packets." She had only briefly scanned the information, but she knew the captain would not be pleased.

"Main display."

Maker complied, pushing the most recent map of fleet positions and a status listing up to the large screen. She wasn't sure who said it, but she had to agree with them.

"Fucking hell."

She hoped Rodriguez wasn't lying about having real liquor on board.

If they survived, they would all need a drink.

CHAPTER 2: THE TAIL

Lost Ninth. Proper Noun. In 2061 a Culler attack on the Pluto surveillance outpost destroyed three Earth military vessels, leaving nineteen thousand soldiers dead. Damage to the dwarf planet was so severe, its orbit destabilized within the year. Pluto gradually broke apart over the next four decades. The devastation to human life and the Sol system was memorialized in the Coalition seal, featuring a nine-pointed star – one point for each of the original planets in the solar system.

Hour 0930
May 5, 2156

An explosion large enough to be heard through his proximity comm went off in the upper atmosphere. The blast wave impacted against the lower hull of the *Scythe* and rocked its trajectory. It was followed by three more in rapid succession. Malak braced himself, expecting additional hits near and around his ship and the *Garrote* flying nearby.

"Primary touchdown site is untenable. Switching to secondary site." Hemah's calm pronouncement coincided with the abrupt swerve of the *Runa* vessel, and Malak followed their progress on his own screen.

On Navi-II, Coalition forces were pinned down in a narrow valley. Culler forces were advancing from the southwest. To the north, two mountain ranges ran parallel to each other, drawing closer and closer until three soldiers could walk abreast, but no more. It continued that way for eight kilometers before slowly widening again. It was a terrible route for withdrawal and offered multiple points for enemy ambush.

On his way to the strategic system, Malak had read the mission reports. The primary and secondary retreat plans for the Coalition had been heavily bombed; casualties had been enormous, leaving only an undesirable hike through the narrow mountains for what was left of three battalions to meet up with the rest of the army. The Cullers had already reinforced their lines with an additional hundred thousand and had a fleet in the system keeping the Coalition too busy to send their own reinforcements to Navi.

The bulk of the Legion was on the opposite side of CSNS creating a wedge to drive through Culler occupied space, but Malak had been less than ten light years away from Navi when the comm came from Thomas. He had been ordered to abandon his mission of destroying strategic resupply posts and instead provide support to the Coalition under attack. The orders had not given him any pause until the *Pale Horse* was leaving ISG, and data from the planet became available. Navi was a heavily occupied system. Malak's orders since his first day of training had always been to keep the Legion in a Blackout. The list of humans who knew of its existence was short and heavily vetted. His curiosity – his suspicion – about the sudden change in policy had been great enough that he had felt justified in comming back to Thomas.

"Are you telling me it can't be done? That we should write off three thousand soldiers as KIA? And that is on just the southern continent!" The colonel's irritation had been palpable even across hundreds of light years. "Navi has four different corporations doing resource extraction. Seven hundred thousand civilians in-system - and strafing runs on the moons already killed most of the hard-labor workers there. Should we lose the researchers and techs too?"

"No," Malak said sharply. More sharply than he intended. "The situation is salvageable, but our presence will not remain clandestine."

Thomas snorted, leaning back in his chair and rolling his eyes. When Malak did not react, he said, "That horse has left the barn – don't you think?" Malak had felt his jaw tensing. He disliked metaphors, and Thomas knew it. "You seem to enjoy ignoring blackout protocol – if your frequency in doing so is any indication. You may not want to come out of the shadows, Major – it may be the end of you. But it is too late for that. You showed the brass what happens when you make your own rules, and they have taken a keen interest in the results. You have the authority to do whatever it takes to complete your mission. Just keep your face off the news feeds and the Coalition will take care of the rest."

Malak had not pointed out that never before had his mission been to directly save humans, and the comm line was closed without any satisfaction to Malak's curiosity or his suspicion. Thomas had not skirted the issue – he had been adamant on more than one occasion that he was disappointed and disapproving of Malak's decision on RB14.

Malak did not see the similarities. Then, he had only considered the lives of those Coalition on the ground once he was certain he had done everything possible to meet his objectives and secure his own people. The entire mission on Navi was saving humans. Malak wasn't certain it was the highest and best use of the Legion's skills.

"Legionnaires, battle-ready." On Malak's order every soldier not already in full armor snapped on their helmets and readied their weapons, copying their commander. He did not express his irritation or concern in front of his subordinates no matter how much he wanted to.

Smierc's voice came through on a direct comm from the *Pale Horse* to the *Scythe* as Hemah began a descent into the atmosphere, "Papa-Hotel is in position. Waiting for orders."

"Silent running until further notice." He noted another two Culler ships dropping out of ISG and heading for Navi-II. "Emergency intervention is your call. Out."

Malak retasked his display to focus on ground troop movements and his two *Runa*, relegating the battle in the space surrounding Navi to the Coalition. There would be nothing he could do about that combat once they landed. Smierc would ideally be able to remain hidden from both sides of the conflict until he was ready to withdraw, but if the fighting drew too close to the *Pale Horse*, she could engage as she saw fit. It would not surprise him if it came to that. Although the SC had formed a reasonably adequate defensive line around the planet and its three moons, Culler forces had already been attacking on the surface for twenty-eight hours by the time the Legion arrived. Two moons were completely dead, and more than a hundred thousand of the enemy had reportedly landed for ground maneuvers on the planet.

That was where the Legion would have the largest impact.

Legionnaires selected for pilot and ship's tactical systems were excellent at their duties, but they were not trained for fleet maneuvers. Malak was honest enough with himself to also admit that humans were often better at ship-to-ship battle. His people had been bred primarily to fight on the ground, and he preferred to play to their strengths. Once the Legion shifted the odds on Navi-II in the Coalition's favor, it would be up to the captains orbiting the planet to take control of the skies.

"Prep for landing," Hemah's voice came over the comm. A high-pitched whistle preceded an impact to the hull, knocking the transport off course until she could correct. "Coming in hot."

Malak secured the straps on his jump seat before the next impact. A Third. Fourth. Then a hail of debris that cracked against the plastisteel viewing window in the helm. He raised the blast shield himself so that Hemah could remain focused. It blinded their physical eyes, but sensors gave them all the data they needed.

Urchins had entered the planet's atmosphere, pursued by a squadron of *Ictus*. The two-man Coalition fighters outgunned the Culler ships, but they could not compete for maneuverability. The Urchins were outnumbered, but they were making deep inroads with bombing runs on a research settlement while the Coalition forces were trying to protect civilians. Any ship an *Ictus* hit that was not completely destroyed was piloted to crash against the buildings and people below. Some of the Cullers ejected to fight in melee combat; most sacrificed themselves and their damaged ships to kill as many humans as possible. For each Culler that was killed, dozens of humans died as well.

The secondary landing site was a few clicks from the besieged settlement on a flat clifftop littered with mining equipment. It would take Malak and his team at least fifteen minutes to get from their transport down to a position where they could begin defending the Coalition retreat. And then they would need to backtrack to reach their original intended target. He panned out the map on his display and assessed the casualty and munitions figures that the troops on the ground were uploading to the fleet. They would be more effective getting as close to the settlement as possible.

"Scrap secondary site. Proceed to new coordinates." Malak pinged his map and transmitted to Hemah's station. "Tactical, engage at will." Af bared her teeth in feral anticipation and began targeting Urchins. Malak switched to comms to reach the *Garrote*. "Team two, proceed to new tertiary site and primary target." On his display, he watched the path of the other ship as it changed course.

Hanako's voice responded from the *Garrote*. "Shock and awe, sir?"

"As you will."

That was the end of conversation until after the *Scythe* made a rough landing; a laser cannon had grazed the hull and destroyed the stabilizers. Af and the tactical officer under Hanako's command on the *Garrote* cleared a two hundred meter radius around Malak's coordinates. Five Urchins were strategically downed, and where they fell the burning debris created a shelter from advancing Culler ground troops. Af targeted a large group, taking a last few strategic shots to clear a path for the *Runa* to disembark. Malak used the time to unstrap from the jump seat and overlay the transport's sensor data onto his display.

Malak's goal had been to take pressure off of the Coalition so that they could round up the civilians and move through a narrow pass in the mountains to a secure position. The data Thomas had sent him was nearly two days old; communications from the system were complicated by significant radiation from the blue star. The situation on the ground was not as dire as reported.

It was much, much worse.

Af and Hanako had brought both transports down at the edge of the security wall separating corporate facilities from the bulk of the 3-D printed concrete buildings designed for housing and local industry. Clumped inside makeshift bunkers and scattered, hiding in the settlement, were fifteen thousand civilians. They were waiting for Coalition saviors that would never come. A wide swath of human bodies to the west was swiftly cooling to sensor sweeps, crushed into the mud by bony Culler talons as they advanced on the settlement and the retreating line of soldiers.

That was the bulk of the Culler army. Several hundred thousand of the enemy had already landed on the planet at a few locations before the fleet arrived. Approximately half had been fighting the Coalition on the southern continent, destroying their opportunities to retreat and gaining ground. Their number was too large and their heat signatures too close together to get an accurate count. The main SC forces were to the north of Malak's landing site. They had fortified positions along the ridge of a mountain range with heavy gun and air support as well as anti-Urchin missiles. As long as the fleet held, civilians and soldiers alike could survive there. More importantly, as far as Confederation politics were concerned, the water processing facility that was the backbone of industry in the Navi system, and one of the largest suppliers to Coalition ships, would remain intact. With planning, they could even stage a retaliation and chew through the remains of the Culler forces if the fleet maintained the blockade. However, in order to reach that secure location, the humans would have to survive the twenty-five kilometer march. The field was not favorable to the Coalition due to Cullers on the west and south, an ocean to the east, and the mountain range along the north. The forest vegetation between the mountains and the settlement was too dense for sensor penetration, so there was no telling what surprises might be waiting there. Malak did not particularly care for surprises.

"Clear!" Af shouted.

Malak was already at the rear hatch, hitting the controls to open it. "Sweep in maneuver teams. Collect and protect." It was a testament to the discipline of the Legion that not a murmur was heard in response to that order – the first time he had ever given it. "Drive survivors to these coordinates and create a wedge line between them and the enemy." He pinged a location on the map in a clearing two-thirds of the way through the forest. A red line, the hold line, he drew between the Culler advancement and that spot. The hatch opened fully, hitting the ground hard enough to send mud splattering into the air. "Go."

He stood aside as his team surged out, a perfectly coordinated line of soldiers fanning to positions behind the downed Urchins and moving under cover of fire from there. The *Garrote* was emptying as well, and Hanako stepped towards him as she followed the soldiers out.

"*Scythe, Garrote,*" his voice rumbled over the comms. Through the thick, humid air filtering into his helmet he could smell the sudden, sharp anticipation of Af and Hemah behind him. Their voices blended with the tactical and helm officers under Hanako.

"Yes, sir."

"Scuttle and move out." They all responded in the affirmative, with an extra growl of satisfaction from Af. Within a minute, both *Runa* were locked down tight, their hatches closed as their crews followed the rest of the Legionnaires.

"Major." Hanako didn't ask questions as she took up his flank, but Malak knew what she wanted to know without words. She wasn't a 27-series, but she was still pack. Still one of his.

"We'll draw fire away from them," he said, meaning the *Runa*, "but if they are destroyed, it will not matter."

"Smierc will land the *Pale Horse*." It went unsaid that if she couldn't, both Malak and Hanako and every other Legionnaire would be dead. It was an unlikely outcome. "After you, sir."

Malak tracked the two-person maneuver teams as they moved through the rubble and the few buildings that were still intact. Just as in training exercises, they formed a staggered line moving north and west. A secondary line followed behind, moving north and east. The first killed Cullers and painted survivors. The second collected the humans and pushed them farther from the fighting. Malak moved quickly, slipping though the rear line and into the empty zone between his people. Hanako followed silently. Cullers, their yellow smudges on his display thick and fast, were painted and fell in quick succession. Each time a maneuver team moved around the shelter of a rubble pile or shelled wall more of the enemy fell. Pale yellow faded as they died and the Legion continued onward. Malak and Hanako had nearly caught up to the forward position when new Urchins circled around from other locations to buzz the settlement.

He crouched, and Hanako flipped an anti-fighter gun off of her back and onto his shoulder. She used him as a tripod to steady her shot. Bombs dropped, exploding in a rain of mud and shrapnel as more buildings collapsed. The door of the closest structure flew open, and a ragged wave of humans surged out – but not fast enough. Hanako fired, smoke curling in Malak's peripheral vision. A projectile fell, hurtling end over end as the ship that had released it exploded in the air. The missile crashed through the roof. Humans screamed, throwing themselves to the ground. An older man at the rear of the group braced open the door and physically pulled another two out behind him before throwing his arms over his head.

Malak remained motionless, the anti-fighter still on his shoulder. He waited.

Nothing happened.

Far off in the distance, the shrieks of Cullers and the dull repeat of weapons' fire continued. The smell of smoke and burnt flesh from explosions and laser cannons was acrid in his nose even through his helmet's filters. The humans were beginning to stand, but Malak waited until his display confirmed: the missile was active but undetonated inside the building.

Along with eighty-three heat signatures.

"Secure the entrance," he ordered Hanako. As soon as she lifted the gun from his shoulder, he was moving toward the doorway. The man there was prepared to go back inside. His deplorable attempt at rescue was ill-advised. Structural integrity of the building was poor, and if the explosive detonated, his civilian clothing would offer no protection. Malak casually shoved him aside, ignoring the pleas as he scanned the building.

"Coalition! Thank God! We thought the fleet had abandoned us!"

Near enough, Malak thought. Certainly, the Legion was the best chance at survival the researchers had, but there was nothing stopping Malak from declaring the mission a scrub and leaving the humans to die. He did not share the same sympathies as the Coalition soldiers. Tears and thanks from civilians did not play on his emotions. If the Legion did not succeed, there would be no backup mission.

It took nearly twenty minutes to clear the building. He left the dead; it would have been a waste of time to dig out the corpses and foolhardy with undetonated munitions so close. The missile itself was half-buried in the floor, indicator lights blinking and protective case cracked. Like a herd of animals, the researchers stumbled out ahead of Malak, falling into the tight groups of survivors already huddled behind Hanako. She had taken position near the remains of a ground transport, her Klim out and ready. Cullers were drawing closer, their shrieks interrupted only by the sounds of projectiles shattering chitin. Hanako anticipated Malak's order, and as soon as the last human cleared the building, she holstered her side arm and singled out the older man that had begun the evacuation. She sent coordinates to his personal tech. He glanced at his bracer, wide-eyed.

"You can't mean for us to head there alone? There are hundreds of Cullers already on the outskirts of the settlement!" His words were heavily accented.

"Thousands," Hanako corrected, "conservatively. Follow the route. Your retreat will be covered."

Malak positioned himself in front of the transport shell, Klim ready while he tracked the movements of his team and the enemy. They were getting closer. It was time to move.

"Covered?" Out of the corner of his eye, Malak saw the man's jaw drop open. "By one soldier? Is that guy nuts?"

"No." Hanako paused, head tilted to the side.

Malak heard what she heard, the crunch of boot on bone. Rapid fire from two separate firearms. Two standard projectiles. Three slag rounds. An abruptly silenced shriek and the snap of a talon. Hemah popped over the top of a low-slung building, her back to him and firing behind her. Af followed, the severed arm of a Culler clutched in one hand. She flipped feet first onto the surface and slid to a knee. She fired with one hand and slashed at an unseen enemy with the bloody claw. Hemah holstered her Klim and pulled two pommels from her pack. With the push of a button, blades extended, the gently curved arcs gleaming in the sunshine. Despite Af's precision work, three Cullers vaulted onto the roof, advancing on Hemah. Malak aimed carefully and took out the middle position. Hemah made quick work of the other two. Her blades met in an x, carving the shoulder and jaw off of her first opponent. She used his falling corpse to push herself into the air in a leap that brought one heavy boot down on an upraised talon and the other into the wide black eyes of her opponent. Her right blade sliced through exoskeleton and bone. One talon clattered to the roof a second before the back of the Culler's head - followed by Hemah's boot and a splatter of ichor.

"He is not here to defend you." Hanako gestured with her Klim. "They are." Af fired twice more and then took a running leap, crossing the narrow street filled with survivors and the burned-out transport. She had turned and aimed again before her feet touched down, and Hemah dropped down to the ground. The man was still staring in awe.

"Forty-seven down," Hemah reported on a direct comm to Malak and Hanako. "This area has been cleared, but fighting is increasing further north. Orders, sir?"

"Move the humans. We will relieve the line and send more back to you. Contact with them is to be minimized." Hemah nodded her acknowledgment to Malak and took off skirting and backtracking along the ragged group to get them moving while Af covered them from the rooftops. Hanako motioned for the human leader to follow them.

Malak did not wait to see if they obeyed, but took off at a slow jog on a course diagonal to that of the humans. He met his first enemy around the corner of the bombed building. It went down easily, his knife sinking into the jaw, just below the armor plate. He drove his fist into the joint of the Culler's arm, at the intersection of talon, fingers, and muscle. It snapped, and his motion pulled the blade behind him, deepening and circling the nerve cord that ran from the brain up to the eyes. It fell without a sound. A second Culler, too far away for melee, got off a shriek of anger and warning before a piercing round took it in the chest. It fell to one knee, and Malak followed up with a slag round through an eye. It collapsed on the ground, twitching and screaming as the molten copper and tungsten exploded from the projectile and left a poisonous trail as they burned through soft tissue.

His display alerted him to incoming enemies. He and Hanako would have their hands full, but they needed to keep moving to redirect the Culler's advance and take pressure off of the Legion's front line. Behind him was the bombed building, before him a plaza one hundred meters wide. "Pull them in," he ordered.

Hanako used his hip as a brace and jumped onto the same roof that the Af and Hemah had recently defended. Malak did not see where she went, but took down three more Cullers before she reappeared on the opposite side of the courtyard. A trail of screaming aliens followed her. Malak kicked open the back door of the collapsed building and then bent on one knee. Hanako jumped from the roof, landing in a neatly tucked roll across the grassy plaza. She was on her feet and running again when the first of the Cullers entered the open space. "Tag," she called through the comm as she stepped on his bent leg. One foot there, the other on his shoulder. One hundred eighty pounds of sleek muscle and deadly intent pushed off of him and onto the side of the building. The twisted supports and broken masonry created excellent handholds on the second and third stories. Malak took down the four Cullers at the front, giving Hanako a decent lead, before retreating into the building.

There were stairs to his right, and he took them three at a time. His long legs ate up the distance so that he was nearly to the third landing before they entered the building. Malak did not bother pausing to shoot. A section of the treads had been destroyed, leaving a two and a half meter vertical gap. He jumped, but from somewhere behind him a shock spear was thrown. It hit his legs, and he barely managed to get a handhold on the tangled roots of reinforcing metal bars that protruded from the wall. He swung his body back and forth, quickly building momentum, and fired down the stairs to cover himself. With no easy way to get back onto solid steps, Malak threw himself straight forward, flying through a hole in the wall and into an interior office. Power was off, and the space remained dark. His night vision kicked in as the Cullers realized where he had gone. They shrieked in pursuit.

"At position," Hanako's voice wasn't even winded through the comm. "Status?"

"Move," Malak ordered.

On his display she did not hesitate, but took off running across the intact portion of the roof, leaping into the air to cross to the next building and repeating. Malak navigated through overturned furniture to the center of the structure, where he reverted to normal vision. The missile had carved a hole roughly two meters across through every floor, leaving cabling and broken bits of masonry raw along the edges. Malak could not get a clear shot at his pursuers, but he fired off a few rounds blindly to give away his location. He holstered his Klim, freeing both of his hands for climbing, and jumped over the hole. Below his feet in a pile of rubble was the undetonated missile. He climbed, hand over hand, occasionally swinging to find a more secure grip.

The grating cry of Culler language bit at his ears as their talons bit into the concrete of the building. They were faster climbers – no need for fingers and hands as they drove their serrated, bony appendages directly into the concrete blocks and crawled up the building. As he reached the top, one of the enemy sank a talon into the meat of his calf. His armor kept it from severing the muscle, but as he kicked out and smashed the creature into an exposed metal bar, the wrenching pain in his leg reminded him that the ceramic weave was not impenetrable - merely highly resistant. His arms strained and burned. With a quick, sharp tug he flipped out onto his back on the roof. Without pause, Malak rolled, pulled his weapon and toggled to an incendiary round. Eight Cullers had already begun to climb up the hole. His display showed an additional fifteen inside the building and ten more scaling the wall as Hemah had done. Malak fired.

He pushed up into a running position. There was a quiet *crack*, barely made out under the distant heavy guns, the screams of his enemy, and the sound of his own breath in his lungs. He pivoted on his left foot, his leg muscle protesting and blood welling out through his suit. *One, two steps.* A boom, a rumble, more movement than sound and then the building was trembling under his feet. *Three, four steps.* The roof was collapsing under him, Cullers crying out, shrieking, screeching, wailing into the sunny sky.

Malak's right boot hit the lip of the roof just as it crumbled away, giving him no traction. Still, he threw himself over the gap between that building and the next. It was lower, and he connected hard with the roof, his shoulder taking the brunt of the impact. Kinetic gel absorbed the worst of it, leaving him with only discomfort rather than a broken collarbone. He did not stop moving until he had crossed two more buildings and met up with Hanako, who was sniping Cullers as they broke around the end of the Legion front line. Through the proximity comm, he heard her deep inhale. She smelled his blood, but did not say anything.

"Next objective. Assess." He sat next to her, pulling out his med kit and sealing the wound before pinching the edges of his suit together and sealing that as well.

"Team One is making progress, but the terrain is holding them up. Urchin air support is utilizing the buildings to block movement and create openings for Culler ground troops." She pinged a mass of the enemy at the far north of the Legion. "These are moving around our people faster than we can advance. Gunnar is on the line. He reports that another fifty thousand are on the edge of his sensor range. It looks like they are redirecting to intercept here."

A tone sounded on his display and new information appeared on his map. The Cullers had landed their ships before the fleet could blockade the planet, and three had touched down to the west of the settlement. The mountain range dipped south there, forcing the aliens to come down close to the research buildings before they could move north again through heavy vegetation to the Coalition retreat position. It was a bottleneck for the Cullers, hemmed in by the landscape and the Legion, but they had superior numbers. Malak's people were equally restricted by the need to defend instead of becoming the aggressors. He turned his back on the urban warfare and faced to the northwest. From above, the vegetation had looked like any thick forest with trees so close together the branches interlocked and created a solid canopy. Although it was still more than a kilometer away, from a side view, Malak could see oddly shaped stone columns, curved and broken in places but still reaching dozens of meters upward. Dense vines snaked up from the ground randomly before leafing out when they reached the top. Malak studied the shape of the columns, the jagged, broken edges worn smooth over time by the elements.

"Papa-Hotel, this is Team Leader. Over." There was a long pause after he broke communications silence, and Malak used that time to extract the long-range rifle from his pack. The same make as Hanako's, the barrel and stock were in four pieces that easily screwed together. Malak only ever loaded armor piercing rounds into his rifle, so there was no need to toggle ammunition. He used the roof ledge as a rest and lined up a Culler in his sights. It would take the Falcon technician on board the *Pale Horse* a few minutes to verify encryption and secure a new line. He fired and watched through the sight as several hundred meters away a burst of ichor exploded from the back of a Culler and it dropped like a stone.

"Team Leader, this is Papa-Hotel. Go ahead." Smierc sounded tense, which was at odds with the humor she found in most situations. Malak squeezed the trigger again and another Culler fell, knocking into the one next to it and tripping a third.

"Papa-Hotel, sending coordinates for air support. T-minus one-twenty minutes. Over."

"Team Leader, Papa-Hotel position will be compromised. Enemy reinforcements have arrived. Over."

Malak only hesitated as long as it took him to breathe. Thomas had said the decision was his, that remaining clandestine was not as important as saving the researchers on Navi-II. If the Coalition was finally ready to use the best weapons they had, without restrictions, then Malak was willing to show them what he could do. More importantly, he was ready to take out as many of the enemy as possible. Why they had attacked in the Navi system so far from the front lines of the war and the bigger shipping lanes was unknown, but the Legion would make their enemy think twice about such a bold move.

Another question remained unanswered as well. Why was the Coalition willing to reveal the Legion? A third question whispered at the back of Malak's mind, *what is so important on this planet?*

"Papa-Hotel, at your discretion. Out." He fired off two more shots in rapid succession before dismantling his rifle. Hanako had hers put away first. "Two man sling-shot," he told her. "Give Team Two time to reposition before we draw them in."

"Yes, sir." Hanako didn't relish the combat in quite the same way as Af or Smierc would have, but she was the equal of any in the Legion except himself or his lieutenants. He gripped her forearm and dropped her over the edge before following, using window sills and broken masonry to lower himself to the ground. The nearest Culler was eighty meters away and advancing slowly through a narrow alley. Its shadow moved like an oil spot across the pale stone.

Malak flashed a grin in his helmet. He was most definitely looking forward to the fight.

CHAPTER 3: DESCENDANT CONTRIVANCE

Homogeneity. Noun. The quality or state of being all the same or all of the same kind.

Ex. In 2031, terrorists attacked the western grain supply by releasing a biological weapon on United States cornfields. Due to the relative homogeneity of seed supply, crop production was devastated. World cereal markets and related livestock markets crashed. Starvation rates in developing nations skyrocketed as exports dwindled. Although seed manufacturers developed resistant strains, the engineered disease spread to Africa, decimating more than 50% of grain produced and consumed on that continent. An estimated 400-650 million deaths are attributed to the attack.

Hour 1400
December 23, 2128

Soledad Venegas sipped his tea and waited patiently for Helen to get to the point. From long experience he was aware that there was nothing he could do to speed up the process. He also knew after having navigated the tangled social structure of Sol Congress for decades that it pleased her when he did not simply ask why he had been summoned. A holographic display of a compound molecule was suspended over her desk, gently turning and displaying a series of written notes in a language he couldn't read. It wasn't Standard English or Portuguese. Definitely not Mandarin.

"I'm so sorry to keep you waiting, Sole," she said. Her voice actually sounded regretful. "I just need to finish signing off on these reports and then I am all yours."

Venegas glanced around the office of the Prime Minister while he waited. A plaque by the door noted that it was one of a suite of rooms originally included in Louis XVI's private apartment. The parquet floor was intact, and the marble fireplace had been restored. Tall multi-paned glass windows overlooked an interior courtyard. Heavy brocade velvet drapes were pulled aside to let in the afternoon light and a view of citrus trees and reflecting pools. In contrast to the 17th and 18th century architecture and painted murals, Helen's very modern desk was made of opaque glass. It was thick, clouded, and an obvious display of the recycled 'working' art that graced many rich corporate offices. She kept the surface clean with only a wide visual display, her tablet, an ornate tea set, and a simply made wooden stand with an antique fountain pen for signing important documents. It was an office that spoke of power, taste, and efficiency. It did not speak of ruthless ambition or judicious consequences, but that was understood by anyone personally acquainted with the Prime Minister.

"Done," Helen stated with finality. She waved off her display, and pushed her tablet to the side, allowing the projection to continue playing. "Thank you so much for coming in today. I am sure you are eager to be home for the session break."

"I am always eager to be home, Helen. My wife would love for you to visit as well. Bring Greg; she misses that boy – and his cooking. Since he finished his agriculture degree we have barely spoken with him."

"I'll let Greg know, but he just received word this morning that he was awarded a grant for a new research project aboard a Coalition ship. Hopefully he will make some friends; I understand this ship is mostly new recruits. And I would love to, thank you Sole, but I have a few things that have to be buttoned up first. Avani Sudarshan has decided to run for a Senate seat, and the committee reshuffling is a nightmare."

"No." Venegas didn't say it with any malice, but he was quite serious. There were few things about politics that he found enjoyable, and the Oversight Committee was not one of them. Helen had promised that he would be able to step down during the next committee reappointment opportunity. He knew her well enough to know she was going to renege, had known it from the beginning, and that there was nothing he could do about it.

Helen became solemn, her usual pleasant smile dropping. "I would not ask it of you if it wasn't the last option."

"Barghest is done. Project Jagd is progressing on schedule and is so black book *I* can barely find it. The next Committee Chair won't even think to look for it. It doesn't exist. There will never be a better time to-"

"This isn't about soldiers," Helen interrupted. "This is more important. I'd give up Jagd and Barghest both if it would ensure success with this."

Venegas sat back in his chair, shocked and not bothering to conceal it. Barghest and its successor Jagd were Helen's most prized accomplishments. She had always asserted that such innovations and risks were necessary for survival. For victory. Despite himself, he was curious. He knew the moment Helen realized it, considered it, and seized on his weakness.

She poured herself a cup of tea. "What is the rate of success with the latest James upgrade?"

"It's hovering at seventy-two percent. Of course, it could be lower. We don't have many translators that are more fluent and able to test it against actual speech. Even then, it isn't fast enough; we're too slow in reacting to their communication."

"That is because you aren't hearing all of it. We went through several subjects to confirm, years of research, but there is an underlying component to the Culler language that the James is incapable of receiving." Helen left Venegas waiting. He rapidly considered several banal options: body language, facial expressions, chronological or locational vocabulary changes. "They produce a measurable electronic field during speech and thought which adds meaning." She paused, waiting for his eyes to focus on hers. "It can traverse subspace."

Carefully, so as not to spill or crush the delicate china, Venegas set down his cup. His stomach fluttered, rippling a bit with an uncomfortable mixture of excitement and dread. "Are you suggesting...some sort of...extrasensory means?"

"I would never suggest, Sole." Helen leaned forward, pressing one palm flat against the smooth glass of her desk. "My people have proven it. Cullers use audible and electromagnetic means of communicating with each other that combine to create a psionic language." There was a gleam in her blue eyes that was unsettling.

The Culler communications had always been difficult to crack. It was nearly forty years into the war before the first break in understanding came. Decades later spying was still practically useless to the Coalition as translation software was nowhere close to infallible, and human translators were so scarce as to be nonexistent. The enemy fleets seemed capable of sending warnings, directions, and valuable intel across vast distances without pinging the standard sensor arrays. Soldiers reported an uncanny ability for two or more of the aliens to synchronize their movements; although one might die fighting humans in a closed room, the next attacker would be prepared for the Coalition's exact numbers and weaponry.

"So you want the Oversight Committee to move funding to SAR to update the arrays?" He knew it wasn't the right conclusion, but Venegas still felt like he was playing catch-up. Whatever endgame Helen had in mind, she was a dozen moves ahead and not slowing down.

She waved a hand dismissively. "Already done. Privately funded and far more discreet than the amount of money and maintenance that would have been necessary if it went through government channels. A rather old corporate family – I am visiting their vineyard next week to confirm the details. Your committee and SAR have a task better suited to the Confederation." She pulled her tablet between them, gesturing at the slowly rotating figure. "This is a polynucleotide, only isolated a few years ago. It is what allows the reception, and – presumably, transmission of electromagnetic wavelengths." She pointed to a section that was labeled with red and zoomed in. Two additional molecules hung off of the edge of the structure, creating a loop. "This contains an entirely new kind of nucleobase, not ever documented in life on Earth. It isn't known to our alien allies either."

"What do you plan on doing with it?" Venegas immediately wished he could pull the question back into his mouth and swallow it. He did not want that knowledge.

"Recreate it, of course."

"You're going to engineer that into humans? You'll be breaking the law, Helen. A law you helped to pass. Barghest was one thing, and while I understood it, you were walking into a very gray area. But this is going too far. No human, no matter how desperate, would willingly agree to Culler genetic insertion! You can't honestly be considering this?"

"Of course not." Helen smiled, and the flop in Venegas' stomach grew wilder. "It is already there." She pinched her fingers together over the image, then flicked them apart. The hologram zoomed out, displaying a long section of a twisted double helix. The red nucleobase glowed like a beacon, small and almost unnoticeable.

"This-" Venegas swallowed and tried to compose himself. There were many things that Helen was, things he did not approve of, but at least she was not playing God. It was cold comfort. "This is human DNA?"

"Yes, very rare. I have the specifics here, but believe me when I say that not only is it present in only a tiny portion of the population, it is getting smaller. It most often associates with some undesirable traits and is being cut out as junk DNA by most reproductive geneticists. They don't know what they are getting rid of." She pushed her tablet to the side, and Venegas had to wrench his eyes away to focus on her. "It is still theory – but highly sound theory – that anyone with this marker could be trained to reproduce not just the spoken language but the psionic component as well."

"You'll need test subjects," Venegas stated, his mind already working on the logistics while his morals were still wrestling over what could have been – where Helen might have taken such knowledge. An unthinkable conclusion.

"Yes, SAR will need funding. And access to the standardized placement tests. I have a team working on it already, and they are confident we can identify the best candidates for training through genetic analysis and primary school psychological exams."

Venegas left an hour later, both frightened and excited by the prospect. A new kind of soldier, one who could bring them closer to understanding their enemy and its motivations. Instead of training to shoot or fly, these children would be trained to speak – with their minds. The entire project would be classified Eyes Only or even further restricted, and he knew that nothing more than the results would ever make it to his desk. But he trusted Helen to do the right thing, to help the next generation of humans to reach their full potential and bring them all a step closer to ending the war. She was driven, ambitious, callous sometimes, but Helen had a moral code that was unbreakable. He had always believed that about her.

The door closed behind Representative Venegas, and Dr. Patay waited a few moments in the reception area before he knocked lightly.

"Enter."

He spoke as soon as the room was secure. "Are we cleared to begin, Prime Minister?"

"Yes. But please keep this out of the records until you receive your official notice from the Minister of SAR. It wouldn't do to have you preempt your own boss."

He smiled, "My boss, of course." He tapped at his tablet. "Those are the updated figures. Phases One and Two are fairly innocuous, but once we move on to Three the incidence of irreversible injury is anticipated to increase."

"And Four?"

"Lethal. Computer modeling shows thirty-eight percent of subjects die during training, and another fifty-one within the first year of field testing."

"Not ideal, but acceptable. We'll need more candidates."

"Of course. I took the liberty of directing a team to assess the potential for genetic insertion. We are probably a decade out, but isolation was the first step. Given a few discreet reproductive geneticists and some carefully worded legislation, we could be targeting up to ten percent of the population in a quarter century."

"Let's keep that in our arsenal, but as a tertiary tactic. We need to assess what other side effects this gene may have, as well as its performance in the real world."

"Yes, ma'am."

Her assistant held the door as Patay left. "Ma'am, I have your son on the line, I believe he has received his departure date for the research grant. And I put in a word to have his physical scheduled with the medic you prefer."

"Thank you, Miguel."

Hour 0930
November 24, Year 2152

"You have had this information for almost twenty-five years." Yardley had to force his jaw to unclench. In the highest office of the Ministry of Science and Research he sat in a comfortable blue chair and did his best to breathe evenly.

"Confirmed for that long, although SAR was working on the theory while I was still employed there before I ran for office. Of course, it took a bit longer after the first candidates were identified to begin thorough testing."

"And you did not feel that was information that the families of those children should be made aware of?"

"No children were hurt, Captain Yardley. I am not some sort of monster. We have only used passive testing on subjects that have not reached their legal majority."

"And after?"

"Well," she took a sip of tea and raised an eyebrow, "they are the property of the Coalition for a minimum of two years. Anything that happens during that time, as long as it is approved as part of the defense efforts, is not optional for them. But do not assume that I do not take their well-being into consideration. They are too valuable a commodity for imprudent methods."

Yardley lost the battle with his anger. His back teeth came together hard enough that he could hear them grind. "Minister, I am not certain you wouldn't lobotomize your own child if you thought it would give you the upper hand."

She smiled. An honest, sincere smile. "We are fighting for more than just survival, of which you have intimate knowledge. When the future of an entire species is at stake, no price is too high. Although, I would note that my son is perfectly healthy. I take full responsibility for my actions, but I will not admit guilt for a harm that was never done."

He struggled. Struggled with the desire to summon his guard and have the woman removed from office. Struggled with the itch in his hand to reach across the desk and slap her self-assured, egotistical face. Helen Maker was proud of what she had done, what she had hidden. Worse, Yardley was certain he had only heard the best of it. He swallowed. "And that was the extent of it? You manipulated SAR into testing for this genetic marker in the hopes that future soldiers could be trained – you've been training communications officers to use this... psionic language?"

"Yes, exactly," she said without hesitation. She began pulling up a new file, ready to brief him on another black project.

Regardless of how sincere she appeared, Yardley knew she was lying.

CHAPTER 4: STING LIKE A BEE

Dummy Bar. Alt. DME Bar. Noun. Daily Meal Enhancement. Dense nutrient supplement designed to provide one soldier with necessary calories for 24 hours of active duty along with essential vitamins, minerals, and immune system boosters. Nicknamed after the soldiers who willingly consume the Coalition's version of hardtack.

Hour 1230
May 6, 2156

It wasn't the alarm that woke her, but the slam of her shoulder into the floor of the C&E break room that yanked Maker from sleep. In the hours since her shift on the bridge had ended, there had been too many alarms for her to pay attention unless it affected the Communications and Encryption offices. ISG malfunctions, gravity repairs, incaporeal leaks, hull breaches, and a million other life and death issues kept Engineering occupied while the rest of the crew repaired individual stations and prepped the transports and fighters for battle. Maker had spent most of the first shift sorting out the comms staff. The C&E Chief had been injured during the fight with the two Culler ships and was still confined to the infirmary. Half of the remaining crew were sporting concussions, broken bones, and contusions; they had all reported for duty.

Maker was proud of them for that. Communications officers were cross-trained as technicians and could supplant engineers and mechanics on smaller jobs throughout the ship. With the chief out, Maker took command, ignoring the more senior second-shift officer who was eager to step aside from the responsibility. She split her people into repairs and their regular duties translating and encrypting data packets to be sent back to Sol. Information from the fleet at Navi came in short trickles through the radiation interference, but each new update brought worse news than the last. The Coalition was outnumbered and barely holding the line around the most populated planet. Hundreds of thousands of private contractors and civilians were trapped there fighting Cullers on the ground, and only a small contingent of soldiers had made it to the surface to defend and organize an evacuation. The Coalition desperately needed the *Khalid* to help turn things around.

Maker snorted to herself as she sat up and tried to focus her vision on her bracer. What they desperately needed was the rear admiral and a dozen more ships. *Fat chance of getting that.* A notification was blinking, ordering Maker to the bridge. She acknowledged it and pushed to her feet. A wave of dizziness hit her as soon as she was vertical, and Maker had to close her eyes and lean against the wall until she steadied. Too many hours without real sleep and not enough time to find a meal were catching up with her.

"Lieutenant."

Maker looked up to see one of the new privates, less than two months out of basic, standing before her with a cup of coffee and a forehead wrinkled from worry.

"We finished the secondary dish alignment, and there is a new data packet coming in. ma'am, can I...can I get you anything?"

"Is there any more coffee?"

A more seasoned officer, one who had instigated the initial prank war against Maker when she was first stationed on the *Khalid*, pushed past the rookie and held out a full cup and a nutrient bar. "Extra salt, just like you like it," he said with a straight face.

Maker took a sip. There was almost enough sugar in it to cover the bitter taste of the coffee, and it was wet enough to make the nutrient bar digestible. She smacked her lips and replied with an equally dry tone, "Needs pepper." The private looked confused, and Maker took pity. "Inside joke, Fuzz. Don't worry about it. Sergeant." The older man nodded and walked beside her on her way through the comms stations. "Make that data packet a priority. Pull a crew off tertiary repairs if you have to, but the Captain is going to need that ASAP."

"Yes, ma'am. Do you want us to keep pinging the relay system?"

"Your call. You know the stress levels better than anyone else. Just note it for the records if you decide to forgo procedure, and I'll sign off on it later. I'll be on the Bridge if you need anything." She hit the door control and stepped into the corridor.

"Let us know if *you* need anything, Ma'am," he nodded seriously, and a few others who had been on the *Kahlid* while she was a supervisor in comms looked up from their stations and did the same.

Maker waved her unopened nutrient bar. "Anyone who can find one of these that tastes like steak and won't chip my teeth gets an extra day off this week." There was laughter from her crew, and Maker felt some of her tension ease. They needed a break, even for a few minutes, before they arrived at Navi. The doors closed and Maker straightened her shoulders and forced herself into a brisk walk. She had choked down a third of the hard, dry bar and most of her coffee by the time she entered the bridge. The primary crew were in the middle of first shift, and Jones was still in her chair, deep in conversation with Ben-Zvi. Maker went to stand at attention and wait her turn, and realized belatedly that she was still holding her cup and food – both banned from the bridge. *If I'm this tired now, I'll need stims to make it another eighteen hours.* A mechanic working on the console closest to the door opened her tool box and gestured. Maker quickly disposed of her contraband with a nod of thanks. The ship shuddered again, and she had to brace one hand on an auxiliary station to keep from falling.

"Comms," Jones looked up from the tablet Ben-Zvi was holding. "Get me a status update from Engineering. I want those tremors locked down before we exit ISG."

"Captain," Soon spoke up from his station. "I would suggest we focus instead on the secondary hull fissures. From the latest data, it looks like we'll have a few hours once we enter the system before we'll be in firing range of the enemy. We can use that time to repair the gravity drive."

"I respectfully disagree, Captain," Giradot interjected from his place at the ancillary engineering console along the rear wall of the bridge. He looked irritated, as if the debate was inconveniencing his day. *Get in line, asshole,* Maker thought. "Waiting at the edge of the system until we have orders from Sol is our best course of action. Until communications has received confirmation that we are to enter this conflict, it is better to reserve the *Khalid* to protect this sector should the fleet fail at Navi."

"Your input is noted, gentlemen," Jones replied. Her voice gave nothing away, and Maker could only wait and stare at the back of her neat braid until she was called upon. "However, we have no way of knowing if Sol has even received our latest update – is that correct, Lieutenant Maker?"

Maker started, surprised to find herself involved in the debate. She had taken over repairs in the chief's absence, but she wasn't the ranking officer. She glanced at the lt. commander manning the primary comms station; he had seniority. He nodded for her to go ahead. "Ehm, yes, ma'am. C&E has sent the packet twice and continues to ping the closest relay, but radiation interference is high and repairs to the tertiary comms dish are not yet complete."

"But if they were, you could boost the signal and reach Sol, could you not?" Giradot was pressing her for an answer, and Maker knew he wouldn't like what she had to say.

"It is possible, sir, but the tertiary repairs will not be completed before we reach Navi."

"How long would you need?" This came from Ben-Zvi, who shifted her weight with impatience.

"Time is not the issue, ma'am. We don't have the parts. Engineering could probably scavenge what we need, but they are on other priorities and – my best guess – they'd have to take circuit boards from the external sensors to make it work."

"Flying blind puts us at a disadvantage, ma'am." The primary tactical officer was older than Ben-Zvi or Jones, and he looked like he had seen every battle since the invasion. His prosthetic hand twitched over the console, allowing him quicker reaction times. It wasn't good form to disagree with the Chief of Intelligence in front of the captain, but from the look of tactical's scarred face, Maker doubted he gave a shit.

"Agreed." Jones tapped out a few commands on the console to her right, and the main display was overlaid with the most recent update from the fleet. The globes of blue light representing Navi's binary stars pulsed with radiation; twelve planets, three within the wide habitable zone, rotated around the suns. The outer three planets and an icy disc of dust were devoid of activity. Closer in, the number of ships was so dense that Jones had to magnify the view to allow individual objects to be discerned. "As you can see, the Cullers continue to grind down the fleet. We are holding for now, but losses are high and eventual defeat inevitable. Assuming the rear admiral received my request for additional resources, we should obtain reinforcements in twelve to fifteen hours."

"Even if they can last that long, the casualties – have they been calculated?"

Ben-Zvi answered Soon, "Losses among the fleet will mean little to the ground troops. With the civilians to evacuate, they are taking enormous personnel casualties. I estimate three hours until the Cullers break defenses on the surface." She listed numbers for civilians and soldiers that would die. Maker swallowed hard. It wouldn't be the largest single defeat the Coalition had ever taken, but it would be substantial.

"We will exit ISG within the system, here," Jones painted a dot on the map and continued talking as if she had not proposed one of the riskiest maneuvers a *Sidus*-class was capable of. *Too long serving with Yardley*, Maker thought. "The majority of the fleet is on the distal side of the planet. We'll approach the attacking ships from the proximal side in order to drive a wedge in their formation and give our ground transports the opportunity to launch before they can react to our presence. I anticipate heavy damage to the *Khalid* and want every fighter out of the docks within twenty minutes of interstellar travel. Lieutenant Maker," Jones waved her forward and Maker stepped up beside the Captain's chair. "I reviewed the comms logs. You translated and anticipated the Culler action with a minimum thirteen-second lead on the James. Can you do that again?"

Maker could feel sweat starting to bead under her arms. *No pressure.* "Yes, ma'am."

"Good. Pull up comms on the ancillary console and provide support to the lt. commander and his second. We have one opportunity to surprise the enemy. Do not disappoint me, Lieutenant." The weight of Jones' gaze was heavy, and Maker felt for a moment as if every life on the *Khalid* rested there.

"Yes, Captain."

Jones turned back to the main display and addressed the entire bridge. "Get to work."

The ancillary console needed a few more repairs, and Maker did them herself so that the mechanic could move on to more complicated work. She was grateful for the distraction. There were few situations when anyone had viewed her ability with the Culler language as an asset, and Maker had a very short list of the number of times when she had come out of combat no worse off than she had gone in. Since she had been promoted to serve on the bridge, there had been many skirmishes, countless number of orbital support missions while ground troops had deployed, but never had she been asked to track and listen to so much alien chatter during combat. Her head was unusually clear, but she knew it was only a matter of time before it began to ache.

Her prediction became true within minutes of exiting ISG. A stray shot, intended for another target, sailed through what had been empty space to collide with the suddenly appearing *Khalid*.

"Friendly fire," Soon announced calmly as the impact alarm sounded. "Rail projectile to hull plating, exterior measures holding." At her back, Maker could hear the two comm officers and beyond them the rest of the bridge crew.

"Transports three, five, seven, and nine away. Docking bays fully open in eight seconds."

"*Emici* squadrons two and six prepped and ready. *Ictus* one through four have launched. Targeting enemy now." A display to the side of Maker's main screen mirrored the primary display. A flood of blue and green dots representing the *Khalid's* fighter craft swarmed into the empty space between the ship and the rest of the fleet. Culler ships lit up in yellow as weapons were locked in on them. Purple dots representing the transports moved toward the planet, bringing support troops to the ground battle.

"Two *Citrine* are turning, Captain."

"Aft guns prepped."

"The nearest *Red* first," Jones ordered. "Let's give that *Khutura*-class and the *Saladin* some breathing room. Fire." Maker pushed away the urge to open the *Saladin's* comms and check on her cousin's ship. Instead, she restricted her comm bands, isolating the frequencies the Cullers used. With a brush of her hands, the fringe frequencies – used during emergencies and for restricted communications – were pulled out and set to background noise. Everything else she closed down, leaving the two bridge officers to monitor those.

The chatter was not as overwhelming as she had anticipated. Although multiple ships were sending out communications at the same time, they followed a logical pattern rather than the jumble of voices and data packets each Coalition ship emitted. Still, the familiar shriek and grate started a throb at the base of her skull. Whether it was actual pain or anticipatory, it hurt all the same.

Human reinforcements have arrived.

Where there is one, there will be more.

Retask to destroy?

Maintain pressure on the defenses.

Target the refineries. Maximum casualties.

On the surface, Culler troops spoke less, but their conversation was more chilling.

Leave the dead. Not fit to eat.

Humans moving ahead, some have survived.

Find them.

Flank them, disable the young to slow the herd.

For two hours Maker did her best to keep the *Khalid* a step ahead of the Culler movements. Aside from two persistent *Citrine* that the *Ictus* kept busy, they were mostly ignored by the enemy who only increased their efforts to break through the Coalition line. Jones continued to order aggressive attacks, but the only gains the *Khalid* made were the successful launches of troop transports. Maker's eyes were beginning to feel the strain. The pressure in her head was building, but she grit her teeth and focused. Thousands of her fellow soldiers would die. Hundreds had already died in a single day. Her headache was nothing in comparison. She turned down the volume on the enemy comms just for a moment to give her ears a break. Maker pressed the heels of her hands to her forehead, willing the pain away so that she could concentrate again.

"The colonel is in position," the lead comms officer said behind her. "Captain, she is requesting a direct channel."

"Go ahead."

Maker watched out of the corner of her eye as Jones took the call on the main display. Ben-Zvi looked tough enough to chew glass, but her backdrop was chaos. Hastily erected medical structures were overflowing with wounded. Coalition soldiers huddled in groups, dirty and slumped with exhaustion. Those that had made it to the surface before the blockade were a sharp contrast to the fresh troops Ben-Zvi commanded. Her companies were setting up new defenses and organizing attack groups.

"The Cullers knew just where to hit," Ben-Zvi began without greeting. "Estimated death toll on the residents is at four hundred thousand. Preliminary numbers put the refugees from the moons at twenty thousand." No one dared to interrupt, but there were several sharp inhales among those listening. Navi-II and its moons had a population of almost three quarters of a million civilians. Half were already dead. "We are currently hemmed in at the rally point. To the west is our extraction location. I can defend it with what I have – even if we lose orbital defense – until reinforcements arrive from Sol. But it will mean abandoning the pass and the technetium stockpiles and refineries on the other side. If there are any more survivors, they'll never make it through the Cullers in those mountains."

"You have ground command, Colonel. Be advised, the *Khalid* will continue to try to break the offensive, but we are making little headway. Do not anticipate any ships becoming available for evac. If you need an airstrike, we will do our best, but consider the *Khalid* and your forces to be on their own."

"Very good. My decision stands, Captain. Coordinates..."

Through the muffled screams of Cullers, a whisper, a regular crackle of static caught Maker's attention. She sorted through the comm lines, looking for it. It could have been interference. The computer wasn't identifying it as anything else, but it didn't sound right to her. The fuzz and pulse of the signal were smoother. Almost lyrical in cadence. She muted all but the wide-band Culler comms and pulled apart each of the ancillary frequencies. Her fingers danced across the display as she worked.

There. Found you, she thought with satisfaction.

Right on the edge of the Coalition spectrum was a single ship-to-surface comm. It was encrypted, but the code looked familiar. The *Khalid* shook with a direct impact from a laser cannon. Maker needed to return to monitoring the enemy, but the back of her neck was tingling.

"Maker to C&E," she opened the line even as she turned up the other channels. The new signal she held open as well, passively listening.

"C&E Lead here, go ahead." Maker recognized the voice and

double-checked it against the computer's notification.

"Sergeant, I am sending you a signal that needs cleaned up. Break it using the attached cryp file. This is a top priority."

He hesitated, "Data packages?"

Maker knew what he was asking. The coded information from the rest of the fleet was always the first priority for the department. It was what the captain based decisions on regarding which ships to support and which to write off as too costly to save. Overriding that directive could be a court-marshal offense. The ache behind her eyes dulled; the hairs on the back of her neck rose.

"On my authorization. Maker-Four-Zero-Seven-Tango-One. I need a clean signal yesterday, Sergeant."

"You'll have it." He closed the comm, and she went back to her own job.

"Tactical! Urchin squad turning on our port side, one hundred thirty thousand clicks! They're covering an Amber – repositioning to coordinates...sending to you now." Maker fed the information to the weapons and comms stations. Comms retasked *Ictus* to intercept the Amber while tactical focused on the new enemy fighters coming at the *Khalid*.

"Lieutenant Maker," Soon sent updated maps to her display. "I need a read on these two ships. Picking up increased heat signatures."

Maker focused on the signals coming from those ships. "Reserve soldiers...Transports repaired..." She closed all but a single ship comm and the ancillary line to get rid of background noise.

...distract. Maximum devastation. Complete loss acceptable.

Enemy command identified. Destroy.

"They're sending more troops to the surface. And-"

"Comms, get me the reserves. I want the remaining *Emici* launched and those transports brought down. Full-"

"Wait!" Maker spun around and interrupted Jones, but she didn't have time to second guess the outburst. "They've isolated the *Saladin* and intend to take her out."

"You're certain?"

"They've been looking for the command ship. They say they've found it and are targeting it now. Expecting heavy losses on their side."

"Helm," Jones snapped, "find me a course through this mess to the *Saladin*. Comms, notify Captain Eumaeus to prepare for assault. Tactical-"

A tone in her ear notified Maker of a waiting message. The sergeant had come through. She opened the file and read through the transcript as decryption ran on the active ancillary line.

"...damaged. Require repairs to short range weapons."

"Papa-Hotel this is Team Leader. What is your position status?"

"Undetected, Team Leader. Do you require immediate assistance?"

"Negative, Papa-Hotel. Remain-"

The recording cut out with the sound of heavy artillery and the dissonant screams of humans and Cullers. Maker watched the signal in real time even as she opened a link to the sensors station. Soon and his second chair had not been scanning for additional Coalition signatures, but a broad system sweep when the *Khalid* first exited ISG would have been performed automatically. She raced through readouts searching for anything out of place. The enemy ships were still ordering new positions, but Maker downgraded those feeds to text only so she could concentrate – relying instead on the James to alert her to threats.

Navi-II had three moons. Two were on the distal side of the planet. One of those had been immolated, the atmosphere set on fire by the Cullers – killing everyone on the surface. The other was barely holding its orbit after intense bombing and would need artificial stabilization to keep from breaking apart over the next few years. The third moon was currently between the planet and its suns. It was tapped out for resource extraction, and the small outpost there had been evacuated early in the invasion – leaving it mostly untouched by enemy fire. On the opposite side of the moon from the *Khalid* was a nearly dark heat signature. Maker highjacked a small portion of sensors, praying Soon wouldn't notice, and ran a new scan even as the ancillary line came to life again.

"Papa-Hotel, this is Team Leader." Gravel and glass tumbling over themselves. A deep voice that demanded respect. Maker would have recognized it anywhere. "Break position and provide orbital support to these coordinates." Numbers flashed across her display, and Maker began decoding reflexively. "Full spread."

"Team Leader this is Papa-Hotel. Coordinates received." There was a pause. "Appears to localize on your signal, Team Leader." Sensors confirmed it was a Coalition ship, a *Cicuta* class. It did not have any match in the registry.

He ignored the question and Maker felt her stomach flip uncomfortably. If the *Cicuta* fired where he directed, he would be targeted as well. That class didn't have the precision of a gun ship like the *Khalid.* "Papa-Hotel. Begin count of ten minutes on my mark. Mark."

Maker redirected the sensors to the planet's surface, looking for the coordinates of the air strike. It was covered in dense vegetation. A few miles to the West, a massive heat signature was closing. The speed and movement could only indicate

Cullers. Maker focused on the coordinates again. It required a lot of processing power, too much to go unnoticed by an officer as perceptive as Soon, but she had to know. The computer picked up anomalies in the vegetation and stripped away the image to see what was underneath. Maker had to dig her fingers into the console to keep from falling in shock. Thousands, maybe tens of thousands of people were hiding in that forest. The Team Leader would be with them.

He was Legion. She knew that, had known it since RB-14 when he saved her during the sand storm. Known it since she heard his voice over the comms. Cold. Professional. Efficient. She had seen his unit do incredible things – things no other Coalition soldiers could have done. Things not even the Raiders could have pulled off. They had destroyed the Culler base on VK10 and given the ground troops enough time to pull out. They had defeated a hoard of attacking enemies on RB-14 and saved her people.

Ben-Zvi and the Coalition were going to abandon the pass. The civilians stranded on the other side, cowering under the cover of a forest, would be left to face the Cullers alone. They would be slaughtered.

*Unless...*unless the Legion could save them. It wouldn't be enough to merit support from the *Khalid*, but the technetium stockpiles might be. The element was incredibly rare in the Sol system and essential in the processing and manufacture of plastisteel and ship plating. Losses would be in the trillions – worth more to the Coalition than civilian lives.

"Maker!" Soon's voice whipped across the bridge like a physical knife, cutting into her thoughts. "What the hell do you think you're doing? Get out of my sensors!" He tried to lock her out, but Maker sprang into action, capturing the data at her station.

"Lieutenant," Jones began with a scowl.

"Captain, there are-" Her defense was cut off by Soon.

"Urchins six hundred thousand clicks and closing! Coming around the far side of the planet. Tactical, conf- Coalition ship! *Cicuta* class, maneuvering from behind the moon."

"Comms, notify them of the incoming Urchins. Sensors, sweep the battle again. Helm, I want to be moving in five, the *Saladin-*"

"Captain," Maker interrupted again, "That *Cicuta* has no short-range weapons."

"Are you questioning the captain's orders, Lieutenant?" Giradot was the one to ask, and Maker barely managed not to snarl at him. She was nearly certain he had interfered with the array outside Alnitak – or at least knew who had. Falling in behind an intelligence officer who was shadier than most was the last thing she wanted to do.

"Yes," she spat. The bridge fell quiet, despite the battle raging around the *Khalid.* Maker felt the blood drain from her face as the Captain slowly turned her chair. "There is additional intel, captain," she spoke as quickly as she could. "Special ops units are on the ground, opposite the colonel on the pass. They have the opportunity to evacuate twelve thousand civilians and protect the technetium reserves but are awaiting air support from that *Cicuta.* Without it, the reserves will be lost."

"Sensors," Jones spoke quietly, eyes narrow. "Verify."

A bead of sweat rolled down Maker's chest, making her twitch. Urchins were closing on the *Cicuta*; the clock was running down to the air strike.

"Verified." Soon reported. Maker exhaled. "Between ten and fifteen thousand signatures are trapped between the pass and a rapidly approaching front of Cullers."

"How many?" Jones' eyes never left Maker's.

"Too closely grouped for accuracy. Computer estimates forty

thousand."

Tactical let out a startled huff of shock, but it was Giradot who spoke, "Even if the lieutenant is correct no unit will survive against that number. It is a waste of our resources."

"They will." Maker ignored the stares and sidelong glances from the rest of the bridge crew and focused on the Captain.

"Urchins will make contact in four minutes." No one responded to Soon's update.

That leaves another four minutes for Papa-Hotel to wipe them out with weapons they don't have and provide the air strike that won't be accurate enough, Maker thought desperately.

"Are you clairvoyant as well as a translator, Lieutenant? You have no way to back that claim." Giradot dismissed her. "Captain, the *Saladin*?"

"Two Ambers and a Red have targeted the *Saladin*!"

"Signals have been blocked. *Saladin* is out of contact!"

"Course plotted, Captain. Ready on your order." The primary helmsman remained focused, but the secondary turned to wait for the captain's acknowledgment. Jones was still staring at Maker.

Maker had no idea if she could convince Jones, but she had to try. "That unit is black ops, ma'am. Give them the assist and they will succeed."

"What unit?" Giradot's eyes snapped to Maker, his posture tightening with anticipation.

"Ma'am," Maker scrambled for anything that could persuade her, "it's classified, but-"

"What unit?" Giradot demanded.

"*Saladin* is taking fire! Hull holding, for now."

"Plotted course is closing, Captain," the helm warned. "Two minutes!"

"Give me something, Lieutenant," Jones said softly.

"I- may I speak to you privately, Captain?"

Giradot made a sound of disbelief. Soon growled in fury. Jones ignored them both and surged out of her chair. She snapped out as she walked to her ready room, "You have sixty seconds, Lieutenant."

Maker barely remembered to secure her station before she ran after the Captain. The door closed behind her with a hiss of the lock. Jones crossed behind the conference table and poured herself a glass of water. "Fifty-one seconds, Lieutenant."

"The unit. It's the Legion." Maker felt like a weight had fallen from her. At the same time her stomach heaved and her mouth filled with spit in preparation to vomit. The realization of what she was doing, of all that rode on the next minute, was overwhelming. She reached out and squeezed the back of a chair, leaning on it for support. Jones turned, her expression carefully blank.

"Keres Legion?"

"Yes. Their leader is on the surface, organizing the retreat of the civilians. He called in orbital support from the *Cicuta*, but their short-range weapons were damaged. They won't stand a chance against the Urchins, and without the air strike his position will be overwhelmed."

"How sure are you that it is the Legion?" Her finger tapped against the clear water glass, making the liquid inside ripple from the vibration.

The back of Maker's neck tingled with a cool brush of air. "Positive."

"Why?"

That question pulled Maker up short. *Because I've heard that voice before. Because it was the lifeline I needed when I thought I would die. Because it gave me hope when I would have given up and then it followed through on that promise. Because he saved me when he didn't have to. Malak. Because I know.* She refused to give voice to those thoughts, the illogical certainty that whispered the truth in her brain. Carefully, she spoke, "I intercepted the Team Leader's signal on VK-10."

"This is the person who ordered the evac?"

"Yes. Yardley told me not to report it." Jones nodded, clearly remembering the farce she and Soon had participated in. "Then at RB14-"

"It was the Legion?" Jones cut in. "The Legion defended the base there?"

"Not defended. They were there on another mission, I think. Two squadrons. Two. Against all those enemies."

"No bodies were recovered among the Cullers. Are you saying they took no losses?" Maker nodded and Jones set down her glass with a clink. "Either you are a liar who should be executed for the damage you are trying to cause in this war, or I am to believe that some exceptionally gifted elite operators are capable of working miracles."

"Only if miracles involve severed spines." Maker belatedly added a measure of respect, "Ma'am."

Precious seconds passed and neither woman said anything. Maker was ready to admit defeat when Jones finally moved, stepping around the table and past her. She followed the Captain back out onto the bridge. "Sensors, keep an eye on the *Saladin*. Helm, plot an intercept course for that *Cicuta*. Tactical, take down those Urchins."

"Captain-" Giradot began.

"Lieutenant Maker," Jones continued as if she hadn't heard her Chief Intelligence Officer, "Get that ground unit on the line. Confirm coordinates for orbital support."

"Yes, Captain." The *Khalid* had far superior firepower to a *Cicuta* and would be able to target with more precision. Maker slipped on her headset and pulled up the ancillary comm line again. "Team Leader, this is *Khalid*-niner, come in." Maker waited half the time she normally would for a response, knowing that they were cutting things close. The *Khalid* was already repositioning. Short-range weapons were focused on the Urchins and tactical had locked firing solutions.

"Team Leader, this is *Khalid*-niner. Papa-Hotel is taking fire. We are moving to assist. Confirm coordinates as requested." The line was open and live, but he did not respond. Irrationally, Maker felt anger rising. Twice she had tried to help the Legion. On RB14 she had saved his life. The Culler whose skull she had crushed with her own helmet would have gutted the Team Leader if she hadn't been there. The least he could do was respond. *For fuck's sake.* "Malak! Confirm the damn coordinates!"

She practically shouted into her mic, and she knew the other bridge officers were staring. Her breath was coming fast, fear and adrenaline mixing with the responsibility for changing the captain's mind. *God, we should have gone to the* Saladin. *They could be destroyed. Seamus is on board. He could die. The battle-*

"*Khalid*," his voice rolled over the comm like a dark wave of tumbled stone. Maker closed her eyes for a moment, letting the relief wash through her. "This is Team Leader. Sending confirmation now."

Maker decrypted the data as quickly as possible and fed it to sensors and tactical. An Urchin crashed into the *Khalid's* hull, making the ship rock slightly as the kinetic shielding reacted.

"Put it on the main display," Jones ordered. Maker turned to watch an image of the surface, the pale green of the forest where the Legion was protecting civilians was dwarfed by the massive red heat signature of the Culler front. "Fire."

CHAPTER 5: WAG THE DOG

ResQFoam^{TM}. Noun. An expanding medical foam designed to stabilize wounds and allow continued activity after trauma-induced hemorrhage. Generic versions issued to Coalition troops are often pejoratively called WuSS Foam, i.e., Wound Stabilization System.

Hour 1030
May 6, 2156

More than twenty-four hours had passed since the *Garrote* and the *Scythe* had landed on Navi-II. An entire day, and all Malak had to show for it was a hole in his calf, a dislocated knee, and eighteen thousand human civilians. *Seven kilometers.* He snarled to himself in his helmet, knowing Hanako was the only person close enough to hear on the proximity comm. Seven kilometers in twenty-four hours. The humans moved at a snail's pace, limping along with injured and children, easily frightened. It was everything the Legion could do to keep them from scattering completely whenever an Urchin strike or Culler-led attack came too close.

Malak snarled again and braced his leg against the crumbled wall of a building. His people had taken out nearly ten thousand Cullers during that time without a single casualty, but injuries were mounting and ammunition was running low. He had been forced to resort twice to calling in an air strike from the *Pale Horse*. Although Smierc had successfully carried out his orders without drawing the attention of the Coalition fleet, the Cullers had noticed and responded. The *Pale Horse* had taken fire during the second orbital support run, and technicians were still making repairs to the *Cicuta*-class ship.

Malak pressed one hand against each side of his knee and forced his weight onto the joint. The ball of his lower leg slammed into the socket on his femur with jarring intensity. He ground his teeth through the pain, ignoring it in favor of sheer frustration. The bulk of the Culler force had been waylaid in the settlement and the mountains to the north, but not even the Legion would be able to hold them there much longer. Twenty-four hours and he had moved the humans seven kilometers. There was another thirteen to go to reach the pass. It was disgraceful. Disgusting. Damned infuriating. Hanako offered him an injection from her med kit, and he waved her off. His own stims and meds had already been spent on civilians to keep them alert and moving. *Wasteful.*

If this latest mission to protect humans had taught him anything, it was that they were desperately in need of assistance, and probably not worth the cost. Malak checked his display for the next target. He plotted out a course that would take Hanako and himself through a thick band of the enemy, relieving pressure from the forward line, but the Cullers were once again gaining ground and surging out ahead of the Legion advance. It was to be expected, considering their sheer numbers and physical adaptations to run over rough terrain. That did not mean Malak had to accept it.

"This is Team Leader. Papa-Hotel, come in." He sent the attack plan to Hanako and reloaded his Klim with additional slag rounds.

"This is Papa-Hotel-actual. Team Leader, go ahead."

"Orbital support requested. Sending coordinates now." Malak began to run, ignoring the one-lane road that led into the forested area and instead utilized the destroyed buildings at the edge of the settlement to conceal his movements.

"This is Papa-Hotel. Coordinates received."

"Fire at will."

A jagged line of Cullers was moving through the debris, searching for survivors and killing anything they found. Malak slammed bodily into the first in the row, catching it by surprise and forcing it into the next one five meters away. He toggled for incendiary rounds and fired while he remained in position, his bruised knee on the ground and his other foot braced for support. Hanako followed him at a run. She carried a salvaged Culler shock staff, and she braced the butt in the ground even as one booted foot connected with his thigh. She pole vaulted through the air, feet first, and met the fifth enemy with the soles of her shoes. Malak came after her, using one projectile to end Cullers one and two, and ignored the next two that had been caught in the incendiary blast. Hanako had already moved on as he passed the crushed remains of a Culler skull. She had braced her own knee in the dirt and was providing cover fire as Malak approached; he used her for a springboard just as she had done with him, sailing through the air to topple the Culler line.

A high-pitched whistle, nearly painful to his ears, was the only warning before heavy artillery from the *Pale Horse* impacted the surface. A wide swath of buildings and a large section of a mountain collapsed into a crater. Four more strikes followed, each punctuated by the maddened, pained shrieks of dying Cullers. Two additional missiles should have hit, but did not.

Malak launched his service blade at a Culler that broke formation to charge him but kept his position on one knee, waiting for Hanako to repeat the leap frog across the enemy. He shot two more before her boot pushed off against his thigh.

"This is Papa-Hotel. Team Leader, come in." There was background noise on the comm signal. Malak rolled to dodge a Culler that had crawled over the roof of the northern most building to drop down on his position. A talon slashed at the dirt where his head had been moments before.

"Go ahead," he grunted. He fired a slag round, but the enemy slipped in the blood of Malak's previous kill. Pink juices mixed with the pale dirt and stuck to his armor suit, interfering with some of the sensors.

"Taking enemy fire. Long-range weapons down. ISG down. Short-range weapons at sixty-two percent."

"Pull back," he ordered, even as he met the screeching Culler's upraised talon with the muzzle of his Klim. He pulled the trigger point blank against the joint between talon and arm. The projectile blew through exoskeleton, sinew, and bone to explode out the back of the limb and burrow into the torso. The Culler thrashed wildly, catching the curve of Malak's helmet with the opposite talon and throwing him off balance. Malak moved with the force, gripping the shoulder on the injured side of the alien, using it as a fulcrum to swing around. As the Culler fell he let go, focusing on his next target.

"Engage the enemy and prioritize engine repairs. Send notification when complete."

"Understood. Papa-Hotel out."

Hanako had cleared the rest of the line, and she rejoined him as he collected his knife and cleaned it. One side of her suit was tacky with grayish pink ichor.

"Sensors are malfunctioning," he noted. "Yours?"

"Spotty." She pulled up a handful of grass and used it to wipe splatter from her helmet. "We're out of high ground, sir. The orbital support has given us some breathing room, and the clearance team is currently circling back around to regroup and move again. Orders?"

Malak toggled back to his map. He and Hanako were between

the forest and the settlement while the clearance team had been sweeping along the northern edge, just below the mountains. Cullers had infiltrated the rocky terrain, using their agility to their advantage. They couldn't move in very large groups, but the high ground combined with the element of surprise was dangerous to the humans plodding along just to the south. Team One was giving up ground to the advancing main force, but they were making the Cullers pay for every step. Every fifty meters that the enemy advanced, they lost dozens to pressure sensitive mines and precision strike Legionaries. At the rate the humans were moving, it would take another three days to hit the pass. Malak's people were good, but even they needed ammo and a few hours rest to keep up a defense against those numbers.

"Call in Team One. I want them back here double time to set up a perimeter defense system at the edge of this forest. We'll use the cover to our advantage and buy Smierc time to make repairs."

"Yes, sir."

At the top of the hour, Malak and Hanako circled back to meet with Team One, providing relief as they set traps for the pursuing Cullers, then returned to the rear guard for the humans. Relief from the blackness of night under the leafy canopy was just beginning as Malak threaded through the tall white columns.

"Report." He paused at the knoll of a small hill, looking down over the retreating mass of engineers and technicians, geologists, metallurgists, chemists, and what was left of their families. The dulled black of Af's helmet was visible in the distance, a sharp contrast to the bare heads and shorter stature of those around her. Hanako fell to one knee at his side, protecting his back.

"We've lost twenty-three more to injuries. The ground here is too soft; each time we have to dip into a valley they are sinking into swamp. What the bacteria in the water isn't infecting, the fish are biting into. I estimate we have dropped our pace again."

Malak was aware of the problem. His own boots and suit were coated in slimy muck up to his knees. Only the sporadic, small hills gave relief from the exhausting work of trudging through the mud. He braced one palm against a column. The sensors in his suit were only half-functioning, but they projected an analysis of the structure onto his display. Oydroxapatite, calcium, phosphate, potassium chlorate. Trace amounts of magnesium, sodium, cesium, technetium. Composition analysis suggested organic osseous tissue.

Bone. Columns he had assumed were stone or petrified wood were actually bone. Malak surveyed the area again. Their placement wasn't random but they were positioned in what might have been curved rows, interrupted only where another row intersected, as though one enormous animal had fallen on top of another and been left in place to decay. Plant matter had taken over at some point, utilizing the structures to climb toward the sun, creating a grave of leaves.

"Suggestions for faster movement?"

It was Hemah who responded with a sigh. "Unless we can get on firmer ground, they aren't going to move faster. I could *carry* a human quicker than they walk."

Malak pulled up the map on his display while Af spoke, "They can't take another night under here, sir. Their clothing can't compete against the lower temperatures."

Another two kilometers ahead, the bone forest had been cleared to make room for refineries and storage units. The area would provide cover and allow the humans to rest and regroup before pushing the final distance to the pass. It pained Malak to even think it, but he needed more soldiers. Even a few human companies would have been an enormous help in securing the exit for the civilians. Gunnar's comm line activated.

"Team Leader, enemy is congregating in mountains to your north. Appear to be staging for an assault. Permission to engage?"

"Negative." Malak had to bite off a snarl. He knew Gunnar wanted to go after the Cullers and kill them where they stood. Malak wanted the same, but if the Legion was drawn farther from the forest, they wouldn't be able to maintain a secure perimeter. "Maintain distance. Paint targets and set munitions for assault defense." A data packet, patchy and too encrypted to have been sent directly from the *Pale Horse*, was received by his comm unit. Malak verified its security and ran decryption. New orders from Thomas. There were three scientists among the civilians that were to be protected at all costs. Images of two were included, but the third had been corrupted by the radiation from the system star. Malak spit out a curse in his helmet and growled as well. Thomas' tone implied he wasn't happy about the directive or having it issued so late into the mission. That did not console Malak.

He should have known. The Coalition had lied, to Thomas, to the Legion – to him. They would not have sent their most elite units just to save civilians – no matter the number. No, the Coalition had risked Malak's people to save *three* humans. This was why the Cullers were poised to win the war. The Coalition cared less for their survival and success than they did for petty politics.

"Sir," to her credit Hanako did not flinch at his growl, "I'm picking up movement behind our position. Estimated time until Culler engagement, two hours."

He signaled to Af and Hemah. "Get them up," he bit out. "Get them moving along this line." Malak sent new coordinates that would lead the group to the firm ground at the edge of the bone forest – within range of strikes from the mountains. "Double time." He stalked though the crowds of humans, ignoring the way so many flinched from his path – and so many more called out thanks and sought reassurance. He did not respond to any of them. His display flashed when he pinged the personal communicator of one of the three scientists.

"Where is Dr. Patay?" His low question had nearby humans pulling away from him. The scientist answered in a trembling voice.

"He was still in the lab when the first strike hit. I thought he got out, but we haven't seen him."

Malak breathed deeply through the filtration system in his helmet. The damp mud and rotted vegetation of the swampy ground reminded him of Culler flesh. The stink of unwashed, frightened humans was strong. The female scientist was sweating, despite the chill in the air. She smelled bitter, like cortisol and epinephrine. *Lies.* It didn't matter; it was no more than Malak should have expected. He spun away, grinding his back teeth together in an effort not to turn and snap at the weak little woman. He considered, for a brief, enjoyable moment, turning and shooting her. No more lies. No more orders.

"Team Leader, this is Papa-Hotel. We are secure, but there is increased Coalition activity in the near vicinity. The hull has been moderately damaged. Still require repairs to short range weapons."

"Papa-Hotel this is Team Leader. What is your position status?"

"Undetected, Team Leader. Do you require immediate assistance?"

"Negative, Papa-Hotel. Remain at your location. Connect me to Falcon support." He reached Hanako at the same time that the humans began to move. With a signal, she followed him back toward the Culler line.

"Team Leader, this is Falcon support. Go ahead."

Malak transmitted the chemical composition of the bone

forest and what his sensors had identified about the area. "Suggestions?"

There was a long pause while the tech looked through the data. "Suggestions for what?"

"Munitions."

"Oh. Ah. Just a…"

A stray Culler emerged from over a small hill twelve meters away. Malak did not hesitate to launch his tomahawk, separating the jaw from the chest and dropping the alien. Hanako had already moved ahead, taking out another scout, before the technician spoke again.

"Definitely flammable," the tech finally confirmed. Malak retrieved his weapon and skirted around Hanako, moving in alternating sweeps with her to poke holes in the Culler offense. "I'd estimate one hit from an orbital cannon would take out about a kilometer radius on initial impact – within the first ninety seconds. Secondary fires and structural collapse would increase the damage significantly over time. Depending on local wind and-" Malak cut the comm and checked his map. The brief rest had helped the civilians; they were moving faster and didn't have far to go before they would all be in the narrow, rocky clearing between the mountains and the forest. His sensors flickered as he silently cursed the sticky cling of Culler fluids and mud that interfered with his technology.

With additional soldiers - another hundred Legionnaires or three hundred experienced humans - he could draw the Cullers deeper into the forest and maintain adequate protection for the escaping civilians. He didn't have another hundred Legionnaires. He didn't have even one to spare – and he certainly wasn't going to waste any of his people on protecting the Coalition's scared scientists. Every one of his soldiers would be necessary for the mission to be successful. Malak knew that, and he understood the ramifications.

"Hanako," he spoke through the proximity comm, and she severed the nerve core of another Culler before giving him her full attention. "Maintain rear patrol, within three hundred meters of the retreat." He double-checked his ammo stores and pulled his tomahawk and service knife. "On my signal, order Af and Hemah to break cover and make for the refineries. Team One will meet you there and work with Team Two as you continue to the pass."

"Sir," she began, but he cut her off by opening a line to the rest of the Legion ground forces.

"Hanako has command until further notice. Team Leader out." He nodded to her, and she returned the gesture before crouching and gracefully leaping to the next hill, continuing northeast to follow the civilians. Malak turned the opposite direction.

It was dark under the thick canopy, and the setting sun made the shadows longer and heavier. Malak breathed deeply, controlled. Cullers used shadows to their advantage. Their quick movements and uncanny ability to sense their enemy scared human soldiers. The fear was born from the humans' personal experience, but the Legion – they had been created in the minds of men. And the mind was capable of producing terrors far greater than existed in the universe. Malak was everything that human beings found frightening. They had named his ancestors from their oldest fears.

Barghest. Hellhound. Grim. Death.

This was his purpose. Malak let the responsibilities of his position slide away: the fury over the Coalition's obfuscation, the disgust at the wasteful tactics of the military, the weight of his duty to protect his own. He rolled his shoulders, adjusted his grip on his weapons. This was his purpose. To kill.

Adrenaline began to pump through his veins as he ran. Sensors picked up a cluster of the enemy seconds before he was upon them. They were moving along a narrow stream of water, picking their way through the mud on limbs well-suited to difficult terrain. Malak jumped straight down, bringing his boot into the eye socket of the middle Culler in the group of five. He used the body as firm ground, planting his heel and kicking out with his other foot to knock aside a shock staff. That one stumbled backward, running into the last enemy in the line. The Cullers shrieked. Malak spun, hearing the crunch of exoskeleton under his boot. He planted his weight again and then lunged forward. His momentum carried his service knife in a slashing motion up the inner thigh of the creature. It screamed and fell, talons thrashing, but Malak met the closest elbow joint with his tomahawk, severing it cleanly.

He pushed forward again, digging his knee into its chest – directly above the nerve cluster. It went limp and Malak rolled with it, landing in water but keeping to his feet and managing to duck under the swing of another shock weapon. He used the weight of the small ax to balance himself and flicked up his right hand, lancing the alien at the hip socket. Once the tip of his blade was under the outer shell, he twisted and pulled up, slicing through the thick artery there and cracking the bony covering until the lower portion ripped away. Pink ichor sprayed across his face plate.

Malak did not wait to watch it collapse, but turned again. The last two Cullers had regained their footing and were charging, their shrieks echoed by other groups farther away. Malak's James reported that they were calling for reinforcements. He sheathed his tomahawk and met the shock staff with his gloved hand, grasping it near the center of the shaft and throwing his weight into it. The Culler predictably lifted the weapon to try and shake him off, and Malak jumped to follow the movement. As he flipped over the Culler's head, he slammed his knife into its eye. The last Culler ducked Malak's boots but was too slow to turn around before he had landed behind it. He threaded his arm around the Culler's bicep, under the arm and behind its back, gripping under the edge of its opposite jaw in a modified arm bar. It struggled, slashing out with its free talon, but Malak stepped onto the reverse knee joint and used the additional height to fling himself to the side, tearing the arm loose and cracking a portion of the bony covering on its face. As it fell, it cast the attached talon wide, seeking to stab Malak. Instead it sank into the still breathing chest of the Culler that had been directly in front of it. Both were mortally injured.

Malak retrieved his knife and surged up the farther bank of the stream, deeper into the Culler lines. He didn't stop to rest, didn't pause except to verify position and approaching heat signatures. He just killed. For thirty minutes he moved farther from the rest of the Legion, the shrieks of dying and angry Cullers in his wake. His James confirmed they were flooding the forest, homing in on his location and swarming to surround him. His sensors continued to short out, made worse by additional damage he had taken. Between eight thousand and twenty-five thousand Cullers had packed into the forest, encompassing him. He crouched behind the protection of a moss-covered fallen bone and one of the standing structures.

"Papa-Hotel, this is Team Leader." He didn't wait for acknowledgment. "Break position and provide orbital support to these coordinates." Malak sent his own location up to Smierc. "Full spread." If one shot would take out a kilometer radius, a full spread should decimate everything - from the outpost all the way to where the civilians were retreating.

"Team Leader this is Papa-Hotel. Coordinates received -" there was a pause, " - appears to localize on your signal, Team Leader."

Malak knew what Smierc was saying. *You won't survive.* He knew the chances were slim. He had already considered it a hundred times since he had left Hanako. It wasn't suicide. Malak wanted to live, to lead his people in the defeat of their enemy. There was a chance, a very small chance, that he could outrun the blast but it was all he could get with the resources available. "Papa-Hotel. Begin count of ten minutes on my mark. Mark." Malak cut the transmission and fired two incendiary rounds into the nearest Culler group before standing and moving. His heart beat steadily; his breath came easily. He ignored the pain from the hole in his calf and the strain on his muscles from the prolonged fight. He ignored the stitch in his side from a broken rib and the pull on his forearm from a long, shallow talon cut that his armor had sealed. He needed to move.

"Team Leader, this is *Khalid*-niner, come-in."

Malak's steps faltered. He knew that voice. The stumble cost him a few precious moments, and a Culler closed on his left. He fired his last slag round and regained his footing. *She should not be here*, he thought. *She should not be able to break into our comms. Again.* Malak picked up speed to jump across a narrow draw, tossing a frag grenade below him. The explosion and strangled screams followed as he continued to run. He snorted to himself, almost, but not quite, amused. *Where else would that fool be but where she doesn't belong?*

"Team Leader, this is *Khalid*-niner. Papa-Hotel is taking fire. We are moving to assist. Confirm coordinates as requested."

The *Khalid* was a *Sidus*-class. It would have superior targeting and fire power to the *Pale Horse*. If the *Khalid* performed the bombardment, it would increase his chances by as much as eighteen percent. But he would have to break comm silence.

Malak could hear the snap in her voice, the demand for a response. He pivoted around a dense clump of bones and charged straight into fourteen Cullers. He was moving too fast to stop and knocked down the closest enemy with his momentum. There was no time to deal with them individually; the countdown on his display reminded him of a definitive deadline. Malak did not wait, but pushed forward, ramming his fist into the elbow joint of the second Culler and shooting a third. He snapped two knees and lost his tomahawk to a tangle of carapace and talons before he was free, flinging his last grenade over his shoulder and sprinting northeast and away from the blast site.

The flashing taste of her frustration ghosted across his tongue before her voice shouted into his comm. "Malak! Confirm the damn coordinates!"

It was the second time she had used his name. Malak skirted two lines of aliens scouting through the forest and had to remind himself that they would die even if it wasn't at his hand. He wondered how she had come by that information. She had cracked the encryption on his comms; there could have been a number of other security breeches. *She is a risk.* To herself and the Legion if she had any details about their mission. He could not deny, however, that while she was abysmal at physical combat, she had shown high aptitude with tech, and her unusual tactics had worked in the past.

"*Khalid.*" Again, he could almost hear her shoulders relaxing, smell the rush of serotonin in her relief. He pulled up the coordinates and re-sent them, this time to her directly. "This is Team Leader. Sending confirmation now." He estimated he was still a full click from the outer limits of the bombardment and increased his speed. There was a line of the enemy between him and his destination. Malak altered course, running up a small hill and jumping for a broken shaft sixteen feet off the ground. From there he sprung up to slam his feet into a standing bone, feeling the shudder and give of it beneath him. The Cullers had seen him, were lifting their shock weapons and scrambling to follow him. He turned in midair, pointing his Klim back to the enormous bone that supported the forest canopy overhead, and fired.

He was expecting a flash and the collapse of that one structure – enough to hopefully distract and disorganize his pursuers. Instead, a shock wave caught him. His eyes were still open as his back slammed into another bone tree, breaking through it and flinging him farther. A wave of fire, white hot and roaring, chewed through the forest. When he hit the next tree, his kinetic gel failed, and he blacked out to the sounds of Culler screams and the smell of burning rotten flesh.

CHAPTER 6: BEGAT

Oort Siege. Proper Noun. A series of Culler attacks against the Sol Coalition in 2090-2091. Culminated in the successful test of the Oort Defense Station System (ODSS). Nine weaponized space stations at the far edge of the Sol System were activated and utilized along with the Coalition Fleet to destroy six hundred twelve Culler ships. 1.6 billion human lives were lost. It is considered the second greatest success in the War, after the Expulsion.

Hour 0730
January 2, 2138

"I know, sweetheart, and I am so sorry I had to cancel our plans. These corporate negotiations are important to the coming budget, or I would have put them off. We'll do something special, just the two of us, when I get back."

"But it won't be my birthday anymore." Nine-year-old Clara Maker was bordering on whining, but the sad look in her big eyes demonstrated that she was truly upset. Helen nodded sympathetically at the video screen. Her trip had been scheduled for more than a year, and the plan had her inspecting progress at the *Project Jagd* facility and returning to Earth well in time for Clara's party. Unfortunately, even the most preciously calculated experiments were capable of developing unexpectedly. There had been technical issues with the artificial wombs, and so decanting the thirty-four series was delayed by nearly three weeks. Helen glanced out the window as the ship slowed and the gas giant Struve D came into view. It was several factors larger than Jupiter and had hundreds of moons. The complex orbital interactions and debris ring would have made any pilot think twice before attempting to get close. It was an ideal location to hide a black book operation.

"So, really, it will be as though you have two birthdays this year. And that is not something to be sneezed at, is it?" Helen watched Clara nod, resignation coloring her good manners.

"Yes, Grandma."

"Wonderful, and if you check with your father, I believe the present I had messengered over-" there was a squeal from the other end of the call loud and high-pitched enough to make Helen's assistant look up and her personal security guard wince. "All right, that's enough. Have a good day, Clara."

"Thank you! Love you!" Clara made a kissey-face at the camera before the call ended.

"Everything all right, ma'am?" her assistant asked tentatively.

"Fine, fine." Helen waved her off and watched their destination draw closer. It was one of the larger moons, slightly smaller than Venus. The atmosphere was thick with dark purple-gray clouds. The main continent would be chilly and wet, and Helen had dressed accordingly in expensive wool trousers and matching sweater. Her thick coat and gloves lay on the seat beside her; she planned on touring the grounds of the facility while she was there. The landing procedure went smoothly, and within an hour Helen was escorted into a large office that had grown cluttered over the years. Dr. Martinez was watching a video feed as she came in.

"Madam Prime Minister, I apologize. We're in the middle of a test and-"

"No, please. I'm early. Don't let me interrupt." She set her bag and coat down and studied one of the many original drawings on the walls. The paper was old; the torn edge where it had been removed from an actual sketchbook was easy to see under the glass. A boy of nine or ten was crouched on the edge of a rock. His face was upturned, a look of intense excitement on his features and a long tail hovering in the air. It was quite good, and might have indicated a career in the arts for Dr. Martinez if all of her models hadn't been classified military property.

"I can have someone bring refreshments – are you on Sol Standard, or a local Earth time?"

"Sol Standard – too many years in Versailles." She moved on to another art piece while Martinez sent a message to her staff regarding a breakfast tray. The next image was a printout of a digital drawing. It was done in heavily saturated pigments, dark and moody in a style reminiscent of watercolors. A boy, his body wiry in the way of young teenagers, stood in the center of a semicircle. His face was set, his eyes dark and serious. Two other boys, one very tall and the other heavily muscled, stood to one side of him while two girls were on his right. The first had rich brown hair that melded into the shadows at their backs. Her shoulder blended with that of the center boy until their clothes and bodies meshed in washed out strokes. At the far side, slightly apart from the others, was a shorter girl with a long, red ponytail. Rather than listening to the center boy, her face was turned to the viewer. Her lips twisted in a smirk, and her green eyes seemed to glow.

A young person in generic professional clothing entered with a tray and left again. Helen poured herself a cup of tea and handed a coffee to the doctor.

"Oh, thank you, ma'am." She tucked a tablet under her arm and pointed to the video display with her cup. "You may be interested in this – they're coming up on the latest command test." The camera captured a wide swath of thick, grassy meadow that had been set up like an obstacle course. It took a moment for Helen to recognize the figure on screen; it was his tail that finally gave him away and reminded her of the reports she had read when *Project Barghest* was in its infancy.

"We have had some significant downtime while we wait for the decanting, so in addition to the commercial research we do to support the facility, I have authorized more work on a-" Martinez smiled to herself, "-pet project, so to speak. That is Bee out there now."

"From the..." Helen had to think for a moment, "twenty-two series?"

"Yes. They experienced some aggressive aging issues, but Bee was stabilized. He now ages similar to the average human. He is chronologically thirty-five." Although the man moved with an easy sort of grace – emphasized by the swish and flick of his tail – his appearance was that of a person in their seventies. Perhaps even older. "My predecessor, Dr. Gillian, was adamant that he and any other subjects deemed not viable, but stable, should still have a certain quality of life if we are able to provide it for them. Bee was an essential component to the training of series twenty-six through thirty, and is working with thirty-one through thirty-three now. I have hope that he will be able to continue to serve in that capacity for many years. But today-"

Bee made a sharp motion with his left hand and an explosion of grass and leaves streaked across the screen. Whatever was on the training field was moving too quickly for Helen to identify, but target dummies were knocked over in rapid succession as it approached Bee. A growling sound came over the feed and the thing abruptly stopped. Helen leaned closer to the screen.

"What is that?"

"Do you like it?" Martinez was smiling, obviously pleased with the results of whatever they had been testing. "It is a *Micas Immanis Minutus* – not the original species, of course, those are far too large and aggressive for our purposes. Gillian kept a small breeding pack at Erasmus Station for genetic samples. Once we finalized the sequencing for the Legion, we needed to find a new use for them under Project Jagd. Our xenobiologists felt they had been in captivity too long to be released into the wild."

"It is smaller than I imagined." It stood still and Helen could get a good look at the creature. Its head was even with Bee's bicep, and she estimated it weighed as much as a small pony. The fur was a creamy caramel. With its short snout, pointed ears, and forward jointed knees it looked like a cross between a jungle cat and a bear.

"Yes, that was part of our genetic modifications. We wanted them to be easier to handle and more economical – you wouldn't believe how much one of the full-size ones can eat." Martinez zoomed in on the two figures and put a finger to her communications implant, speaking quietly, "Bee." The man and animal both stiffened at the sound of his name. "Go ahead and start the game." She gestured for Helen to watch and spoke at a normal volume. "Pre-Invasion Earth forces often used animals as companions for soldiers. Trained them to search out bombs, guard buildings or units, attack and immobilize enemy combatants."

A pattern of low growls and huffs came over the feed.

"My great uncle was in the last Middle-Eastern conflict. He had a dog...a malinois, I believe."

"Then you're familiar with the utility. Really, this began as more of an effort to keep the staff occupied during downtime and give the subjects some exercise, but I think there will be some economical and valuable applications." On screen, a metal door set flush with the ground opened and a platform began to raise. Secured to the four-by-four area was a Culler. It was extremely angry and extremely violent. "We haven't tested on-command kills yet, so this will be interesting." She tapped on her tablet and the restraints fell away from the alien's legs and talons. It shrieked and dug in its lower claws, the sound of curling metal loud even through the speaker.

The Culler charged at Bee and the test subject, but neither moved. It got within fifty meters. Twenty-five. Ten. Helen glanced at Martinez from the corner of her eye, but the woman did not blink. At the last possible second Bee repeated the slashing motion of his hand and the animal surged forward. It was over in a moment. The Culler was a twitching mass of pink-grey, pulp and the subject was pressing its head up into Bee's outstretched hand, searching for praise.

"That went rather well, I think." Martinez took a long, satisfied sip of her coffee and tapped her implant again. "Good boy, Bee. Excellent work. You both deserve rewards, and I'll see you after lunch." Helen couldn't miss the way the man almost vibrated with happiness – not unlike the animal he was petting.

"I haven't eaten yet this morning," Martinez continued, shutting off the video feed. "If you would care to join me, we can go over the next eight-quarter cycle and then we can head down to the incubation levels. We're anticipating decanting to begin around ten hundred hours or so."

"How long will it take?" Every decanting was unique. Helen seated herself at one of the two chairs around a small worktable. Martinez cleared away some drawing samples and a box of what appeared to be children's toys, then relocated the tray of food.

"Oh, the bulk should be completed within the week, but with the delays during implantation with this series, we expect a few to lag. We may not be finished for another week after that."

"Well. I had hoped to see every individual, as usual. If things look like they will take that long, I'll need to make some additional adjustments to my schedule."

"Of course, Prime Minister." Martinez handed her a plate with fresh fruit and a small pastry. "And once they have all been moved to the Early Childhood Barracks, we can maintenance and recalibrate the artificial wombs for the thirty-fives. Barring any unforeseen problems, the *Project Jagd* target population of five thousand should be mature and ready for the field by 2156."

"Hm." Helen nodded and swallowed a bite of Danish. "Tell me about your changes to the training program."

Hour 1130
November 24, Year 2152

President-elect Yardley pinched the bridge of his nose. Whether he was feeling incredulity or anger, he couldn't decide, but it was giving him one hell of a headache. Helen Maker had created an elite band of special forces, utilizing banned GMH technology and what he could only guess were highly suspect psychological conditioning techniques. And those same units had been operating among the Coalition without public knowledge for twenty years. She had explained there were fewer than fifty people outside of the base the Legion operated from who knew of their existence. Yardley wasn't even sure where to start.

"This Legion-"

"Keres Legion," Helen Maker supplied for him. "I have no doubt that the Minister of Defense will give you a much more comprehensive briefing than I could. Oversight of military operations was never my purview."

"I believe there are quite a few things, Minister Maker, that were never your *purview* but seem to have been arranged by you regardless of that fact. Things like authorization and permission and legality don't seem to have affected your actions for quite some time." He was angry, he decided. So furious that there weren't words, weren't expressions adequate for it. If he had been speaking to a fellow officer, he might have put his fist through their face. As it was, he ground his back teeth together and tried not to yell as he stared down the placid woman across the desk from him.

"Captain Yardley, while I could debate issues of morality and governance with you all day-" she smiled and it was a condescending, amused thing that set his blood boiling, "-I believe we have more important matters to discuss than actions that cannot be undone."

His knuckles were turning white where he gripped the arms of his chair. "Is there some other horrendous clandestine project I should know about? Are there any other laws you have broken – ethical lines that you crossed - while spending trillions on black book research and operations?"

"Sir," she chuckled and he nearly came out of his seat. "This meeting is going to run long as it is. And you have other places to be today. However, there are a few other items we should touch on before you start planning your new Cabinet." She flicked her fingers across the surface of her desk, bringing up a holographic screen and forestalling his initial reaction to tell her to go fuck herself. Video of soldiers – too young to be anything but rookies but moving in such perfect sync they couldn't possibly be new recruits – began to play.

"*Project Barghest* was, as I said, dismantled with the successful formation of Keres Legion. However, their great promise – which has been exceeded by their performance – led to *Project Jagd*. I think you will find we are more than ready for the next phase of this war."

CHAPTER 7: RING THE BELL

Yemen Mass Suicide. Proper Noun. In reaction to the revelation that aliens exist, 512 men, women, and children gathered in an open field to commit homicide/suicide. Similar, smaller movements by religious cults claimed more than 5,000 lives across the globe in the year 2056.

Hour 1600
May 6, 2156

"Hit confirmed."

"Secondary blast wave damage being calculated..."

"Colonel Ben-Zvi on the line, ma'am."

"Calculate route to *Saladin*. Put Ben-Zvi on the main display."

If Jones felt any of the sick nerves and fear that splashed around in Maker's stomach, her calm expression didn't betray it. Ben-Zvi's face came up on the screen even as Maker tried to concentrate on the disarray in the Culler comms. It was difficult to ignore the itch to patch into sensors again and confirm the Navi civilians and the Legion were okay. *Malak is fast,* she reminded herself, *with ten minutes he could have probably run all the way through the pass and into Ben-Zvi's camp.* She did not think about why she was concerned for one soldier whose face she had never even seen when thousands were probably still in danger. Her skin felt too warm. Her head was sore.

"Captain," the Colonel began. An indistinct shout in the

background had the veteran frowning and pointing off screen to someone. "Our sensors are picking up aerial bombardment, but the heat has blinded us against reassessing enemy movements on the ground. Can you confirm numbers and movements?"

"Captain," Soon interrupted. "Sensors confirmed secondary damage 2.83 kilometers from impact point. Preliminary review estimates thirty-six thousand terminated targets. Civilian signatures are holding steady and continuing en route to pass."

"Good news." The colonel's eyebrows rose. "We'll be able to hold this position longer – hopefully enough for them to make it here and prep for extraction."

The junior sensors officer called out a warning, "Urchins targeting us! *Emici* moving to intercept."

"Give them all you can," Jones advised Ben-Zvi. "Special ops are covering the civilians to your location."

"Acknowledged. Good hunting."

The main display reverted to the battle before them, and Maker turned back to her console, doing her best not to be distracted by the continued silence of Malak's comm line or the inexplicable ache between her shoulder blades. Jones directed the helm to bring them into position to assist the *Saladin*, and the two officers at the comms station had their hands full relaying information on ship damage and fighter positions. The battle in orbit of Navi had shifted, with the Coalition chipping away at the initial Culler advantage – using their momentary distraction against them. Maker listened as the Cullers all but ignored the turning tide.

Find them!
Ground forces in pursuit destroyed. Numbers low.
Send More!
Humans flanking!
Listening, listening!

Find them! The ones! Alive. Bring them or you won't be good enough to eat!

"Cullers launching ground transports!" Maker notified her Captain and pinged the two Amber class ships that were about to send reinforcements to the surface. The enemy wanted captives. Specific prisoners. It flew in the face of everything the Coalition knew about Cullers, but with all that Maker had seen in the past few years she could believe it. The only questions were who, and why.

"I want two squadrons on those transports. Not another ship touches down." Comms acknowledged the order and began dispatching more *Ictus*.

Tactical and helm were arguing loudly.

"I need room, dammit!"

"Then give me something to work with!"

"Helm," Jones warned, "I need us alongside the *Saladin*."

"Can't do it, ma'am. Fighter movement is too thick, and that Citrine will clip us if we-"

"Urchins have locked on to our hull! They're drilling into the aft section, between decks eight and nine."

"Comms, send the reserve to meet them. Helm," Jones' voice never lost the cool, calm edge, but it still conveyed a warning, "get me in position or find someone who can."

"Yes, Captain!"

"*Emici*, redeploying-"

"-eight, seven, and twelve, say again. Say again."

"Locked on target. Firing when-"

Her head was pounding, her heart racing, and her gut churning.

The reserve were the newest recruits, led by the oldest, most experienced soldiers on the ship. At least half would die when they met up with the Urchins trying to board the *Khalid*. Engineering was on decks eight and nine; Rodriguez would be there, exhausted and overworked and not armored or armed to stand a chance against shredding claws. Her cousin, Seamus, was on the *Saladin*, and its status as point ship in the battle made it a target. Three massive Culler battle cruisers had surrounded it and continued to press its defenses. If the *Khalid* couldn't provide support, the *Saladin* wouldn't be able to hold out much longer. Gonzales and Kerry were on the surface with Ben-Zvi, and if the Cullers took control of the surrounding system, then Navi-3 would be lost.

"*Rommel* breaking through distal enemy line," Comms notified the Captain. "She's targeting those Ambers."

And Lin Yamamoto was captaining the *Rommel*.

Maker couldn't listen to the updates and do her job. Maker turned on the noise cancellation for her headset. It was dangerous, not being able to hear what was happening on the bridge, but she relied on text readouts to alert her for important maneuvers or incoming hits. She focused on the Culler communications and breathed evenly to prevent hyperventilation.

Capture them or it will be your shell!
Hull breech, losing-
New target, the voice listed off the coordinates for the *Khalid,* moving to flank.
Provide cover, find them! Find them!
Too many lost-
Sending reinforcements-
-bigger trash! Attack the surface so-
Cut it open!

She sent a message to tactical, pinging the Amber that was

preparing to launch ground reinforcements, but Maker didn't bother to speak. She focused instead, trying to narrow her band and pick out the Culler that was giving the most orders. It wanted three humans from the surface, but she couldn't tell which three – or for what purpose. She eliminated communications lines one by one, sending them into the background until she had what she was looking for.

Orders stand. Bring them or die, by the trash or by talon!

It called out names for other Cullers, or possibly ships, Maker couldn't be sure. Another voice, too faint to be heard, was speaking in the background. She strained her ears, eyes closed against the agony that was curling around her brain, squeezing with each shriek and screech. *-locked.* She had it, and more. The image of a ship, a Coalition ship, sprang into her mind. It looked sharp and brutally bright against the darkness of space. A score of Urchins, prepped to rip through the hull, suddenly veered away.

Fire.

It took nearly four seconds for Maker to understand. The ship she was watching fired upon an unseen enemy, launching another squadron of fighters under the cover of the rail guns. The view shifted, rising, spinning, even as a burst of a laser cannon cut through the distance towards the Coalition ship. There was only the brief sight of the insignia and the name painted on the hull and Maker cried out a wordless warning.

Too late. The impact rocked the *Khalid* and knocked her back from her station, slamming her against the main communications console. Her uniform provided little insulation between her spine and the unforgiving edge of metal. The secondary comms officer barely held to his feet, but the supervisor tumbled to the side, his elbow connecting hard with the top of Maker's head. Jones was yelling orders. The bridge went dark, then flooded with the reddish glow of emergency lighting. An electrical fire erupted hear the helm, the shower of sparks creating blinding white spots in Maker's vision. Fire suppression systems functioned quickly, leaving a cold cloud of retardant chemicals floating along the floor. The display screen strobed a sickening, tilted view of the battle, bringing the room into alternating sharp relief and hellish fog.

Someone was gasping for air. Maker rolled across the floor, trying to find her balance and avoid the stumbling feet of the other comms personnel. Her headset was still on. Distantly she wondered how it had stayed on her head, and how she could hear anything through the noise cancellation. On hands and elbows she got to the edge of the station, gripping the stair railing that descended to the lower level where helms and tactical were located. The display screen flicked off, but the weaker emergency lighting did nothing to stop the spinning of Maker's head. Her boots continued to try to magnetize to the floor, but her legs wouldn't obey her commands. Tactical was working, shouting furiously, but she couldn't hear anything but the desperate sucking and a buzz in her own ears. Her eyes rolled to the side. Not able to focus, she tripped over the blood-hued vapor slowly settling to the floor. The secondary helmsman was dead, blackened and stiff at her still-smoking console. The display flashed again, the reflection startlingly white before it winked out once more.

On the floor, slowly revealed by the settling suppressant, was the primary helmsman. He was the source of the wet panting. It was all Maker could hear. His eyes were wide and white against the sooty, reddened skin of his face. Below his chin, the color became darker, red snaking and cracking into garnet and burnt mahogany. One wide brown hand – too healthy and whole to belong with the rest of the body – clutched at the crumbling flesh of his neck, desperate to breathe. It didn't do any good. His chest was peppered with holes where searing hot bits of shrapnel had exploded from his console and passed right through him. Maker could see an even-shaped wound just to the side of his heart, and the seared edges of lung tissue.

Her gaze flicked back up to his face, but his eyes were fixed. His mouth no longer gasping for air.

"Maker!"

Sound returned in a thunderclap of dissonance. A strong hand gripped her bicep and tugged her upright, leaning her against the railing even as the room continued to tilt unexpectedly. Bretavic gave her one more squeeze, making sure she wouldn't fall again, then slipped past her to the helm. He was not gentle as he moved the primary helmsman out of his way.

"Helm, defensive maneuvers!" It was Soon who was giving orders from the sensors station while his second tended to Captain Jones. One of her shoulders was pinned to her chair by shrapnel. *Two for one*, Maker thought wildly, knowing that it had probably come from the explosion at the helm and may have even passed through the dead helm officer first. Blood was running down the Captain's face and soaking the her uniform. Maker was certain Jones wouldn't survive.

"Circuits are shot," Bretavic responded. "I need a new station."

Tactical cleared their primary seat and Giradot, the fingers of his left hand blackened and stiff, moved back to work at the engineering console near the rear of the bridge. Comms was working furiously, directing the *Khalid's* defense teams to breeches where Cullers were attempting to board the ship. A technician raced onto the bridge and popped open an access panel next to the malfunctioning display. Secondary comms was yelling into their own line, ordering *Emici* into position and checking positions with the rest of the fleet. Only one side of Maker's headset was working.

Direct hit.
Fire again. Then retarget main threat.

The *Saladin*. The display flashed, then flickered out. When it came on again it was dimmer but steady. The lead ship for the Coalition forces was surrounded by Cullers. Urchins had bored into the hull in nearly a hundred places. Scorch marks and floating debris were all that remained of the aft bay doors and landing pad.

"We need to move in." Maker didn't realize she had spoken aloud, but the ensign tending to Jones shot her a horrified look.

It was obvious. Above Soon's commands and the frenzied shouts of the officers behind her, above the furious efforts of tactical and the sound of scraping vibrations in the hull as another Urchin locked on, she could hear it.

The port side is weak. We need to protect it until the mission is successful.
"Charge all weapons again, and keep that enemy ship away!"
"I obey First!" One hit and we will be lost. No others are ready to take command. First cannot fall. Can't fail. Need the targets. Can't fail.

With perfect clarity she could see the spot, see the diagrams of a ship in front of her four digits. The commands to launch more Urchins. The damage to the gravity drive – too close to atmospheric filters. She could feel the urge, the need, the all-consuming compulsion to succeed. To kill. They would destroy the *Saladin*, and in the ensuing chaos, escape with their captives. That was the plan.

But the battle could be ended. Now. In the Coalition's favor. One hit. One massive impact to destroy the Culler lead ship and take out their command, the *First*, and they would flee.

Cullers never ran. Never. But they would. Maker knew it, felt it. The aliens were incapable of fighting if the lead ship was destroyed.

"Move in," Maker said calmly.

"What?" Bretavic asked, not even turning to look at her as he worked at the new helm right next to the charred corpse of the secondary helmsman.

"Closer," she repeated. She carefully stepped down and crossed the space to lean against the back of his chair. "We need to ram them. Here." She opened the tactical display over that officer's objections and highlighted the aft area of the ship. It only looked lightly damaged, but Maker knew how weak it was.

"Stand down, Lieutenant," Soon snapped.

"They're going to fire again, and they're targeting our weapons. We don't have time to maneuver away, but-"

"Lieutenant-!"

"Controls are sluggish, Commander," Bretavic interrupted. "Maneuvering is limited."

"Hit them and they will go down." Maker lowered her voice, "Trust me, Bretavic. Right there."

"Lieutenant Maker, you have earned yourself a court marshal! Get the hell off my bridge!" Soon snarled and gestured to the exit.

"Helm won't have time." The junior tactical officer didn't look at her, but kept his face on his own screen, barely moving his lips. "Their laser cannon is nearly charged. They'll fire again before we can close the distance and get out of their weapons lock."

Maker felt fear. It was familiar and expected by now. The cold slide of sweat down her aching back and the clench of her stomach didn't distract from what she knew she needed to do. "How much time do you need?"

"Comms, get me an MP!" Soon ordered. "I want Maker in the brig!"

"Yes, sir," comms replied. Maker ignored them.

Bretavic frowned, then sighed. "Twenty seconds. Twenty-five would be better."

Maker opened up a wide-range communications band over the bridge comm system and pulled off her headset. She stood back on shaking legs and pushed sweat-slicked hair off of her face. Her mouth opened, and she screamed.

"First! First, I see you! I see the trash you have dragged here! You are weak. Too weak to lead, too weak to fight. Too weak to live!"

There was a long silence. No shot hit the *Khalid*. No laser cannon fired. Every eye on the bridge, all but Bretavic, stared at her. Maker didn't have any time to feel self-conscious, to worry if she had made the right decision.

One of you? How is it possible? The one called First answered, his tone equally shocked and enraged.

"You dare to take one of mine? You dare to challenge me? You shall watch as I rip the shell from each one under your command." Bretavic was moving, the *Khalid* repositioning, but he needed more time. Maker took a risk. *"You will not be First, but Last! I will cast you down like the trash you are. Too weak and pathetic to claim any right! Failure! Defeat! This is your name!"*

No! It is not, the One cannot be! I will kill you!

"Weapons," Soon stuttered, flicking his confused and angry face down to his console and back to Maker. "Weapons charging. Targeting us. Maker, what have you-"

The laser cannon fired, but it did little damage. Bretavic had closed the gap inside weapons range and was gaining speed quickly.

"You can try," Maker shrieked, her throat quickly growing raw. *"It will not be so."* A grating cry of fury and denial came through the comm from the Culler ship as they recognized what the crew of

the *Khalid* could clearly see. Impact was imminent.

"No!" Soon's eyes widened and he flung himself around his station and towards Maker. "No!"

She could hear more Cullers in the background. Whispering, wondering. She knew their fears and added them to her distraction. Her throat was raw, but she managed one more threat.

"They will not be pleased."

The *Khalid* slammed into the Red Class at the same time that Soon hit Maker with a flying tackle. Sparks shot across the room and the groan of impacoral gel in the hull quickly gave way to the grind of metal twisting and torquing under immense pressure. Emergency alerts sounded and the fire suppression system went off again, but Maker couldn't focus on anything but the heinous and panicked shrieks of Cullers in her ears and the weight of Soon on her face and chest. Another console blew out, and Bretavic was thrown back over them, bouncing against the steps to the upper console level. Jones let out a sound of pain – loud enough to be heard over the shouts for bulkheads and atmospheric seals. Maker pushed at Soon, but he refused to move, holding his position as sparks flew around them and he shouted for the crew to prepare for impact.

Impact? The thought circled Maker's abused skull. *We already-*

The explosion shook her teeth in her jaw. Gravity stuttered, then increased to slightly above normal. The inner hull began to crack, sending globs of hardening impacoral gel dripping into the bridge where they smashed, denting the floor or anything else they hit. Soon let out a groan and fell heavily against her, then another, smaller explosion rocked the *Khalid*. Comms was yelling for *Ictus* and *Emici* to form up and perform strafing runs. Other ships were queuing up requests for information and status updates. Maker could barely suck in air past the weight of the Commander on her, but before she passed out she heard the Ensign clearly,

"The *Saladin*, her bridge is gone!"

CHAPTER 8: SUBVERSION

Excerpt from the *Sol Coalition Field Manual for Special Operations (Roger's New Rules of Engagement), Section Five: Taking Prisoners.*

Do not.

Hour 1730
May 6, 2156

Malak sat up, clawing at his chest and throat, trying desperately to breathe. Grief overwhelmed him. His stomach turned over, his eyes stung with wetness.

Just as suddenly as he had woken, the overwhelming sensation was gone. Malak blinked, staring unseeing at the dim interior of his helmet. Never before had he been so completely consumed by emotion. Even when Giltine had been lost, he had been angry and forgotten his control, but he had not felt fear. Not shock or the freezing sorrow that had brought him to tears. It took several moments for his surroundings to register in the wake of so much feeling.

The bone forest was burning.

Few of the white columns still stood, and those that did were charred and fragile. As far as he could see into the distance, the canopy of vegetation had been converted to a soft rain of ash. Culler bodies – no more than twenty meters from his position, were blackened and crisp. Malak had only escaped the initial blast radius because the sonic boom of the impact had thrown

96

him clear. He would not remain safe for long, however.

Although the ground was soft and wet in the hollows, the small hills burned easily. Even as he concluded that he needed to move, another spark drifted to the rise where he sat, quickly igniting the short grass and dry, fallen canopy leaves. Malak rolled to the side and stood, then hissed against a flare of pain from his back. Once he acknowledged the injury, it was difficult to ignore. The skin across his spine was tight and dry – too hot when he removed his glove and hovered his palm over it. He turned carefully to look at the bone tree that had halted his brief flight. It too was black and smoldering. The sensors in his suit were not working, but from his own careful movements he estimated that not only was his back burned right through his armor suit, but he had one or more cracked vertebrae and ribs as well. His head was also throbbing although the pain was lessening. He considered that he might have a concussion.

Injuries would have to be ignored for the time being. He needed to move before the ground under him was engulfed in the growing flames. Malak began a careful walk, stretching his muscles slowly and testing his agility. Each step sent a fresh slice of pain into his back, but the headache was almost gone after ten meters, and his legs still worked properly. He picked up the pace, heading in the general direction of the pass. He would move faster through the wildfires in the forest than if he followed the line of retreat and had to deal with enemies along the foot of the mountains. A quick inventory revealed that he was ill-prepared to meet any significant Culler resistance.

His tomahawk had been lost before the aerial bombardment. While he last remembered his Klim in his hand, it wasn't there now and had not been anywhere near him when he woke. His service knife was still strapped to his leg, but the rifle he usually kept on his back was nothing but melted nylon straps and a hard lump of what had been the barrel. He wondered if the impact and heat of the burning tree had ignited his ammo and done the damage to his spine. On his belt he found no painkillers. No antibiotics. No anti-fungals. No steroids and no stimulants. One dosage of WuSS foam had survived, and he paused to bend awkwardly and inject it along his spine. The sudden firmness brought relief from the pressure on his lungs and the pinched nerves of his spinal cord, but several playing card sized flakes of gummy, seared skin came off against his fingers. He did not feel anything when his flesh fell off nor in the place where it had been on his back. There was little he could do about it.

He dealt with his most immediate concerns as best he could. Malak picked up the pace to a jog, then a dreary run when nothing in his torso seemed to be shifting. The kilometers had never passed so brutally slow. Each fall of his boots jarred his entire skeleton, increasing the hot pulse in his recently dislocated knee and the hole in his left calf. The flames continued to grow behind him, clogging the air with smoke that smelled of green wood, bone, and spoiled meat. With his sensors and communication systems destroyed, he had nothing but his thoughts to occupy his mind.

Why was the Coalition so determined to protect Dr. Patay and two other scientists?

Why were the Cullers so intent on taking this outpost from the ground? Why not bomb it while they still had superior numbers – before Coalition reinforcements arrived? Usually ground movements by the Cullers were because the terrain did not allow for orbital bombardment or because they had been caught resupplying. Why now, in this system, engage in a prolonged battle when the Cullers had nothing of value on the surface?

How did Maker know his name? Almaut was relentless about information security, and Parshav routinely scanned Coalition and civilian databases for anything specific on the Legion and then deleted it. How had she found out his identity? She had displayed ingenuity when it came to communications, but this was the second time she had broken Legion encryption.

The thoughts continued to swirl around in his mind, finding no answers, only conjecture and more questions. Three Cullers died under his knife as he ran, all already injured by the spreading fire or the initial blast. Otherwise, the forest was silent save for the crackle of flames until he reached the far eastern edge. Twilight was fast approaching, the mountains casting long shadows over the human retreat.

Legionnaires made up the rear guard for the humans; thirty meters separated each soldier from the next as they herded the exhausted civilians toward the technetium refinery. The storage tanks were partially buried underground, but the cooling towers for the plant rose in squat rectangles above the mass of humanity seeking shelter among the buildings. Just beyond, following the pipelines that lead north through the pass, a Coalition forward base had been established. Malak would need to head there to coordinate the defenses of the human soldiers so that his people would be free to hunt down and press the Culler forces.

He hadn't made it more than ten meters out of the forest when the first of his people spotted him. From the distance, Malak couldn't tell who it was – not without his tech, but they obviously sent out a comm to the others. Legionnaires paused in their movement and looked his way. Every single one nodded deeply, baring their necks before continuing with their assigned duties. From farther in the crowd a lone figure sprinted toward him. The humans parted around Hanako, and she closed the distance to him quickly. Every human eye was on them, but nearly a half-kilometer separated him from the larger group. Hanako was gesturing, and Malak shook his head to indicate he couldn't hear. They removed their helmets to speak.

"Sir," she began. He could smell her relief. Happiness. Barely restrained excitement. "I thought...it's good to see you, Malak."

"Hn," he grunted. Just for a moment, he relaxed enough to speak in the deep chuffs and sharp sounds they had learned as children. *Good job.* He expressed his own satisfaction at rejoining the pack. She grinned, fangs on display. "Who is in charge of the Coalition on the ground?"

"A Colonel Ben-Zvi, sir. Gunnar is with her now." Hanako paused for a moment. "It seems they were expecting us, sir."

Maker. He huffed out a snort that was equal parts irritation and resignation. He had announced himself to the Coalition when he accepted her communication – her assistance. It had most assuredly saved his life, but that didn't stop him from regretting the necessity. Or from resenting her intrusion into his mission.

"Take me there. And call ahead for new equipment. This suit is no longer functioning adequately." He stepped forward, just a beat ahead of Hanako, and she made a low, keening sound when she caught sight of his back. She quickly contained herself, but that brief noise was telling. He couldn't feel anything, but it would have to look irreparable to make the battle hardened soldier voice concern.

Hanako lessened the tension with another report. "We located Dr. Patay as well. He had slipped to the front of the group and was trying to commandeer a field comm bag. I assigned one of the thirties to watch him and the other scientist. Until you decide what to do with them." She didn't have to say what they were both thinking – it was a waste of valuable manpower.

They both snapped their helmets into place, and Malak followed Hanako through the humans a kilometer across the refinery complex to the Coalition base. As always, civilians moved out of his way in a hurry, but he did not miss the whispers and gestures his way. More than one human he vaguely recognized. Those he had pulled from buildings or escorted to the main group stared after him in shock. He was suddenly grateful that his proximity comm wasn't working. Smelling unwashed, fearful, sweaty humans was bad enough – he had no inclination to hear them as well.

The forward base was indicative of the kind of leader Ben-Zvi was. Only the bare necessities had been constructed: two heavy gun platforms, a triage and surgery station, and a small, unassuming HQ. He could see two basebots at work increasing the height and thickness of staggered walls designed to create pinch points for the inevitable Culler attack. There were no tents or shelters of any kind for the refugees, but areas had been designated for rest and hydration before civilians were sent on up through the pass to the relative safety of the extraction point.

Here, among the human soldiers guarding the walls and standing sentry over the base of the mountains, the disparities between them and Malak's people were startlingly obvious. Hanako was as tall as most males in the Coalition, and she was average among the Legion. Malak stood another fifteen centimeters above her, and his shoulders were nearly twice as broad. Even without comparing the shape of their ears and teeth, he and his pack stood out as different. The humans had noticed as well, although few seemed to have reacted with the fear or revulsion that Malak had long expected. He could smell their interest, their excitement. He had never considered himself particularly adept at dealing with human motivations – he had Smierc for that – but it seemed as though the soldiers were eager, even pleased, to see the Legion. It was baffling. But then, perhaps they would have reacted the same to any force that had saved so many of their own.

It was a relief to drop the puzzling issue as he stepped past a Coalition guard and into the base headquarters. Three humans were inside with Gunnar, who had obeyed orders and kept his helmet on to conceal his features. At a sensor and communication console in the corner sat a middle-aged man, headset on his ears, who was constantly throwing furtive glances over his shoulder as he routed information and compiled data for the commanding officer. Another man, taller and older, lieutenant's bars on his cuffs, stood between Gunnar and the colonel. *Ben-Zvi.* Her name was familiar, but it took him a moment to place her. *Zulu's commanding officer. VK10.* Malak felt his lip curl in a snarl and both Gunnar and Hanako straightened to attention. This was the woman who sent green soldiers under Zulu's – *Maker's* – command to infiltrate an enemy base. A fool who threw away other fools. If she noticed the new tension in the room, she did not show it.

"*Khalid* told us to expect you. I didn't believe it was possible, but I was assured you would make it through, civilians intact. Excellent work..." She paused, her eyes looking over his uniform for rank insignia. Finding nothing but the patch for the Keres Legion, she continued briskly, "I have triage set up. With your people assisting, we should be able to move everyone through the pass in six hours. I estimate losses of only fifteen percent. You will split your soldiers into two-"

Malak gestured to Hanako, shaking his head.

"No," she said for him. "We have different orders."

"Excuse me?" Ben-Zvi's voice was like ice, but she did not have the opportunity to say anything else as Hemah entered, carrying a new armor suit and helmet. It was standard issue Coalition, apparently the largest she could find. Malak could tell already that it would be a tight fit. She handed that, a replacement Klim, extra ammo, and a med kit to Hanako. Her shallow bow and tilt of the head before she left wasn't missed by Ben-Zvi's narrowed eyes.

Gunnar, without prompting, knew what Malak would require next. "Lieutenant, Comms, let's take a walk."

"I did not-"

Gunnar cut her off, "Classified, ma'am. Your ears only." He

waited, hands easy at his sides and as nonthreatening as a Legionnaire could appear to a human, until Ben-Zvi gave a nod to her subordinates. Then Gunnar followed them out, shutting the door behind him.

"This better be fucking important."

Malak ignored her, feeling every bit as tired as he ever had. His stomach was cramping with hunger in a way it hadn't since his early testing days, and the lack of sensation in his back was beginning to concern him.

Thomas had stated the horse had left the barn. It was a nonsensical idiom, like many of the things his superior said, but after years of hearing it Malak understood the meaning. He had committed to this mission and saving these few thousand humans and he did not do things halfway. Malak crossed to a low table designed to project maps and leaned against it, then removed his helmet. Ben-Zvi, to her credit, did not visibly react. Her heart, however, began to beat faster, and Malak could smell the increase in adrenaline.

He flipped his knife out, studied the layer of dried ichor on it, then waved Hanako over.

"How clean is yours? You'll have to cut me out."

"Hm. Yes. The kinetic gel hardened to your skin. Painkillers first?"

"Save them. Can't feel anything." He kept his eyes on Ben-Zvi as Hanako got to work, sawing first through the collar of his armor and then down the back of one arm so she could peel it away. As predicted, the gel had stuck to him, and it took wide strips of burned skin with it as it was removed. That, Malak could feel. He had to breathe deeply to avoid making any sound of pain that might disturb the charged silence between himself and the colonel. Once the upper half of his suit was off, Hanako silently went to work with antiseptic and an emergency skin graft.

Ben-Zvi broke first.

"So this is the infamous Legion. Lead by a tuber." Her expression was hard, but she gave nothing else away.

"Hn." He wanted to get straight to the point. Discussions of force numbers and positioning, strategy. However, his long, slow learning process of dealing with the Falcons advised him to set the command structure straight first to establish a working respect, or things would end badly. "Is that a problem for you?" Hanako's subdermal syringe found a spot that still had a few nerve endings, and he could not prevent the twitch of his shoulders as cold fluid splashed across burned tissue.

"You were on VK10. You stole Lieutenant Maker's comm codes."

Lieutenant. She had been promoted. It was not surprising, somehow. Despite terrible odds and superiors that seemed determined to throw her into impossible situations, she had survived. The Coalition would reward that. Malak was more impressed – grudgingly – by her tenacity to defend those under her command.

"If I *was* there, that would be classified above your pay grade."

"If you were," Ben-Zvi countered with narrowed eyes, "you saved the lives of more than three battalions of my soldiers." She waited, but despite his decision to meet with her, he was not willing to confirm Legion movements. It was notable, and contradictory to Coalition precedent, that she was more interested in lives than protocol. Hanako began abrading loose skin and he had to clench his jaw.

"Maker called in an airstrike a few hours ago," she switched topics suddenly and Malak had trouble determining her intentions. *Not good*, he was certain. "My captain took a big risk on Maker's recommendation – it seems she took a big risk on you. Why is that?" When he still didn't respond, she continued,

"They broke off defending one of our own, the *Saladin*, to make that strike. My last report shows significant damage to both ships. *Khalid* rammed a Red Class – lost an entire deck to a hull breech. The *Saladin* lost her bridge."

"She survived?" Malak cursed himself the moment the words were out of his mouth and blamed his lapse on the punishing pressure Hanako was using to adhere a graft to his back.

"The ship, or the lieutenant?"

He offered no response, but she studied his face and seemed to relax as if she had found one.

Ben-Zvi continued, "You are good at what you do...Soldier. Do you have any suggestions for how we might salvage this situation?" Suggestions, not orders or commands. Ben-Zvi might not be hostile, but neither would she give him even a fraction that she did not feel he had earned.

That was fine with Malak. Hanako stepped away, finished with her first aid, and he reached for the new lightweight undershirt and armor jacket. One glance at the pants confirmed they would never fit his legs. The shirt was surprisingly comfortable, the tight fit pressing his back together gently. The jacket barely stretched over his shoulders but was long enough to seal to his own pants. He double-checked his rounds, attached weapons and the remains of the med kit to his belt and started his system booting up with Legion codes.

"I understand technetium shouldn't be exposed to oxygen."

Ben-Zvi leaned back into her heels, a quirk to her lips indicating humor or capitulation. Malak couldn't tell which.

"You Legionnaires really like to burn things down, don't you?"

CHAPTER 9: NOTIFICATION

DARS. Noun. Docking and Restocking. Refers to putting a ship in at a station or base to resupply and make crew changes. It is generally accompanied by a crew leave rotation.

Ex. It has been so long since we had a DARS scheduled, the galley is serving soylent for dinner.

Hour 0800
May 11, 2156

Maker waited with Kerry at the airlock quietly, watching a repair crew work on an exposed water reclamation node. The *Khalid* was like a flayed body. Half the hull panels that hadn't been lost in the combat were shorn off in the collision with the Red Class. Impacoral fluid had crusted over the wounds - a thin, brittle barrier between the crew and space. Deep gouges from laser cannon cut through two decks, exposing nearly fifteen percent of the ship to cold vacuum. Inside, it looked just as bad. Pressure fluctuations and power surges had hit almost every system, blowing circuits and lines throughout the ship. Engineering still wasn't accessible without a full suit and helmet, and the port side fighter bay was quarantined due to a fire that flamed up whenever oxygen was reintroduced. Cullers had boarded in several locations, and the melee combat had taken a severe toll on soldiers, crew, and the *Khalid's* décor. Maker purposefully avoided glancing at the bloodstained flooring around Kerry's feet.

As bad as it looked, the *Khalid* was in better condition than the rest of the fleet at Navi. It had made a logical meeting place for the post-battle strategy session, especially given that the lead ship, the *Saladin*, had no bridge and had lost half of her crew quarters. Maker shied away from that thought and focused on Kerry's face. They hadn't spoken since he returned with Ben-Zvi and priority refugees from the surface. Maker had been busy in comms, and Kerry had been working as manual labor with mechanics to clear debris. He should have been on a rest rotation, but had instead volunteered for escort duty with her. He had always been an overprotective sort of friend, which was endearing – right up until it wasn't.

She sighed. "Just say it."

Kerry scowled.

"I know you are dying to say something – just get it out before the delegate arrives."

"Who's doing what now?" Rodriguez plodded around the corner with a smile that belied the fatigue lining his face and the graceless slump of his shoulders.

"Nothing," Kerry said at the same time Maker answered,

"I did my job, and John is irritated about it. What are you doing here?"

Kerry took a deep breath to argue but Rodriguez beat him to it.

"You should be more careful, Clara," he mimicked in his most serious voice. "You are my best friend in the whole universe and I couldn't live with myself if I had to tell your father that your little munchkin body was horribly mangled and you will never be able to experience that handsome Rodriguez boy."

"I didn't say-" Kerry was cut off.

"I'm an adult and a trained officer." Rodriguez continued in a painfully high-pitched voice, "and I'll do my job – and anyone else - however I see fit, gosh darn it." He switched back to his regular tone. "Then Maker will tense up like an alcoholic at Oktoberfest – there she goes. Might even stamp her tiny foot – no?" He waited a beat then whined, "But it is so adorable! Kerry will get the big, sad, puppy eyes – yep, just like that." Kerry scowled again. "And you will both forgive the other and do your secret club handshake or whatever it is you two kids do when you're alone. We're all hunky-dunky."

"Hunky-dory," Maker corrected tightly. It was taking everything in her power not to stomp her foot in frustration. And then to follow it up with shoving her boot down Rodriguez's ever-running mouth. If he hadn't looked like sleep was only a passing acquaintance, she might have done it regardless of how right it would make him.

"That sounds stupid. Are those even English words? You're messing with me now. Don't mess with people who are this overworked. It isn't nice. You go to hell for that."

"Same as lying?" Maker asked through a sharp smile.

Rodriguez frowned, "Don't think so, or I'd already be there." He glanced around, wide-eyed, at the destruction of the *Khalid*. "Oh. Wait."

"You believe in hell?" Kerry asked with surprise.

Rodriguez, predictably, ignored him. "There's supposed to be a mechanic and a Class II Engineer coming over with a replacement resistor assortment. We're trading for our spare hydroponics gray-water converter – which isn't a spare so much as the only working one in the fleet, but we can limp back to dock with our food reserves, and *Saladin* is going to be here at least another week before she's safe to tow anywhere. I have to inspect the supplies and make the trade before I can take a shift break. Wake me when the transport gets here." He pressed his back against the wall and slid to the floor, promptly closing his eyes. He was snoring within a minute.

"It's pretty bad in engineering," Kerry ventured softly.

Maker exhaled hard and took his olive branch. "Pretty bad everywhere. Sorry I didn't let you know when I was released from the infirmary. Bretavic knew I was out. I guess I figured he would pass the word along."

He nodded. "I overreacted. Just didn't hear anything from you, and comms wouldn't release the casualty list."

"How'd you get back so quickly, anyhow? Thought they'd assign you to corpse detail." It wouldn't be the first time. It wasn't that Maker wasn't grateful that Kerry had been on the priority transport; he deserved the same rotations as any other soldier.

Kerry shrugged and glanced away. "We good?"

She nodded. "Can we agree not to tell Rodriguez about this? He'll be insufferable."

"I'm the best," the sleeping mechanic mumbled.

Maker snorted out a laugh; even in sleep the man had a high opinion of himself. Kerry grinned. Quiet resumed, punctuated by the occasional snore, with a new lightness until the proximity alert sounded for an incoming transport. They docked without any issues, and Maker checked their security code before Kerry manually opened the hatch. The squeal of malfunctioning hydraulics was loud enough that it woke Rodriguez and he leaped into a ready position, his hand on his belt where his service weapon should have been. The holster was full of tools and a half-eaten meal bar.

"What the fuck!"

"At ease, Ensign," Maker mumbled, lightly smoothing the back of her hand down his forearm. She gave him what privacy she could to settle down by angling her body in front of him and facing the airlock. A soldier, just as tired looking as Rodriguez but his pupils wide with stims, stepped out first. He checked the corridor and his eyes roved over her group efficiently and with no emotion. The delegate came next.

"Welcome aboard, Commander Neils. *Willkommen im Khalid.*"

He answered her in heavily accented Standard English, "Thank you, Lieutenant. It has been some time since I have heard German. *Egal wie sehr ich es benutze, Englisch fordert mich immer noch heraus.*"

"It does not sound that way, Commander. However, Captain Jones wanted to offer you the option of a human translator or access to the James program during the meetings at your discretion."

"I do not believe that will be necessary. Between you and me, even in my day – before Standard English was adopted – German schoolchildren learned English." He smiled, and deep lines curved around his mouth and across his forehead. Neils was easily the oldest person she had ever met still serving in the Coalition. "Although it has been so long since I was stationed anywhere but Intelligence, I'm not certain I remember all the protocol for a fleet command meeting." Maker nodded and tried not to dwell on why Neils, at the ripe age of eighty-seven, had been promoted to the field command of a captain. Damage to the *Saladin* was still being assessed, and large sections had not yet been cleared for survivors or bodies, but currently Neils was the officer with the most command experience.

More than thirty years prior he had served half of a tour as the executive officer on board a *Rungo* class. It spoke volumes that he was best the *Saladin* had left to offer.

"I am sure it will come back to you, sir. If you will follow me?"

Neils fell in step beside her. Kerry brought up the rear while the stone-faced soldier remained sentry at the transport and

Rodriguez waited for his parts. Everywhere they went, tired men and women were hard at work to get the *Khalid* back into fighting shape. Cargo ships bearing supplies and emergency crew replacements were still two days out and the nearest reinforcements were twelve hours away. It was unlikely the Cullers would manage another attack in that time, but Jones preferred to be prepared for every eventuality.

"This is the ship that rammed a Red Class, is it not? I was assisting in medical during most of the battle, but I had heard the rumor."

"Yes, sir. Unfortunately, we weren't able to prevent the damage to the *Saladin*."

"It was a difficult decision for your Captain, I am certain. But I trust that the gains justified the losses."

Maker wasn't certain. Not about the justification. Not about the captain's decision. It had not been Jones, after all, that ordered the maneuver. Jones had been barely cognizant at the time although she backed it after the fact. Maker had suggested it. Bretavic had carried it out. She didn't even remember the aftermath. Soon had tackled her. Her back had been hurting. Her eyes felt hot. Then she had woken up in the infirmary and the battle was over. She had sustained minor cuts and bruises, a mild concussion, but no damage to her spine despite the phantom sensation of heat and pain. By then, Navi had been cleared of Culler ships, those not destroyed had fled – the first recorded incident of an enemy carrier running from a fight. The civilians on the surface were safe; all those that made it to the extraction point had survived – so far. They would be ready when the evacuation ships arrived. Ben-Zvi would return to the surface as soon as the meeting was over to command a portion of her ground troops and those of a few other ships to maintain defenses and hunt down the few remaining Cullers on the surface. A portion of the technetium reserves had even survived.

Coalition number crunchers would no doubt rejoice when they heard the news.

Niels was still speaking, "Although we took heavy damage, it would have been worse if the Red Class was successful in its plan."

They passed an exterior window on the path, and Maker doubted Niels' sincerity. Or his sanity. The *Saladin* had been moved to a LaGrange point between one of the moons and Navi-3, so that it would not have to utilize engines to hold an orbit during repairs. If the *Khalid* had been flayed, the *Saladin* had been drawn and quartered. Her command deck was gone; a massive chunk of the three decks below it was destroyed as well. Neither of the main hangar decks were operational. Transports and fighters were reduced to using a small lower repair bay and airlocks to gain access to the ship. Urchins had drilled so many holes in the hull the *Saladin* could have doubled as the galaxy's largest cheese grater, and her starboard exhaust ports were melted closed. Only one communications transceiver had survived at all, and it wasn't capable of enough signal strength to get out of the local star system.

As they entered the lift, Maker changed the subject. "The captain's ready room had some micro-breaches, so the conference will be held in the Officer's Mess, sir."

"At least we will be closer to the coffee." He raised his eyebrows. "You do still have coffee?"

"Of course, sir." They arrived on the correct floor, and Maker gestured for Niels to follow her. "The *Rommel* brought over tablets to replace those lost or damaged, and a tech is on standby to sync one to your personal codes if you are in need."

"Excellent. I'm certain mine will turn up eventually, but that will make discussions progress more smoothly. As a comms officer, I am sure you have..."

Maker tuned him out as they approached the mess. Soon was standing in the hallway, along with Giradot and Lin Yamamoto.

Her spine straightened. Dealing with Soon was always an exercise in biting her tongue – more so since her latest defiance of his orders. She didn't trust Giradot any further than Kerry could throw him. The last thing the situation needed was her mother. She stopped several yards away so as not to interrupt their conversation, but Giradot immediately turned to her, an expression on his face she couldn't identify but which made her uneasy.

Maker wanted to hand off her charge as quickly as possible. "Commander Niels, this is Commander Soon, the XO for the *Khalid*. And Captain Yamamoto of the *Rommel*, and Sub Commander Giradot, SIS officer on board. Sir," she addressed Soon and hoped he would be more interested in getting rid of her than dressing her down in front of an audience. "Commander Niels, Acting Captain of the *Saladin*. Is there anything else, sirs? Ma'am?"

"Are you *asking* for orders now, Lieutenant?"

Niels gave Soon a strange look at that comment, but politely declined to comment. Giradot shook his head and struck up a conversation with Niels, leading him into the mess. Yamamoto smiled, but it was the way she gently gripped Soon's forearm as she spoke that caught Maker's attention.

"Not at this time, Lieutenant. However, after the meeting, if your off-duty schedule allows-"

"It won't," Maker cut her off. Soon stiffened, mouth open and ready to tear her down, Maker was certain. "Ma'am," she tried to add some professionalism to her response. "Mandatory repair shifts for all personnel."

Yamamoto did not appear phased by her rudeness. "I saw the

casualty lists. Would you care to-"

"No."

"Lieutenant!" Soon's rough bark accompanied by the vein throbbing in his forehead were clear indicators that he wasn't going to tolerate her attitude. Kerry shifted his weight behind her, and Maker had the wild thought that if he punched Soon in the face, they'd never make the Thursday night poker game. "You will-

"Lieutenant Maker." A strong, bold voice from behind her interrupted Soon. Ben-Zvi strode down the hall, her short hair still dripping from a shower and temper sparking in her eyes. She continued, "A word, Lieutenant. You-" she flicked a thumb at Kerry, "- lock down this corridor and lose the next ten."

Maker saw his eyes slide to hers, but he snapped a salute at Ben-Zvi, "Yes, ma'am." Soon looked almost eager for a show, and Maker resigned herself to being disciplined in front of the two people she least wanted to see her weaknesses. What, exactly, she had done to upset the Colonel so much was a mystery, but would no doubt be revealed in precise tones. Probably with a side of unpleasant extra duty or permanent record notations.

"I need a moment, Soon."

"If you insist." Irritation made the Commander frown. Yamamoto was not so easily dismissed.

"Colonel, I must protest. Cla-"

Maker sucked in a breath, anger flaring up. Never had Yamamoto revealed their relationship openly. It was a matter of medical record, of course, and a few of Lin's most long-standing subordinates knew or could guess, but Maker had always believed that the one thing she and her mother agreed upon was that their connection was private.

Salvation came from an unlikely source. "Protest all you want,"

Ben-Zvi said flatly. "Take it up with my captain if you like, but on this ship, I outrank you. Clear the corridor." Yamamoto stiffened as if she had been slapped, her eyes narrowed, but she turned without another word and entered the mess, Soon right behind her.

"Ma'am," Maker began once they were alone.

"How long have you been in contact with Keres Legion?"

Maker blinked. *What*? "Excuse me? Ma'am?"

"Drop the bullshit, Lieutenant. How long has SIS had you running C&E for a blackout operation?"

"They haven't," Maker blurted. "The SIS? They never..." She clamped her mouth shut, finally getting her shock under control so she wouldn't say more than she should. She'd already said too much.

Ben-Zvi leaned back into her heels, arms crossed over her chest. "So that's how it is, then?" Her gaze was on Maker, but she was speaking mostly to herself. "Allmaks? Gafor? No, Thomas. Only George Thomas would have the balls. About bloody time." She snorted. "Giradot must be salivating over the spectacle you made."

"Ma'am?" Maker ventured, when Ben-Zvi remained quiet for a long moment. *What does she know?* Her heart was beating a little too quickly.

"Met a friend of yours," Ben-Zvi transitioned abruptly. Maker's head was spinning. Gonzales and Kerry had been on the surface, but a couple of privates wouldn't merit a colonel's attention. "Excellent fighter. Good tactics. Could stand to blow up fewer things, but to each his own."

Maker blinked. *She can't be...*

"He came out looking just as...*handsome* as he went in. For what it's worth."

Oh god, she is. Maker could feel sweat forming in the climate controlled air. She had suspected that the Legion weren't straight humans, not with their size and skills. But if Ben-Zvi had seen proof, things were going to get much more difficult. The SIS was already suspicious, and Maker had sat through more than enough interrogations and debriefs with them to last a lifetime. If Ben-Zvi filed an official report, Maker would spend the rest of her tour behind one-way glass, lying until her face turned blue. And the others - she couldn't let Rodriguez and Kerry, Bretavic and Gonzales get dragged into this. It had been her choice to open the channel to Malak, her choice to reveal his position to the bridge crew on the *Khalid*.

"Tell me one thing, Lieutenant." Ben-Zvi didn't move, but Maker suddenly felt physically threatened. The rank of Colonel wasn't handed out at carnivals, and there was no doubt Ben-Zvi could take her down if she wanted. "Where does your loyalty lie?"

"My unit, ma'am." Maker answered without hesitation, even knowing it wasn't the answer the Coalition preferred. The tension did not ease.

"The next time you have information regarding my field of battle, you will report it to me. Directly. Not the SIS. Are we clear?"

"Yes, ma'am."

Ben-Zvi nodded shortly, then left for the meeting. Maker sagged against the wall as soon as the Colonel was out of sight. Her brain was churning with all that had been implied in that brief conversation. It was Kerry who brought her back to reality with a gentle elbow to her side.

"You good?"

"I think I need a drink."

"Rodriguez will be pleased."

* * *

Hours later, when Maker had finished her shift and taken a brief, very cold shower, she sat in her quarters waiting for her sub-communications time slot to begin. The call connected with a ping, but the screen remained blank for several long moments.

"Hello? Clara? What's going on? Are you okay?" Her father was slightly off-center from the camera, his face creased from sleep and his pale gold hair sticking up in different directions. He was wearing a thermal shirt – she had forgotten how cold it could still be at home this time of year.

"Greg?" A woman's voice, rough with sleep, mumbled in the background. Maker blinked.

"I'm sorry, Dad. I didn't know you had company – but we're on restricted sub-comms and I couldn't-"

"It's okay." He shuffled, the camera flashing at the ceiling as he picked up his tablet and moved. "Go back to sleep, Raine." *Raine.* The elementary teacher. Maker hadn't realized they had moved past the occasional date. The familiar walls of the back staircase slid by and then the red brick surrounding a massive stove fell into the background as Greg propped the tablet up on the kitchen island.

"Okay, tell me." He looked more awake now, but no less mussed.

Maker tried to sound lighter than she felt. "Is she sleeping over now? Nice job, Dad."

"Clara." It was the voice of her youth. The one that said she should stop stalling, give in and get it over with.

"There was an engagement. A big one. I can't say where, but the report should be released to the press tomorrow. It was...it was pretty bad." She took a deep breath, feeling the tightness growing in her chest, the overwhelming guilt that she should have done more, couldn't have done more. If she hadn't convinced Bretavic to ram the Red Class, the bridge on the *Saladin* might have survived. The rest of the ship would have been lost, but the bridge would have been intact. Greg was still waiting patiently. "You should go over to Aunt Amelia's. She'll need you there tomorrow."

Maker had to stare at the wall behind her screen to keep the sting in her eyes from liquefying.

"Seamus. He didn't make it."

CHAPTER 10: PACIFICATION

Excerpt from the *Sol Coalition Field Manual for Special Operations (Roger's New Rules of Engagement), Section Six: Logistics.* If you must resupply in the field, scout the supply location first.

Hour 0900
May 14, 2156

Smierc looked up, surprise evident in her scent and expression, when Malak entered the conference room. Almaut only nodded deferentially, listening to a communication and typing on his tablet. Skoll and Kapeziel hadn't arrived yet, but Thomas was pouring himself a coffee and standing behind his usual chair.

"How's the back?" Thomas asked by way of greeting.

Upon arrival at the base, seventy-six excruciating hours after they had left the Navi system, Malak had undergone multiple skin and bone grafts, nerve generation treatments and stem transfusions to repair the damage to his spine. The scarring was likely permanent, but he had full range of motion and with therapy would regain his former strength. The scattered patches of extreme sensitivity and numbness were less than ideal, and his entire body still ached as if he had been hit by a *Khutura* class, but he wasn't dead. And his head had stopped aching once they had entered ISG, so at least he didn't have to deal with treating a concussion.

"Fine," he grunted. Smierc used her foot to push out the seat between her and Thomas, but Malak only caught and held it in place. After days lying on his stomach he preferred to stand. And the pressure of the chair back against his skin would have made him want to howl. Most of his injuries were covered by his uniform or already healed, which was fortunate given the curious and furtive inspections he had received from every member of his pack and most of the Falcons. He didn't need to add to the speculation on his recovery by displaying evidence of how serious the wounds had been.

"Well, isn't that a relief?" Smierc drawled. "Now we can add to your legend. The thirties are already gossiping about your supposed rise from the ashes. To see you wholly uninjured-"

Skoll entered behind Malak and swiftly clapped him on the back in greeting. Malak flinched and bit off a snarl and a curse. Skoll blinked in surprise. Smierc laughed.

"Our untouchable leader. *Great Alpha,*" she chuffed. Malak clenched his jaw, but didn't bother reprimanding her for deviating from Standard English during a meeting. Smierc did what Smierc wanted, and it was not as if Thomas wasn't aware the pack had another language. Skoll looked apologetic, but Kapeziel came in behind him and frowned at Smierc.

"We could shove some ammo down your back and light you on fire, see how you fare."

"You do know how to show a girl a good time." Smierc laughed at the look of disgust on Kapeziel's face. While the two weren't genetically related as members of the same series were, they might as well have been cousins, and Kapeziel reacted accordingly to the suggestion of intimacy.

"You've spent too long in Deep Dark; it's deteriorated your brain. Not that you had much to start with." Kapeziel followed up with a reprimanding hiss, and Smierc nodded shallowly in acknowledgment of his superior rank, but she never lost her grin. It was good to see her in a pleasant mood. Malak's beta had taken on more solo missions and other responsibilities since Giltine had been lost; having her back on base and at his side was a comfort he would never openly admit.

"Good news first," Thomas began to forestall any further arguments. "SAR is sending us the new stealth equipment, and with it a ship that it has been installed on." Malak raised an eyebrow, but when Thomas met his gaze the Major kept his thoughts to himself. Such generosity always had a price.

"Another *Cicuta*?" Kapeziel looked pleased. Sharing the *Pale Horse* among the five divisions of the Legion made for complicated logistics and often less than ideal weapons deployment.

"Yes, the newest model. Coalition forces won't see this one for another six months to a year. The *Han* is the concept ship. Specs say she'll run eight percent more fuel efficient and with a twelve percent reduction in water loss. There are upgrades to the impacoral compound, outer plating, ventilation, and core systems siloing. And SAR was gracious enough to instruct the shipyard at Europa to bump up the standard crew sizing by a half meter. They're playing it off as a misunderstanding that won't be a part of the mass specs, but I toured the ship before I left the station. Legionnaires will finally have to stop complaining about stooping for doorways and contorting to fit in bunks."

"I won't know how to sleep without my elbows touching my knees," Skoll said good-naturedly. The scar tissue on his cheek gave his smile a feral look.

"The stealth tech hasn't been tested on this model yet, for obvious reasons. But they are eager for you to put it through its paces and see how it holds up over a larger ship. Since we have a little breathing room after the Culler retreat from Navi, I've reassigned a few downgraded threats to the Raiders so you have plenty of time to-"

"The bad news?"

Thomas acted as if he hadn't heard Malak. "This technology worked so well on Legion *Emici*, SAR is going to deploy with the Raiders in the next year, and after that the rest of the fleet will see stealth fighters. SAR also submitted another request for test data on the kids-" Malak stiffened, his spine protesting, and both Skoll and Smierc opened their mouths with ready protests - "but I took the liberty of telling them where they could shove it. Hope you don't have a problem with that?"

Malak nodded sharply. There were three children that had been born to human and Legion couples. A pair of twins and a recent addition that was less than a year old. They integrated well with the half dozen pure human children that lived with Falcon parents at the base, but there was no denying their parentage – or the interest of the few Coalition scientists that knew of their existence.

Thomas reviewed several potential missions that were in a holding pattern until new intel could be confirmed. He was ready to dismiss the group when Almaut finally disconnected the comm he had been on and spoke up.

"What about the wormhole generators?"

"What about them?" Thomas didn't blink, his expression gave nothing away, but Malak knew his scent. Irritation, resignation, frustration. There was something going unsaid.

"It has been long enough; they should have cracked it by now," Almaut complained, then added as an afterthought, "Sir."

"As of last week, they didn't have an update for me."

"If SAR can't figure it out, we should take another stab at it." Almaut turned to Malak – clearly trying to convince his Alpha rather than ask permission from the senior officer in the room. "Laureaux and I have been going over the data we took after the devices were retrieved. The new guy-"

"Halver," Skoll supplied.

"Halver," Almaut continued smoothly, "has done some work in applied subspace insertion and I think if we commit serious time to-"

"SAR is working on it." Thomas didn't say to drop it. He didn't growl or bear his teeth, but he might as well have with the tense set of his shoulders and jaw. Almaut glanced from the colonel to Malak.

"Hn." Malak changed the subject by reaching forward, biting back a wince as flesh stretched, and flicking his tablet to send data to the wall screen. A dark-skinned man, in late middle-age or perhaps in his early sixties, was captured in an unflattering government ID photo. "This is the man SC wanted specifically protected during the retreat. Hanako said he tried to break away from the group before they reached safety."

Almaut pivoted with the conversation smoothly. "Dr. Patay. I started some digging. I haven't done anything overt yet – nothing to catch unwelcome eyes or ears, but you should know whatever he was doing at Navi – it goes high. Maybe even higher than our cover. To get much beyond his bare bones service record, I may have to access a few secure systems."

"Do it."

At the head of the table, Thomas clenched his jaw, but did not countermand Malak's orders. The rest of the meeting went smoothly enough, breaking only when Johnson, the clerk Thomas had foisted onto Malak, interrupted with stammering apologies that there was a priority communication for the colonel. Malak let the rest of the group go; first shift had already ended and his lieutenants had more duties to complete before they could return to their quarters. Only Smierc, with less formal responsibility for supervision of the Legion and the paperwork that went with it, left with a grin and a pointed comment about getting in some relaxing exercise. Skoll voiced his envy. Kapeziel frowned. Almaut tried to bribe her to take some of his workload.

Malak slipped out before he could be drawn into the discussion or, worse, approached by the clerk that was still far too frightened of him considering how long he had been stationed on the base. As had become his custom, he found that he could get a great deal of work done on his tablet while walking the long corridors.

Patay, the scientist that the Coalition had been so insistent on protecting, concerned Malak. He had to wonder what could possibly make one man so valuable that orders – from General Batma personally – would be issued to put the Legion into direct engagement alongside regular SC troops. The existence of the Legion had been an open secret since VK10. That much was obvious given the speculation on the news feeds and the gossip the Falcons brought to base after every leave. Until Navi, however, it had been a secret that was ripe for denial, twisting, or spinning however would best serve the needs of the war. And the politicians. *Always the damned politicians,* Malak grumbled to himself. In his decades of service, and even the years he spent as a research subject before that, Malak had seen nothing that made him believe that the Coalition leadership would give up a secret – or advantage – unless they absolutely had to. And even then, it would be grudgingly and with maximum cursing and threatening.

It stood to reason then, that whatever Patay knew or was capable of, it was more valuable to the war effort than the Legion was.

Malak paused at a corridor intersection and reconsidered that thought. It wasn't pride, but simple mathematics that led him to believe that the Legion was an incomparable method for not just deterring Culler advances but dislodging the aliens' hold on systems lost to the Coalition in the early years of the war. There was no doubt in his mind that Keres Legion was the single most effective weapon humanity had ever wielded.

Anything that the Coalition valued so highly was dangerous to the Legion. Exposure made them vulnerable to what history proved was fickle human opinion, while at the same time making it harder for the government to terminate Malak and his people should they become a liability. That would make the people in power nervous, even paranoid, and more eager to take a chance and cover up their illegal genetic experiments at the first hint of bad press. Malak could imagine very few uses for Patay that would make him so important. None of them were appealing. All of them were unbelievable. And it seemed to be an unlikely coincidence that the Cullers had happened to pick Navi, out of all of the border systems, to attack just when such an important target was vulnerable there.

Malak needed information.

Unfortunately, that seemed to be the commodity in shortest supply for the major. The list of questions in his mind was growing, but answers were elusive. He still had no confirmation on the purpose of the Culler devices that had cost his people so much. Malak still grieved for Giltine. He still reviewed weekly automated reports from the beacon relay left in the sector where she had been killed although he did not discuss them with anyone, and none but Almaut knew he was still waiting, still looking for a signal that had no hope of being sent. Malak had larger concerns than the death of one Legionnaire – much as it hurt him to admit it. It was embedded in his very genes, in the first word, first action, that had shaped his entire life: protect humanity. Whatever the purpose of the wormhole devices, it would be the end of the minor squabbles and general stalemate between the two warring forces. Regardless of their intended use, the Cullers would have technology that could change the course of the war and make the Coalition long for the days where causalities could be counted in the millions. But without knowing the exact purpose, there was no way to know when or where it was likely to be used – or how to defeat it.

The stealth technology, and another ship under his command, had the stench of a primed gun aimed at his kidney. It wouldn't kill him, but when the shot came it would leave him angry and sick and in need of immediate medical assistance. The Coalition did not give resources without expectations, and the bigger the gift, the higher the repayment. Malak wanted the new *Cicuta*, and the stealth to go with it, but he wasn't sure he was willing to take the gut wound he was sure would follow behind it.

What about Maker, his traitorous mind asked slyly. The unbidden image of her pale face, streaked with blood and dirt as she swayed on her feet and ordered him to save her squad, pulled his mouth into a scowl. He had done his best to ignore her and the lapse in judgment that had compelled him to save her the last time they met, but hearing her voice at Navi had brought all of his indecision about the reckless human to the forefront again. She was everything a human wasn't supposed to be. Smaller, weaker, lacking the basic combat skills every soldier needed to survive. She was also braver and more selfless, more determined to protect those who were her responsibility than he had ever expected. *Bravery*, he questioned, *or stupidity?* Malak snorted and turned toward the nearest lift, traveling down to a storage level where he ran less risk of having his thoughts interrupted.

Whether she knew the potential consequences for her actions, the danger she repeatedly put herself in or not, Maker posed a larger enigma for Malak. She had known his name. He had reviewed her record, again, while he was trapped in the small infirmary bay on the *Pale Horse*. For hours while the medic had supervised his grafts, Malak had lain on his stomach and read through every line of information Almaut had dug up on the communications officer. There was nothing in her file that indicated she would have the clearance or contacts to know anything about the Legion. Malak was willing to allow that she was intelligent enough to break into their comms – more than once, but no sensitive or identifying information was ever repeated on even an encrypted line. Still, somehow she had learned not only his name but his plan to destroy the forest on Navi.

A warmth bloomed at the base of his skull, threatening a headache, and he was reminded of the pain during his time on the surface after he had blacked out. Maker had known he was on Navi, had used his name and likely revealed the presence of the Legion to her commanding officer, if not the entire bridge crew. Possibly the Coalition fleet now knew that Keres Legion had undeniably saved the civilian population and most of the technetium stores and provided essential support to the main surface forces. Malak had revealed himself to that colonel, Ben-Zvi, because Maker had already pulled back the obscurity of the Legion. The only secret that might still remain was that more than just Malak were unsanctioned genetic experiments. *Assuming she hasn't already learned of that as well,* he thought. He did not understand how she could know, or the scope of her knowledge, or what she would do with it. And yet, he was irritated by his own lack of concern over that. Without ever having spoken more than ten words to her, he was certain she would not give away any of his secrets unless it was necessary to keep them from danger. Or protect her own people. His mind circled back around to the question of who she was and what kind of human could so radically depart from every lesson, formal or in the field, he had learned about the species.

"It's stuck!"

"It can't be stuck. Unstick it!"

"We are in so much trouble."

High-pitched voices, barely held to a semblance of whispering, broke into Malak's thoughts. He slowed his step and pulled in a deep breath. *Three. Two pack. One Adopted pack.* The sweet, mild scent of children was not hard to place since there were few on the base. *Lata. Winnifred. Babasheb.* It could be certain that where Lata and Winnifred were, trouble was not far behind. And Babasheb would follow trying to hide the mess.

"Baba, we're only in trouble if we get caught." Malak recognized Lata's bossy direction of her twin brother. "So keep your nose up and let us know if anyone is coming."

"Lata-" Babasheb began but was cut off by Winnifred.

"We'll fix it, Baba, don't worry."

"Winnie, hand me the static shield, I think I almost got it."

Malak stepped around the corner, directly in front of a wide-eyed Babasheb and less than fifteen meters from the two girls and a partially opened cargo unit. A container clearly marked as 'Chocolate, 50 grams, Quantity 100' sat on the corridor floor. Lata had her hand and face inside a control panel, while Winnifred stood behind her with a flashlight and a toolbox that had definitely not been issued to a child. Malak had the strong suspicion that it had been appropriated from the twins' father. There was absolutely nothing about the situation that any of their parents would approve of. Malak was also fairly certain that they must have skipped out of their lessons early to get all the way to a sublevel and break into a cargo container. Babasheb let out a small, sub-vocal whimper, pleading with his Alpha for mercy.

"Baba, don't worry so much!"

Lata's order had Winnie looking over her shoulder to see what was the matter, her human ears not having heard the sound. Blue eyes went wide in her pale face, the spring of atrociously orange hair haloing her expression of shock.

"Ma-ma- Major!" she squeaked.

"Majorly annoying," Lata muttered.

Malak widened his stance, crossing his arms over his chest and narrowing his gaze. "What," he said quietly, "is going on here?"

A yelp and a hollow smack sounded from the control panel and then Lata was scrambling to stand next to Winnifred, her mouth gaping and one hand rubbing her skull. Malak could almost hear the excuses tumbling around in her head. He could not help but be amused. And a bit envious. At the age of four he and his entire series spent their waking hours in classrooms learning Culler anatomy and simple battle strategy and in training to turn their bodies into weapons. Although the twins were nearly as physically and mentally mature as Malak had been at the same age, capable of keeping up with nine-year-old Winnifred, the similarities ended there. The Legion children knew nothing of killing, fighting, and defense beyond the natural instincts to protect those they cared for. Lata quickly displayed those instincts.

"It's my fault," she blurted out. "I'm sorry Major. Winnie and Baba told me not to. Please don't tell on them."

Malak stalked over to the container of chocolate, flicking the clasps with the toe of his boot and looking at the neatly stacked squares of candy inside. None had been taken yet. He recalled a similar mission, decades ago, where he and Smierc and one other had sneaked out of their dormitory and stolen a case of nutrient bars and the components for their first rudimentary comm system. They hadn't been caught – but only because Bee had found out before the guards and had covered for them. Malak had taken Bee's punishment for all of the children: sixty days of extra training sessions. For two months he had fallen into his bunk long after the others were asleep, exhausted.

It had been worth it. If Dr. Gillian had discovered the theft, they all would have suffered worse than merely exercise. And more serious, there would have been new experiments. Malak leaned down and plucked out four chocolate bars, ignoring the pull of new skin on his back.

"For a good plan," he said, tossing the first bar to Lata. She immediately handed it to Winnifred, confirming Malak's suspicions that the older girl was the one to figure out where the goods were stored and how best to get at them without getting caught.

"For setting a perimeter." He tossed her a second chocolate, which she caught. She frowned at it, but then gave it over to her brother – obviously not certain that he deserved it since he hadn't warned Lata of Malak's approach.

"For not respecting the skills of your team." Malak held up the third bar, making certain that all three children were paying attention, then dropped it into the case. Lata, four years old, strong enough to remove a wall panel and smart enough to know how to override the circuits behind it, sucked in her lip. She remained quiet, but her eyes grew damp. It was a hard lesson to learn, responsibility, but Malak's way of teaching was kind in comparison to his instructors.

He held up the fourth candy. "For returning tools to their proper owner, in like condition." The parents – except for the Legionnaire that was the twins' mother – would probably have required that the children admit their wrongs and apologize. Malak was neither human nor their parent. He was their Alpha. The responsibilities that came with that role were different. "Reward in advance." He held the chocolate out to Lata, but did not let go until she met his gaze, "Use stealth." The child nodded, her eyes still wet but a smile twitched at the corner of her mouth. All three smelled surprised and a bit more prideful than was probably merited.

"Smierc is training in H7. Go distract her when you are done."

He chuffed at them to get them moving quickly, and they ran off down the corridor amid giggles and poorly made purrs of happiness.

Malak sighed to himself. At least Smierc would not have any more time to relax than he did. The knowledge was satisfying. He closed up the container, used his foot to kick it back into the storage room, and then resealed the door. It took only a few moments to clear the security log, but Malak found his steps lighter for the next hour, imagining how the unfortunate soldier assigned to the next inventory would try to explain the shortage of three chocolate bars.

The small indiscretion against Coalition regulations had him eager to avoid more of the useless and time-consuming rules and requirements. Before he had returned to his office, Malak decided that he would personally take the new ship on its test run. The reports and forms that were due to his superiors could wait.

Those that could not wait, he could delegate.

Smierc seemed to have time to spare.

CHAPTER 11: OCCUPATION

Kill Box. Noun. 1) A three-dimensional target area, defined to facilitate the integration of coordinated joint weapons fire. 2) Any position which can be fired upon from more than one combatant and generally having limited, or no, points of egress.

Hour 1900
May 11, 2156

"I have Stankovich. She has fingers like knobby steel rods." Rodriguez slid neatly between Bretavic and Maker on the bench where they were waiting for their physical therapy appointments. "Who'd you get?"

"Mind your own goddamn business," Bretavic growled. He had been in a foul mood since Navi. Fouler than usual. It could be partially blamed on double shifts at the helm and partially on the muscle strain that had him hunching his shoulders in pain. "No one is trading you."

"Dahl," Maker responded, in hopes that it might stop another spat between the two men. Rodriguez was just as overworked as either of them, and his normal level of cheerful disregard had been in short supply. Thursday night poker had been canceled due to their storage bay having been converted to emergency evac bunks for civilians.

Also, roughly a quarter of the usual players were dead. It was depressing as hell.

"Maker," Rodriguez turned big, brown eyes on her. His oft-used pleading pout was made more intense by a bruise on his forehead and a fat lip from some unknown injury. "Clara. You are a lieutenant among mere privates. A goddess among weak mortal men. A paragon of wisdom and soft skin the color of sweet cream. My friend, my compatriot, love of my life-"

Kerry growled as he exited Auxiliary Medical, having clearly heard Rodriguez launching into a truly bloated round of flattery.

"Apple of my mouth, sugar in my-"

"It's apple of my eye," Maker interjected.

"That can't be right." Rodriguez brushed her off. "Crisp, succulent apple officer of my mouth, please, please have mercy and switch with me."

"You're lucky Auxiliary survived the battle and that anyone is getting therapy. So quit bitching." Bretavic checked his bracer again as if looking would make the time until his appointment pass faster.

"How's your hip?" Maker asked Kerry, noting that he seemed to be walking with less stiffness.

"Better. I have another appointment next week and a whole list of stretches. Said they would have prescribed something if we weren't running low on supplies. Remember to ask about your back and-"

"Clara-" Rodriguez dropped to his knees in front of her, grabbing both her hands tightly in his- "if you will switch with me, I will give you whatever your heart desires. My firstborn. My unending love. Torrid physical union. Malt liquor. Riches beyond-"

"Hooy morzhovy," Bretavic spat in Russian and punched violently at his bracer. "I'll switch with you if you'll just shut the fuck up!"

Maker raised her eyebrows at the language while Rodriguez frowned and slowly stood. "You don't have to do that, Bretavic."

The sergeant glowered and muttered unintelligible Russian. "I was only joking around. And Maker doesn't mind. She's not even hurt."

The door to Auxiliary Medical opened again and an orderly stepped out. "Bretavic, Petr?" She rattled off his service number and eyed the group with barely restrained impatience.

"I switched with Dan Rodriguez." Bretavic gave the other man a shove toward the door. "I'll take his slot."

"That's an hour wait," the orderly warned even as she stepped aside so Rodriguez could enter.

"It's fine."

Rodriguez glanced over his shoulder once, his eyebrows drawn together, but he didn't say anything else. Maker wasn't sure how to soothe Bretavic's obvious irritation. It was Kerry who broke the awkward silence in the waiting area.

"Weren't you scheduled with Wilson?"

Maker turned on Bretavic with raised eyebrows. Wilson was easily the most avoided of all the therapists, doctors, and nurses on the *Khalid*. He had a serious thing for pressure points and didn't think a patient was done until they cried. No one saw him if they could get out of it. The stress lines from overwork and the constant pain from his shoulder eased for a moment as Bretavic smirked.

"Yes, and Stankovich has been asking around about poker night. I think I might invite her to come next week."

"You sly son of a bitch," Maker blurted. Then laughed. And laughed. Bretavic and Kerry joined in and they were loud enough that another group waiting for treatment yelled at them to keep it down. She had to wipe tears off of her cheeks. "You realize that now we're going to have to hold that party he's been asking about."

Bretavic shrugged, then winced at the movement. "You were going to agree to that anyway. This makes it less annoying."

As her own name was called, Maker supposed he was right.

Two hours later and she was ready to get back to work. Dahl, who leaned more toward Swedish massage than intense trigger point pressure or dry needling, had eased the tension from her muscles and drained away the near constant ache in her skull. No reason for the lingering twitches and tenderness along her spine was found. Maker had followed up physical therapy with her first hot shower in days. She was only allotted five minutes, but it had been sheer bliss after a week of water shortages and frigid temperatures. By the time she strolled into C&E to review the workload before her shift on the bridge she felt better than she had since the attack. Walking into the chief's office, she had only one thought,

Of fucking course.

Commander Soon was seated at the desk she had been using since the chief's injuries removed him from duty. He did not look up when she entered but continued looking through the C&E files he had pulled up on the desk display. The door closing behind her sounded like the shut of a coffin.

"Considering you have the department with the least casualties, I expected your workload to be better managed."

It wasn't a question, but Maker had to bite down on a rebuttal. It was true that only five percent of the C&E personnel had died at Navi, but it was also true that she had assigned her people to run extra shifts relieving engineering techs all over the ship in addition to the massive workload of managing data packets and comms in the wake of the battle. It was also true that they were more efficient than they had ever been under the chief – in or out of battle conditions. Every muscle that Dahl had relaxed coiled up with renewed tension.

"Is there something I can do for you, sir?"

"Unfortunately, it seems like I have to do something for you, Lieutenant." He finally looked up, and Clara was struck by how blank his face was. She had come to expect either disappointed irritation or malicious amusement from Soon.

"Sir?"

"Your little stunt with the Cullers has caused quite a stir. It seems there is concern that the enemy might have taken your conversation personally. What was it you said to them again?"

Maker flinched. Soon knew exactly what she had said. She had provided a transcript – correcting what the James had translated – to Captain Jones. Soon was only trying to remind her that he didn't speak the language – and that he found it disgusting that she did.

"Well," he drew out the word, "whatever it was, Command seems to think that you drew a lot of attention from the Cullers. Apparently the decision has come down that translators with your...proclivities may be at an increased risk for targeting by the enemy. The Brass has concerns for the safety of communication officers like you." He sat up straight, smoothing his jacket. "Until further notice, all Comms translators rated Culler-three or higher will be accompanied by security outside of their quarters."

Maker was stunned. Disregarding the fact that the number of translators in the fleet with a rating of three or more for the Culler language was probably in the low double digits, it was a tremendous commitment of Coalition resources. An unnecessary commitment, as there was no possible way for the Cullers to identify her or anyone else unless she spoke to them face-to-face. It would also be a fantastic invasion of her privacy. An annoyance that would make her stand out negatively among the crew – just when she felt she had overcome the handicap of her own genetics.

"Sir-"

"Do not interrupt a superior officer, Lieutenant. As I was saying, although the Brass have never had the particular experience of meeting you, they have determined that you are worth diverting valuable soldiers from their essential duties. As XO, it fell to me to select a minimum of three lucky individuals to trail after you during each shift and make certain you don't shut your finger in a door or trip over your own feet. I hope you appreciate how difficult the decision was for me to choose the right talent for the job."

Maker swallowed. Whatever Soon had done, she was certain it was worse than she could imagine. He stood, brushing his hands against his pants as if touching her desk had made them dirty.

"Third shift begins in three hours. The first hapless soldier on your detail will meet you on the bridge. Endeavor to display some semblance of respect for those you are pulling from imperative duties and try to be on time."

As if I asked for this, she thought wildly. Then, with more indignation, *As if I have ever been late for a shift.* She said only, "Yes, sir."

Once the door had closed behind him, Maker sat heavily in her chair and let out a desperate chuckle. She had thought she had escaped the worst possible consequences of her actions when Jones supported the decision to ram the Red Class with nothing more than a stern glare. She was already living with the knowledge that her actions had gotten her cousin killed. Now all the respect she had earned would be overshadowed by the special – *ridiculous* – treatment as if she were some precious resource to be guarded rather than a volunteer that had worked her ass off for the position she was in. And Soon had chosen her guards.

He might have picked the most annoying, most poor performing people on the *Khalid*.

Or the biggest bigots.

Or possibly some other poor souls that he hated as much as he did Maker.

Just two more years, she reminded herself. Two more years until her tour was up. *On the bright side, statistically you have a thirty-seven percent chance of dying before you serve the full tour.* Maker dropped her head onto the desk with a groan.

Hour 2200
May 11, Year 2156

He straightened his uniform before answering the incoming video call. The woman on the other end was older, her hair white and professionally styled, and wasted no time on pleasantries.

"SIS is making a move and they intend to use Clara to do it. I hope you are in a position to take care of matters."

"Yes, Ma'am. Her security detail has been assigned just as you desired."

She raised an eyebrow. "I did see that the documentation of compliance had been filed with Administration. Some...interesting choices were made. I do hope that my granddaughter will come out of future situations better than she did on RB14-7."

Sweat beaded on the back of his neck. That mission had not gone as planned and Clara herself had been a part of the problem. "Ma'am-" he tried to explain his failure, but she interrupted him.

"Or VK10-48."

"I wasn't positioned at the time to-"

"Enough excuses." Blue eyes narrowed across light years and he felt the cut of her gaze as if it were a physical thing. "You have been given an opportunity – many opportunities – with only one small requirement attached. One. Is it beyond your capabilities to meet my expectations?"

He swallowed. "No. Ma'am."

For a long moment, she continued to stare at him. Then suddenly she relaxed back into a chair and brought a delicate tea cup into view and took a sip.

"You understand I am not disappointed in you, young man. I, of course, know that Clara can be difficult to ride herd on. A strong, willful individual. I would prefer that will not be broken prematurely, but her survival is more important should it come to that." She took another sip of tea and he nodded, cautiously. "Although," she continued, "I will be most disappointed if that girl does not live through the machinations of the SIS. Most disappointed."

"Is there anything you can do?" He dared to hope that the entire situation might be resolved before he would have to act openly.

"Do not presume," she said calmly. "You have your orders. And, young man-" she paused again, smiling sharply- "I do not have to remind you what can happen if I am disappointed."

"No, Ma'am."

It was several minutes after the communication was ended before he could turn his loathing into something productive. He still had a job to do.

CHAPTER 12: SHELL GAME

Excerpt from the *Sol Coalition Field Manual for Special Operations (Roger's New Rules of Engagement), Section Two: Gathering Intelligence*

Utilize your surroundings and appearance to conceal your movements and intention...Deception is the foundation of all great military maneuvers.

Hour 2100
May 18, 2156

"Hey, stop apologizing. This is the best assignment I've ever had on-ship."

Maker poked her head out of her bathroom, toothpaste foam gathering on her lips, to scowl at Gonzales. The other woman was lounging on Maker's bed, flicking her fingers over a tablet as she skimmed articles.

"Usually ground troops end up cleaning weapons and doing grunt work for Engineering – or, best case, swinging security patrols on third shift. It's all boring as hell, heavy labor, or heavy labor and boring as hell. Guarding you-" she made air quotes with one hand- "on second shift? I'd think Soon was trying to get into my pants by giving me this assignment, but I don't screw assholes and I'm not sure he has the requisite parts anyhow."

Maker spat and rinsed her mouth. "What about that med tech from Titan Station last year? Sammy? Susan?"

Gonzales snorted. "Serena. Yeah, she was an outlier. Real piece of work. But an absolute angel between the sheets. Forget about that. In fact-" she sat up, stretching her neck. The bones popped in a way that made Maker wince- "forget about Soon. He thinks he's screwing us both over, but the only way this would suck was if anyone gave two shits that Command wants to protect lobster mout- uh, um, translators. Which they don't. No one we want to talk to anyhow. C&E all know you are the only thing keeping that place running. I heard the chief is looking at disability discharge, and your cowardly buddy on second shift asked for a psych eval – angling for emotional distress. Rodriguez says Engineering is ready to kiss your feet for volunteering your people to provide relief support, and that Raider you've been banging put out the word that his whole crew backs you – no questions asked."

Maker blinked at that and leaned against the sink, her fingers slowing as she braided her hair. She had only seen Gorm in passing since the attack, just enough to verify that his whole unit made it through – not without injuries - and that they were on the *Khalid* until new orders came down. She liked his team. She had hoped, after her assignment with them was over, that she had earned some credit from them. For him to pass word around the ship that the Raiders trusted her was a big deal. It said a lot more about how the rest of the Special Forces group felt about her than it did about how much Gorm liked that thing she did with her tongue. She probably owed him a thank you. Maybe owed his whole unit a thank you. She wondered absently what it would cost to have her dad ship steaks to an entire platoon.

"No one who you give a shit about thinks this is anything more than stupid bureaucratic bullshit thought up by desk jockeys that have never been out-system," Gonzales continued. "So what if you have Soon's butt monkey outside your door while you sleep? You have me and Kerry while you're awake, and we are the – the – what did your dad call that wine Rodriguez sent for Christmas?"

"The cat's pajamas."

"Yeah. That. We are the fucking cat's pajamas, so to hell with Soon's butt monkey and to hell with a-holes who think you have any goddamn say in what Command does or doesn't do and to hell with fucking Soon, for that matter. You are a good soldier, Clara. And a good friend-" she made a face- "For an officer." Maker laughed and pinned her braid up onto the back of her head. Gonzales continued, "So could you at least be happy for me in my excellent duty assignment?"

Maker did not tell Gonzales how Taav – Soon's butt monkey - had made it a point every night to override her door lock for armed checks of her room at least twice while she was sleeping. She did not repeat the slurs Taav had used regarding her genetics, her Culler language abilities, and – in a form of misogyny that was so archaic it was almost impressive – how her gender must surely prevent her from thinking about anything other than penises. She did not express her fervent desire that, should Cullers attack, it would be while she was sleeping and that she would wake with enough time to watch the aliens slice open his gullet before she was killed. It had recently become one of her fondest fantasies.

She did not mention that he had insisted she have daily time on the range and that she start carrying her Klim outside of her quarters. If he told one more crew member to maintain a two-meter distance from her, she was going to shoot him herself.

She pulled on her uniform jacket and waved Gonzales toward the bathroom.

"You still want to use mine?"

"Hell yes." Gonzales swung her feet to the floor and grabbed the bag she had stashed by the door earlier. "If I had even half the brains for it, I would take a shot at the officer's entrance exams just to get a private bunk."

"I tried to leave you some hot water, but there's probably only a couple of minutes left – five if you go lukewarm."

Gonzales snorted. "I already get to shower, by myself, and on duty too. Lukewarm water is a gift. I'll be out in a jiff."

"Take your time. I don't need to be anywhere for another hour or so."

Maker went through her mail and packed up her laundry before Gonzales was ready to leave. Once they were in the corridor, Gonzales dropped her friendly demeanor and followed behind and to the left of Maker, her side-arm exposed on her hip and her attention on their surroundings. Maker had to give her credit; it was a bullshit assignment, but Gonzales took it seriously. At least when they were in public. The staff in C&E mostly ignored her new shadow, and presented work orders and problems that needed a supervisor – despite the fact that the second shift supervisor was sitting in his office. Maker spoke with everyone on duty and helped out on a few difficult translations and one encryption that was confusing the software.

"No. You're right," she told the ensign assigned to the data packet. "It's definitely a civilian signal. The extra garbage in there may be interference from a quasar, or their own internal systems malfunction, or..." she checked the star maps for the general area of origin and pointed it out to the rookie officer. "Yeah, they're probably in this emission nebula cluster. It's a bear to navigate through but cuts some serious time off of the trade lane to Shichang Outpost. Run it through cleaner Theta-one, then the usual scrubbers. It should help." She listened again for a second. "And you'll want the James – unless you speak French?"

Ensign Chakrabarti shook her head. "Will it be accurate enough?"

"Oh, definitely. The James knows French like you know racquetball, Ensign." The younger woman smiled but still looked worried. Maker concentrated on the signal for a second, closing her eyes to block out the garbled static. "-*mauvais fonctionnement. Veuillez noter que nous nous occupons des réparations, mais ne vous approchez pas.* Sounds like they had to stop to make minor repairs, but they are warning other ships away because...they have a computer virus. Shouldn't be anything we need to worry about, but once you have it cleaned up, send it on up to the CIO's office for assessment."

"He's got a backlog," Chakrabarti warned, "it'll take him a week to get to this."

Maker handed back the headset and winked. "You think he reads his own mail? Don't worry about it. I'm sure it will be flagged noninterest."

Two others requested that she review their work before Maker left for the mess. She was starving, and with the new duty schedule, she would be working third shift with a green recruit on their rotation through comms. M'Benga had been moved to first shift due to deaths and injuries.

"You're really good at that," Gonzales noted as she stood beside Maker.

Maker paused in her meal, trying not to feel self-conscious about dunking her DME bar in hot coffee while her friend loomed over her. "It already tastes like nail clippings and stale cardboard; soaking it at least makes it go down quicker."

"No, I meant with the radioheads. You're really good at that."

She shrugged uncomfortably. "I took a couple of languages when I was a kid. Studies say that makes it easier to learn more."

"Yeah, I'm sure anyone could do it." Gonzales rolled her eyes. "It's not just that. You were good with the kid – the Pakistani kid. Friendly, but she still respects you. Not a lot of officers are like that."

Maker finished off her coffee and rose, dumping the remains of the DME bar in the recycler. "Well, I've been around Soon enough," she said in a low tone so they wouldn't be overheard by anyone else in the corridor or lift, "I certainly have a great example of what not to do."

Gonzales barked out a laugh and was still grinning as she followed Maker onto the Bridge where Gonzales would be relieved by Kerry. They both reigned in their amusement when they saw Giradot waiting by the comm station for them. The recruit that Maker had been training for the past two nights was shifting his weight and looking like he might throw up from nerves. It wasn't every day that the Chief of Intelligence dropped by to chat. Kerry hadn't arrived yet.

"Sir?" At Maker's polite inquiry he turned to face her fully, and the private very nearly sagged in relief from being out of scrutiny. "Is there anything I can do for you?"

"Ah, Lieutenant Maker, just who I was looking for."

Maker stiffened, and she sensed Gonzales tensing behind her. He continued,

"Your personnel record shows that you speak French. Is that correct?"

"Yes, sir." She waited, ready for the unwelcome task she was certain was about to be assigned. *Maybe Giradot needed his memoirs proofread. Please, let the Cullers take me before that happens.*

"Excellent. We have received a recorded distress signal from a civilian ship that is having difficulty. They aren't responding to requests for additional information, and they are only a few hours off of our trajectory, so I would like to send a team to offer assistance."

"Sir?" Her question was weak, and all Maker could think about was how she had been the one to clean up that damn message. It was her own fault that she was getting the post.

"I've already sent a pilot assignment out. I'm sure this will turn out to be nothing, but it's always best to have someone experienced you can rely on. I believe you have worked with Sergeant Bretavic before? I had to pull some strings to get him for you, what with our staffing situation." Giradot smiled as if they were sharing a fun secret, "It pays to be CIO."

Why would Giradot pull any strings for a junior officer that contradicted him in public?

And why the hell was Giradot up late on second shift reviewing his own low-priority comm contact alerts? He had an assistant for that. Multiple low level grunts in Intelligence were capable of and certainly usually were assigned to handling those sorts of tasks. She was aware that Gonzales had stepped back into her post by the door and wished she were closer. Maker wanted the moral support for the stupid thing she was about to say.

"Sir, doesn't protocol state that as long as a civilian ship shows no sign of distress, the Coalition is under no obligation to respond?" Maker didn't get it. Giradot was the last person – maybe second to last after Soon – that she expected to give a shit about the safety of civilian traders dumb enough or desperate enough to leave the verified shipping lanes. She also hadn't forgotten the look in his eye when she contacted Malak on Navi – or the number of Culler 'interrogation' recordings she had translated directly for him.

"You do know your regs, don't you?" He smiled again, but this time tighter. Less believably. The private had crammed himself into the corner of the comms station, hemmed in by his own console and the door to Bridge Medical. He might have been trying to activate a stealth mode as still as he was holding himself. "I can't divulge my reasons, of course, but Coalition intel integrity takes many forms. We'll be best positioned for a

Runa launch in-" he checked his bracer- "ninety-two minutes. You had better get moving if-"

The Bridge door opened and Gonzales casually stepped closer to Maker, hand hovering over her service weapon, as Soon strode through. He was closely followed by Kerry. She turned to face them both, careful to keep Gonzales at her back rather than Giradot. The CIO made the skin on her scalp crawl.

"Lt. Commander," Soon snapped. His uniform jacket was open at the collar as if he had put it on quickly. Where his neck was exposed the skin was red with anger.

Maker breathed out softly. The rest of the bridge crew, parts of second and third shift, all suddenly found vital work they needed to keep their eyes on. Kerry took up a position opposite Gonzales but out of her line of fire. He didn't put his hand on a weapon, but his stance widened as if he was preparing to attack. Soon continued.

"I'd like to speak to you in the briefing room. Now."

No 'please'. No explanation. Soon outranked Giradot, but Bridge officers didn't *usually* give each other orders. Or ever. Instead of taking offense, Giradot smiled wider and gestured toward the door.

"After you, Commander." His smile turned back on Maker and her stomach flipped in a way she had never experienced before outside of combat. "I'll be just a moment, Lieutenant, and then we can discuss those orders." If anything, his comment made Soon more furious. His jaw clenched hard enough that even the tech making repairs down at the helm station could hear his teeth grind.

As Giradot walked past, Maker moved to lean on the console. Her fingers accidentally brushed against his bare hand as he swung his arms in a brisk walk. He was pleased with himself. She recoiled as if bitten, nearly falling into the sweating private.

He hates me, she thought, desperately trying not to rub her fingers on her pants to get rid of the sensation of his skin against hers. Then, with a shaking huff, *Giradot hates everyone. Especially Soon. This is probably nothing more than a pissing contest.* Still, she couldn't shake the sensation that she was in a crosshairs. Couldn't shake that alien feeling of knowing she had the upper hand. *Not me, Giradot.*

The door to the briefing room closed behind the two men and the private slid sideways, his hot breath on Maker's hair suddenly welcome against the chill that was overtaking her.

"What the fuck," he murmured.

"Ship politics, fuzz," Gonzales snapped. Her hand was firm on Maker's elbow as she led her closer to Kerry. "Shift detail report, Kerry," she said loudly, then lowered her voice. "What. The. Fuck."

"Soon was coming toward the lift as I was on my way here," Kerry said quietly. "Before he thought I would be able to hear him, he finished up a conversation over his comm. Sounded like Giradot overrode the personnel roster with his security clearance."

With justifiable cause, Giradot had the authority, but Maker didn't think a civilian ship that wasn't asking for help and showed no indication of distress was justifiable.

Gonzales let out a whistle, "Bet the XO just loves having his toes stepped on. Jack-fucking-frost, I hate Soon, but if there was ever anyone to put that smarmy asshole Giradot in his place..."

Maker had to agree. A simple run out to a stranded human ship wasn't a big deal, certainly it was low-threat and would almost be a vacation after the constant repairs and overtime on the *Khalid.* However, she didn't trust Giradot. Giving in to the instinct, she tucked the fingers of her right hand under the hem of her jacket, twisting them against the material almost hard enough to rub off the top layer of skin. A couple of second shift officers finished their detail reports for their replacements and cleared off the Bridge with mutters about avoiding the splash damage that was sure to be coming. Maker wished she could follow them out.

"Private," she called out to her trainee. Maker was proud her voice didn't betray the sharp worry pricking at her neck. "Pull up the repair check list and begin sorting the comm line traffic the way I showed you yesterday." When he didn't move right away, she raised her eyebrows, "There something more interesting you'd rather be doing?"

"No. No, ma'am." He looked almost relieved to have work to concentrate on, which had been the point.

The old veteran at tactical, the one who had countered both Giradot and Soon during combat, spoke from the corner of his mouth, just loud enough for her to hear and in his native German.

"Watch out for that kill box."

She didn't have time to respond or translate for the confused Gonzales and Kerry. Soon stalked out of the briefing room, followed by a languidly moving Giradot.

"Someone ate the canary," Gonzales muttered before straightening and nodding to Kerry. "She's all yours, Private."

Soon barked at Gonzales before she could leave. "New orders. Travel security detail. You. Kerry." Their bracers pinged simultaneously. "Maker, get your station straightened away, and I want a comm replacement up here and briefed in the next ten minutes. Your new assignment will be waiting for you." He did not turn to watch Giradot leave, but kept his narrowed eyes on Maker as she returned to comms and began checking the personnel lists.

"Lieutenant," Soon continued.

She looked up, but did not know what to say when confronted by the overwhelming and barely repressed rage on his face.

"Try to do your job without killing anyone this time."

CHAPTER 13: MISDIRECTION

Catecholamine. Noun. A group of organic compounds used as neurotransmitters including tyrosine. Release of catecholamines is part of the fight-or-flight response, and high levels of tyrosine have been linked to extreme anger, aggression, and violent defensive action.

Ex. Stims are one thing, but if you really want to keep your edge in a fight, a catecholamine enhancer will do the trick. Or give you a heart attack – but we're all going to die eventually, right?

Hour 1330
May 19, 2156

"You aren't trying to wank it, private, no need to be gentle."

Cicuta ships were designed to be fast, flexible, and economic carriers of small ground troop formations and support craft. They only required twenty crew members, were capable of ISG, and could host two hundred soldiers comfortably. Or three hundred uncomfortably.

"No, not that way! The other way. Dammit. Okay, no. I guess muscle isn't going to do it. Let's pull the panel and check the connections."

The *Han* was all of that – but better. Faster in sublight travel, more resource efficient, and with a prototype real-time responsive visual and sensor stealth system that made her impossible to locate unless the enemy physically ran into her. Her floor plan had been redesigned, making it possible for two hundred Legionnaires to sleep in bunks built for their tall, broad frames.

"This is a damn rat's nest."

Unfortunately, as Malak had suspected, no reward came without a price being extracted. The price in this particular instance was a *Han's* maiden voyage fraught with technical difficulties. Apparently the chief engineer on the project was brilliant but left a lot of details out of the schematics for the stealth technology and how it integrated to the ISG.

"I do not know what the hell this idiot was thinking," the two Falcons working on the open panel muttered to each other.

"I know what I'm thinking. I'd like to see him have to explain to the Major how long this is going to take instead of me." She reached back for a tool from her kit, caught sight of Malak standing behind her, and winced.

"How long?"

"Um. Forty-eight hours. At least. We don't have enough qualified techs to run constant shift work."

The second human lifted his head from the access panel and raised both his eyebrows at the Falcon. He rattled off the names of the other technicians on board. "I thought they all finished the modules and certifications Lieutenant Almaut requested.

"Well..." The Falcon glanced at Malak again, then over at Smierc. She answered for him.

"Release of the continuing ed has been delayed due to clearance issues."

"Are you kidding me? They gave us a ship but no way to maintain it. Who do they think would take a brand new prototype out on its first test flight without a full complement of techs?" The Falcon paused, seemed to realize his mistake, and then stuck his head back in the access panel.

That would be me, Malak thought, eyes narrowed. Thomas better be prepared to push those clearances through, no matter the cost, because this won't be happening again. Even if I have to take it up with General Batma personally. Smierc inserted herself smoothly.

"Clearly we have the best of the best with us." She smiled at the female Falcon, and she returned the expression with as much interest as Malak's second usually garnered from humans – even the ones that did know how cleanly she could snap a spinal column. "Is there anything you can do to speed up that timeline?"

"Uh, maybe. We can take a look at a few things, but what I really need are a few more pairs of hands. And an engineer with more experience with these systems."

Malak closed his eyes and focused on not crushing the railing he was leaning on. He almost wished he had stayed at Keres Base to finish personnel reports instead of taking the new ship out for a test run. Almost.

"What can we offer you to assist, Ensign? I would hate for us to be caught out here by a good Samaritan looking to help a stranded ship."

Or he could have left Smierc behind to deal with the reports.

"We shouldn't have to worry about that. I can't get at the code yet, but the ship's automated beacon has been transmitting a fairly good cover. I know it isn't the way we usually do things but –"

"Automated?" Smierc stood up straight at the same time that Malak growled.

"What." He turned to stare at the technician who was still focused on her tablet and frowning at the figures there.

"Yes, automated. We didn't even know it was in the code until it started transmitting. Just like everything else around here it is unnecessarily hard to make changes. I guess the guy who designed the *Han* was pretty proprietorial over his ship."

"His ship?"

"Uh," the Falcon glanced from Smierc to Malak and scuttled to the side, tapping furiously at her tablet. "Obviously not anymore."

"Let me hear it." Malak struggled not to take his temper out on the tech.

She flicked two fingers across the display and a prerecorded message came over the bridge speakers. *"Un virus informatique agressif qui peut se propager par contact physique provoque des dysfonctionnements.Veuillez noter que nous nous occupons des réparations, mais ne vous approchez pas."*

Before anyone could ask, she translated. "I ran it through the James. It says to keep your distance, and that the crew is handling repairs, but there has been an outbreak of a highly aggressive computer virus that is causing malfunctions. It seems to insinuate that it could spread through mechanical contact." She winced again. "Sorry we didn't think to tell you sooner, Sir."

Malak barely bit off a snarl as he stalked away from the bridge and toward his ready room. Behind him, Smierc was handling the technician far more gently than Malak would have done. Malak wanted to take out all of his frustration with the designer on the blameless Falcon. The design engineer did not have any idea how lucky he was to be out of reach on Titian station and blissfully unaware of the genetically designed killer who wanted to wrap a hand around his neck.

"Can you turn it off?"

"We've been attempting to-"

The hiss of doors closing cut off the Falcon's response and Malak snarled at an empty room. Not only was his new ship malfunctioning, but the idiot human who had designed the stealth *Cicuta* had transmitted their coordinates to anyone who was listening. If Malak could have shot the man and thrown him out an airlock he would have.

You can, he reminded himself. *You have the stealth ship to get to Titan and the skills to infiltrate the base unseen. You can do it,* as long as you are willing to file the report afterward.

It wasn't worth it.

He breathed deeply, trying to reign in his temper. Thomas had been impressed with the man's conditionals; he had high security clearance and the colonel had suggested that Malak consider integrating him with the Falcons and taking advantage of his genius. Malak did not approve. He disapproved. Strongly.

He was beginning to think stealth technology wasn't a big enough advantage to deal with the complications.

His back was beginning to ache but he refused to sit. He stood and pulled up reports on the wall display. Skoll was at Keres base and supervising the integration of a new squad of Falcons that were assigned to help work on the Culler devices. Almaut had sent an update on their progress, accompanied by various and overly excited technical descriptions from Laureaux. Kapiezel was still chasing the Cullers that had fled Navi and thoroughly enjoying shredding their ships at every opportunity. All missions were well in hand. Malak was halfway through a report from the Base education center – several rudimentary but enthusiastic drawings were splashed up on the wall, when Smierc entered. He casually closed down the display, but not before she caught sight of what he had been reading and smirked.

"Two days is, unfortunately, a hard milestone for repairs," she said without mentioning the blank wall.

"Send the Falcon tech in charge in."

"No." She tipped her head to the side, her red ponytail swinging like a pendulum. "I don't think your intimidating her would help matters. So no."

"Smierc," he growled.

"Malak," she growled back playfully. "We don't have any urgent missions, so calm down. We can afford the time and it will give the Falcons an opportunity to learn more about the ship and repairs they may need to make in the future."

"Our location has been compromised."

Smierc rolled her eyes and flopped into the chair at the opposite end of the table from her Alpha, "Assuming anyone was listening – a big if – and assuming that their James translated the automated message as anything understandable – which I have my doubts about, then we still have days before something so unimportant as a civilian ship that isn't requesting assistance garners the attention of anyone nearby. We are weeks out from every Coalition ship except a few that are limping back to CSNS from Navi. None of those are going to waste resources on a matter this inconsequential when they are already dealing with heavy damage and casualties. At worst, they'll flag it for review back at the Oort C&E station. By the time anyone is sent to investigate we will be long gone."

"Thomas recommended him."

"Oh, that is unforgiveable," Smierc agreed easily. She laced her fingers behind her head and stared up at the ceiling.

"If we can't get this fixed -"

"I've already given the Falcons permission to contact Titan base and milk whatever information they need from the designer. They've asked for another day to try and figure it out themselves. Apparently, they share your opinion that the man should be mopping a research facility instead of working in one. Our people are good. They will take care of this if you can find a little patience, Alpha. You're getting short-tempered in your old age."

"We are the same age." Malak ground his back teeth together.

Smierc flapped one hand in the air without looking at him. "Let's talk about something more important. I finished reading all of the action reports from Navi. That comms officer on the *Khalid* certainly seemed familiar with you."

"Maker," he corrected before he could stop himself.

Smierc opened her eyes just far enough to look at him slyly. "Oh, is that her name?"

"You know it is. Cut the shit."

"Shit? Me?" Smeirc made a purring, soothing noise in her throat that was interrupted by her own chuckles. "That's hurtful of you to say, Malak. I'm only trying to assess our possible exposure here...What exactly is your exposure to Lieutenant Maker?"

"You are walking a fine line." He clenched his jaw together. The ache in his back had deepened to a throbbing pain up and down his spine. The medical staff had prescribed synthetic opioids until his muscle and bone grafts were finished integrating, but Malak was sharper without them.

"Don't worry. I'm extremely agile." She abruptly sat forward and punched a code into her bracer. A new file popped up on his tablet, marked priority one and confidential.

"What's this?"

"Parshav grabbed a copy of their data packets before we left the

Navi system. Thought you might want to review the after-action reports of a few of the major players. The *Saladin*, the *Rommel*, the *Kahlid*," she said casually. "Oh, and I highlighted the *Kahlid's* captain's log for you. I just skimmed it, but it could probably use a more through examination."

After she left, Malak locked the door so she couldn't simply barge in on him again. He read through the personnel files he had been putting off and completed several reviews before the blinking notification of the new file became too much to ignore. He opened it and searched for the first date after the Navi engagement. That one was brief and just a notation of number of deaths, major damage to the ship, and the need for a meeting with the other captains in the task group. The next one had obviously had more time and thought put into it. It looked like Jones had used her log to draft an after-action report, including some observations that likely wouldn't make it into the official record. She lamented the loss of lives, mentioned her own injury, and discussed the actions of her bridge crew.

Bretavic stepped up and handled himself, and the Kahlid, well. If not for his cool head and steady hands we would not have made it through the battle. Some of his time at the helm is still fuzzy for me – damn head injury – but I've watched the bridge recording and he held it together like a veteran should and with more professionalism than his evaluations would have...

Malak skipped down, looking for notes of interest.

...Giradot is a pain in my ass...

...glad I brought Soon with me from the Pershing. He's hard on his staff, but they rise to his expectations. A better XO is not to be found in the fleet. He risked his life to save one of the junior officers – an officer he doesn't even like. That is the honor and integrity we need in the Coalition...

...Lieutenant Maker – Malak slowed down and read more

carefully - is the best translator I have ever worked with. That is not in question and never will be. As disturbing as it can be to hear Culler words come out of her mouth, she knows her job and her people respect both her skills and her authority. As a bridge crew member...she leaves something to be desired. She and Soon do not get along, which would not be an issue if she wasn't also countermanding the orders of her superiors. Her psych evaluations described her as meek and easily overwhelmed, but I have not seen any evidence of that. When she demanded to speak to me in private, in the middle of a battle, there was nothing meek or overwhelmed about her. Although she holds her confidences close – as an officer should – she gave me enough information to confirm what I had already guessed about Legion activity on previous missions without providing any specifics that would jeopardize...

"Major," Smierc's voice over his subdermal transceiver interrupted his reading. Malak abruptly sat back when he realized he had hunched over his tablet.

"Go ahead."

"We have a ship approaching at sub-light. It is Coalition."

"You shut off the automated message?"

"Yes, sir. But I think you are going to want to hear their response." Smierc sounded suspiciously happy.

"Put it through."

"Unidentified vessel, this is the Sol Coalition transport *Dido*."

Malak knew that voice. His scalp prickled with the memory of a headache.

It continued, "We have been ordered to confirm your situation and offer assistance. Please respond."

His day was already going poorly. Of course Zulu would show up.

"Ignore it," he told Smierc gruffly.

"And if she doesn't give up?"

"Standard procedure." Resolutely, Malak closed out of the logs he had been reviewing and returned to his own work. He hadn't yet received a reply from Thomas on the status of the wormhole device research that SAR was working on. He wanted to compare it to Laureux's conclusions. He began drafting a message, but Smierc used the comm again.

"If that doesn't work?"

"It will work." Privately, Malak had his doubts.

The phantom ache at the base of his skull continued to annoy him as he tackled the endless reports and intelligence briefings that filled his inbox. Information from Skoll and Kapeziel needed to be addressed. The new Alpha for the twenty-seven fours was struggling; Malak scheduled time to work with her. Grief among that group was still strong and was interfering with their ability to perform. He moved them all to base duty until he could address it. Malak stood and stretched, ready for a break to grab a protein bar and patrol the ship when Smierc came to the ready room personally.

"I would never call the Alpha out on being wrong in front of the others..." She arched one brow, barely containing her smirk and pulled up a video feed on the display wall.

Malak watched as a Runa fired a grappler at the *Han*. A grappler. At *his* ship. Did foolhardy Zulu think she was going to tow him? The *Han* was easily eight times larger than the recommended mass limits for a transport that size. She would blow out a sublight generator before she overcame inertia. He growled, "What does she-"

"Wait for it."

Every muscle in his body tensed as the airlock on the *Dido* opened. It was difficult to make out any details even at the highest enhancement, but Malak would have bet his favorite Klim that one of the two small figures latching on to the grappling wire and launching themselves into a tethered walk was Zulu. It was a stupidly idiotic plan to risk a high value, low martial skill unit in open space while tied to an unfamiliar, unresponsive craft. Of all the reckless humans he had ever come across, only she was that foolhardy. Malak dropped his tablet to the table and stalked onto the bridge.

"Ondrea, you have the conn. Smierc, with me." He did not pause, fury building quickly and seeping out in his scent. Malak didn't bother trying to control it. *Let them know,* he thought, clenching his jaw. If only Zulu was capable of recognizing an angry predator when she smelled one. Human senses wouldn't allow it, of course, but as Malak made his way to the airlock closest to where the grappler had attached he planned several ways to remove any confusion for her.

Smierc followed the boarding team's progress on her tablet as she walked beside him. "They've maglocked to the outer hull... moving out of visual...I should pick them up on another camera in a few moments..."

Malak came to a halt in front of the airlock. He stood with his feet braced wide and his arms crossed.

"Do you think you're going to intimidate her?" Smierc was still smirking, flipping back and forth between various sensors and visual sources searching for the two idiots walking across the *Han*. Malak huffed. Intimidation would be a welcome secondary benefit if it worked on Zulu. In truth, he was holding his arms as tight as possible so that he didn't grab her as soon as she opened the airlock and shake her until her head rattled. Or he might throw her back into the Dark. Untethered. Both possibilities had merit.

"Hmm..."

Malak caught Smierc's frown in the corner of his eye. "What is it?"

"There is a malfunction in one of the vapor recycling ports. I'm trying to-"

Sharp, hot pain shot through Malak's shoulder – enough that he grunted and reached for the joint as if he had been stabbed. There was nothing there.

"What's wrong?" Smierc took her eyes off of the screen to stare at him. "You smell of-"

"Where are they?" He ground out. The initial sensation dulled into a throbbing ache, and he cautiously rotated his shoulder. The pain did not increase or change, but it did not diminish either. He was not injured, but he could not shake the knowledge that he had dislocated his shoulder. The corridor was wide enough that he and Smierc and another Legionnaire could have walked side by side, but he still felt uncomfortably squeezed.

"Malak?"

"They're not headed for the airlock." He turned slowly, envisioning the schematics for the *Han* and any tight spaces that might have been near the grapple point which would interest Zulu. Or cause injuries.

"Where else would...oh." Smierc's brow creased and she scrolled through data on her tablet. "The vapor port. Something is blocking flow. How did you-"

Malak spun on his heel and moved quickly through the ship until he found the interior access hatch. As he arrived, the flex of ducting sounded loud in the corridor, followed by the low, long screech of metal on metal.

"Why wouldn't they just-"

The panel clattered to the floor before Smierc could finish, followed by two SC uniforms and a cloud of quickly condensing vapor. Malak's shoulder tightened with another sharp stab. Smierc snapped her surprised mouth closed before either figure could untangle themselves and get off the floor. The taller one had landed on top and its black helmet turned, taking in his audience

"Well. Shit." He sat back on his knees and toes and pulled the other soldier up to sitting by the back of her armor suit. One of her shoulders was hanging lower than the other, the arm cradled in her other hand.

"Malak." Her helmet distorted her proximity comm but her irritation still came through clearly. "Great. As if my day wasn't bad enough."

CHAPTER 14: THIEVES, EVILDOERS, AND BUSYBODIES

Struo. Noun. Cargo ships used by the Coalition for resupply and medical transports, *Struos* like the *Huangfu* carry minimal defensive fighters but multiple modified *Runas* for ship-to-ship and ship-to-surface transports.

Ex. The Struo *class may be slow, but they have enough armor that they can take laser cannon fire without so much as waking the patients.*

Hour 1600
May 19, 2156

"This is ridiculous," Taav complained. Loudly. For at least the sixth time since they had disembarked from the *Kahlid.*

"Your face?" Rodriguez did not look away from the tiny mirror on the back of the commensurately tiny bathroom door. "That's true, but at least you have your personality. Oh. Wait."

Taav made a fist and rounded on Rodriguez, then let out a frustrated huff to find Kerry seated on the narrow bunk between them. Kerry didn't move; Rodriguez continued fussing with his hair, and Taav was forced to let the comment slide or risk tangling with the first GMH to be considered for corporal's bars. Surprisingly, he made the smart choice, but Maker did not think he looked happy about it. She pulled a packet of coffee concentrate from one of the galley drawers and hoped Taav would make use of his bunk. The rest of the *Dido's* occupants would have a much better day if he were asleep. If he didn't get that way voluntarily, there were at least three people on board who would be happy to make it involuntary.

Gonzales leaned against the galley counter, scrolling through her personal tablet. When Maker raised her eyebrows and gestured to the coffee, the other woman nodded.

"Thanks. Maybe it will make the news go down easier."

"What? Are they cutting our pay or something?"

The female soldier glanced at the men clustered near the table. "Grab the drinks and come take a look." She opened the door to the small bunk room and stepped inside.

"What are you looking at?" Taav's eyebrows were drawn together and his mouth turned down, but he was also bracing to stand up.

"Porn," Gonzales answered flatly. "Huge, hairy, man-on-man porn. Very graphic. There might be some farm animals involved. Interested?" Taav made a disgusted noise, but Rodriguez grinned.

"I might be. Adventure is my-"

"Nobody invited you, Fuzz." Gonzales pulled Maker inside and closed the door with a snap. She traded her tablet for a coffee and took a long sip before hitting play. A news anchor was smiling brightly and thanking the meteorologist.

"We'll make sure to follow your precautions, Yolanda. Severe weather is no joke! In other news. The Barrier Reef Reclamation ribbon cutting was completed today with attendees live on-site from the Coalition Congress and local governments. They were joined by some of the most ecologically conscious celebrities that have been leveraging their massive followings to draw attention to the importance of this project. Once the pH of the Pacific Ocean was stabilized through…"

"Sorry," Gonzales muttered. She dragged her finger over the screen. "I backed up too far. Right….here, I think."

"…own reporter on site took the opportunity to ask the question that has been on the minds of all Sol citizens."

The image cut away to an older woman with a press badge and a microphone leaning into the personal space of a man past middle age with heavy lines on his face. "General Batma, is the elite Legion responsible for the remarkable rescue of tens of thousands of civilians in the Navi system?"

Maker sucked in a breath. Batma did not even twitch.

"I am here today to support the hardworking men and women who have restored this invaluable ecosystem, not to discuss rumors."

"General-" the reporter jogged to keep up with the man as he moved briskly away- "exactly how many of the secretive and highly skilled Legion special forces were lost to save lives and protect strategic technetium reserves?"

"The Sol Coalition will release a report on the Navi incident shortly. In the meantime, please make sure to thank our government and private sector scientists who have accomplished so much here. Good day."

"Well…" Maker swallowed a mouthful of coffee. "Somebody is going to get demoted for releasing action reports to the press. Glad I won't be around when Soon sees this."

"So it's true?" Gonzales glanced at the closed door and then back at Maker. "Was the black ops guy from RB-14 really there? Everybody's talking about that stunt you pulled with the Cullers, but I heard you convinced the captain to support a special forces ground unit. Was it him?"

"Him, who?" Maker drank more coffee to stall for time. The reconstituted caffeine tasted like the inside of a well-used combat boot.

"*Don't mince words.*" Gonzales huffed in Spanish. "Seriously? You're going to try to act dumb with me? I was there the first time. Hell, I saw you and Kwidinok when you got back to base after that storm. You told me the Legion-"

"Yeah. It was him."

"How do you know so much about this guy? I mean, if you got a heads up about the Legion from your mother then-"

"No. Hell no. Why would you even bring her up? How do you even know who she is?"

"Uh..." Gonzales shrugged uncomfortably and glanced away. "I guess you've said a few things. And, uh, I saw Captain Yamamoto while I was working security at Oort Station. You look a lot alike. She...she is your mother, right?"

Maker blew out a hard breath and shoved the tablet into Gonzales' stomach. "Yeah, Pilar. Yamamoto gave birth to me. But she didn't tell me anything about the Legion. We don't talk. That is extremely intentional on my part."

"Okay, sorry I brought it up. No need to get violent." She folded the tablet up and stuffed it into a pocket on her uniform. Maker had almost gotten over the old anger that mention of her mother always brought up when Gonzales finished her coffee and ventured, "So how *do* you know about the Legion?"

"The same way you do, bad luck. Like you said, you've been there every time I've run into him – them – too. It's just my shitty privilege to be the one with the comm training, alright?"

"Alright. Fine." She reached out for the door control,

then paused, "Does that mean Admiral Yamamoto is your grandfather?"

"You want me to run through the family tree for you? I told you, I don't talk to-"

"We are approaching direct comms range." Bretavic's voice over the intercom interrupted the argument.

Thank fuck. There were few things Maker wanted to do less than talk about Malak and the Legion. It only ranked slightly higher in her list of conversation topics than the Yamamotos or Rodriguez's sex life. She hit the door controls herself and stalked past the still testosterone-fueled angst in the galley and into the cockpit. Bretavic gestured to the co-pilot's seat and she pulled on a headset. The automated transmission had stopped, and the ship was inert. If she hadn't been able to see it with her own eyes, she wouldn't have known it was there. As it was, even with the sensors on the *Dido* enhanced as far as they could go, the French cargo hauler was silent, cold, and oddly blurry around the edges. It wasn't even generating a gravity field that could be detected.

"Are we sure those readings are right?"

"You're the officer," Bretavic grunted, going through checks to slow down the *Dido* and bring them into a standard reconnaissance position half a klick away. "I'm just here to fly."

"Rodriguez." Maker turned and called back into the ship. "Run diagnostics on sensors."

"On it, LT." To his credit, he instantly ceased antagonizing Taav and slipped into the narrow anteroom between the cockpit and the galley. He typed at the control panel there for a solid minute before pulling a mag-driver off his belt and opening an access port. Mutters and the mechanical click of processors being pulled, checked, and replaced filled the silence.

Maker stared at the cargo ship while she waited. It was similar in size and general configuration to a *Cicuta* class – which wasn't surprising since a lot of civilian ships were repurposed decommissioned military vessels or cheap generic copies of patented designs. There was something odd about the exterior panels, however. It was as if the ceramic plating had been replaced with a material that didn't reflect light or heat but seemed to absorb it. She leaned forward, staring harder. It *was* blurry. Blinking a few times did not improve the image.

"Check the exterior cameras while you're in there," she ordered the mechanic.

The display went blank for a few moments, then popped back up. It was no less blurry.

"Nothing wrong with sensors, LT. And those cameras are so crisp I could use them as a mirror."

Bretavic mumbled in Russian under his breath. In the name of team civility, Maker chose not to translate. She punched in her codes to bring up the comms controls and opened a wide channel to the French ship.

"*Navire non identifié, c'est le transport Sol Coalition Dido. Nous avons reçu l'ordre de confirmer votre situation et de vous aider. Répond s'il te plait.*" She repeated in Standard, "Unidentified vessel, this is the Sol Coalition transport *Dido*. We have been ordered to confirm your situation and offer assistance. Please respond." She muted her end and started a timer for the regulation two minutes she would need to wait to make contact again.

"What are we going to do if they don't respond?" Rodriguez had appeared over her shoulder so quietly she jumped and almost put her elbow in his face.

"*We* aren't going to do anything. I will comm them again."

"And then what?"

That was a good question. One Maker didn't have an answer for. Procedure would have her review sensor logs, determine if there was anyone on the ship, assess potential firepower, and then make a call to either board the French ship or request backup from the *Khalid*. There wasn't anything in the procedures for what to do if there were no sensor logs. Thankfully, Bretavic answered the nosy mechanic for her.

"Then I use your face to realign the internal array dish and see if that helps."

"Whoa, touchy. Fine. Let me know if you need my underappreciated skills again."

Bretavic aggressively closed the cockpit door behind Rodriguez's retreating back. They sat in silence while the counter ticked down. Maker repeated her comm. Nothing. She sat back in her chair and stared at the blurry image. The Raiders had once come across a dead ship while they were between missions. When they hadn't received a response to their comm, the XO had ordered helm to pull them along side. She had opened the blast shield on the cockpit and then run searchlights over the hull doing a visual inspection with her own eyes. Then three of the biggest adrenaline junkies in the platoon had suited up with chemical and environmental hazard protections in place, headed to the closest airlock, and jumped out onto the dead ship. They had pried open a docking ring, depressurizing one section before they could get inside and manually close the emergency doors. After a thorough search they had found a metric shit ton of alcohol missing its required taxation stamps, illegal artificial dopamine, and enough stimulants to power six platoons straight through the Culler front line. There had also been an entire crew of smugglers that appeared to have had a disagreement over how the profit from their cargo would be split.

A violent disagreement.

The Raiders had confiscated the alcohol, set up a hazard beacon to scare away scavengers, and then alerted the CSNS Guard to come tow it to impound. Maker had not enjoyed the drunken leave that followed enough to risk coming into mag-lock distance with a ship she had no sensor readings on. If there were pirates on board who had somehow managed to mask themselves from scans, they would probably be willing to shoot at a single, dinky little Coalition transport to stay hidden. She wasn't particularly interested in blowing an airlock open either; if there were any crew or passengers alive on the French hauler, they wouldn't be for long if it lost pressure.

"Does that look like a *Cicuta* to you?"

"Sure," Bretavic replied. "If it had been armed by a paranoid American and painted by a depressed Russian."

"If I wanted to get a look inside..." What she wanted to do was set a hazard beacon and get the hell back to the *Khalid*. Maker rolled her head on her neck, enjoying the resounding crack, then sighed. What she wanted was to not have Giradot or Soon crawling up her ass about how she had handled this command or questioning if she had done enough. "If I wanted to get inside, but I didn't want to use the front door, where would you send me?"

"I wouldn't." Bretavic frowned, then huffed. "You know who would."

Maker sighed again and summoned Rodriguez to the cockpit, then posed her question to him. He, in what should have been a predictable move but still managed to surprise her, answered with a grin.

"So you like the back door, huh LT?"

* * *

An hour later, the mechanic had lost his smirk. Behind his clear faceplate Maker could see the whites of his eyes all around the iris.

"This seems more like a job for one of the ground troops. I'm an engineer, not a soldier."

"We're all soldiers for the Coalition, Fuzz." Maker checked the harness over his armor and then her own. *This might be the stupidest thing you've ever done, Clara.* She snorted to herself. *Not even close.* It was a little sad that her current plan did not make the top five in that list.

"Still, what is the point of having three well-trained, beefy hotshots on board if not to stand between the officers and potential danger?"

"You're an ensign," Kerry pointed out as he double-checked the grappling mechanism.

Gonzales chimed in over the comm line. "Awe, that's so generous of you to include Taav in with the well-trained crowd. Are you trying to sweet-talk him?"

Rodriguez waved a hand to catch Maker's attention, then pointed at his own helmet. "Can he hear me?"

"Yes, but I have his transceiver muted."

Rodriguez grinned and answered Gonzales. "Yes, yes I am sweet-talking him. I am hoping he is so flattered he follows after me on this mission. Preferably without a safety harness. Or working environmentals."

"You shouldn't be doing this." Kerry frowned at Maker through their respective faceplates.

"I'm in command," she replied, taking a deep breath. "An officer can't ask a soldier to do what they are not willing to do themselves."

"They can. They do it all the time." The bluish tone of his skin looked darker in the red lighting of the airlock.

"They shouldn't."

"So, seriously-" Rodriguez stopped trying to irritate Taav for a moment- "about this duty assignment. I think Gonzales would be much better suited to this, LT."

"Gonzales doesn't speak French."

"Kerry?"

"Kerry won't fit in the hatch, and he doesn't speak French."

"What about Taav?" Rodriguez was desperately eyeing the grappler as Kerry readied it.

"Doesn't speak French, won't fit in the hatch, and also might cut your line on purpose."

"Well, why do I have to go?"

"Because I need you to override the systems and open the hatch. You will fit, and most of the time I don't want to shove you untethered into open space. We've been over this. You're going with me. That's an order, Ensign."

"Yes, ma'am," he replied sullenly, grabbing onto the safety railing while Maker hit the door controls. What little air hadn't already been vented into pressurized storage whipped out past them into the vacuum of space. Resolutely, Maker kept her eyes on the cargo hauler instead of letting them scan over the vast, distant nothing. After having done a walk between two ships in motion, the task ahead of her seemed slightly less frightening. *I need a transfer*, she thought with resignation. *Somewhere boring. Like a cryogyser.*

"Helm, are we in position?" She tapped on the maglocks on her boots.

"Steady and ready, Lieutenant." Bretavic was the only one of them that sounded calm and professional.

"Fire grappler in three…"

"You should let me do this for you," Kerry insisted over his proximity comm. He was too close to her, blocking her view of the other ship and not where he was supposed to be to operate the line. "I'm supposed to be protecting you – we're here to keep you safe."

"Two…" Kerry wasn't moving, so Maker pulled up her controls and took remote control of the mag-grappler.

"Please, Clara. I need to do this for you. You-"

"One." She pressed the command on her bracer and high-tension braided wire shot out of the *Dido*. Bretavic compensated for the reverse thrust perfectly, keeping them in position and ensuring the grappler hit the target. She pushed at Kerry to get him to move so she could get visual confirmation. He didn't move. She switched to proximity. "We both know this security detail is bullshit. So let's just get this over with."

"Clara, I-"

"Hey, LT." Rodriguez squeezed between her and Kerry, forcing the soldier to take a step back or get a maglocked boot across his instep. "If we're doing this, let's do it before I throw up in my helmet. Okay?" He secured their harnesses together and then clipped their line on the grappler. "You want a three count or-"

His shrill exclamation echoed inside her helmet as she threw them both out into space.

It took longer than necessary to reach the French ship. Maker should have backed them up and given Rodriguez a running start, but she hadn't wanted to give Kerry the opportunity to try and talk her out of going. She didn't even know why he was pushing the issue so hard. He had seen her come out alive of worse situations, and it wasn't like Bretavic couldn't swing the

Dido in close if she needed a rescue. She was grateful when they touched down on the hull of the hauler, and she had something else to focus on. Her boots locked to the surface, Rodriguez a beat behind. She unclipped her harness from his and the grappler line.

Then her boots unlocked.

For a moment, Maker was floating away from the ship. It was only a few centimeters, but the sudden sensation of being untethered from anything caused a sense of vertigo. Her stomach flipped over.

"What the-" Rodriguez started.

Her HUD flashed a warning, unknown composite, then the electromagnets in her boots kicked in again and she was forcefully sucked to the surface of the ship. She took a knee while her inner ear recalibrated and her HUD signaled warnings. As usual Rodriguez talked.

"What the hell is this made out of?" He had, smartly, remained tethered and managed to calmly resecure his own boots and then pull a sensor tool off of his belt to examine the hull closer. "Oh I love this. This is...this is ingenious. LT, you should get a look at-"

"We have a job, Fuzz." Swallowing down the sick spinning feeling, Maker reached out to unclip him as well, then opened a comm channel. "*Dido*, *Dido*. This is Zulu-actual, come in."

"Zulu...clear...say...Over."

Maker frowned, then stood to turn and face back toward the ship. The airlock was still open, casting red light out around Kerry's silhouette, barely visible in the distance.

"*Dido*, *Dido*. This is Zulu-actual. Say again. Over."

"Zulu, this is *Dido*. Your signal is weak, Zulu. Can you boost it?

Over." Gonzales was running the comms back on the ship, and while she had done a rotation in comms, and Maker had briefed her before she left, troubleshooting a problem that Maker couldn't diagnose on her own end was asking a lot of the soldier.

"*Dido*, this is Zulu. Negative. What is interfering with sensors must be clouding the signal. We may lose comms until we find the source. Over."

"Roger, Zulu. Standing orders? Over."

"Hold position, *Dido*. I'll contact again in thirty minutes. Comms silent until then. Over."

"Wilco, Zulu. You want us to comm you if we don't hear anything? Over."

I want you to come save my ass, she thought. *Bring the whole fucking cavalry and the cook wagon with you.* Unfortunately, the truth would make her sound like a scared little whiner and not at all like the officer in charge.

"Affirmative, *Dido*. Zulu out." She flipped off the channel and crouched next to Rodriguez again, listening to how even the proximity comm went staticky and weak as she got closer to the hull. "What have you got for me, Rodriguez?"

"The alloy that this plating is-"

"Later. Focus on the plan, Fuzz. Where is our entrance?"

"Don't you mean your back door?" He turned toward her, waggling his eyebrows behind his transparent visor.

"I mean our entrance. Now get your game face on-" she gestured to her own opaque helmet- "and get me inside this ship."

The hatch looked smaller in person than it had on the schematics. Rodriguez did not seem concerned, so Maker held her complaints as he hooked up his equipment and overrode the ship's system to gain access. Water vapor escaped in a quick burst, then he gestured for her to go first. Maker cursed, going head first into the narrow pipe. She had more room than Rodriguez given how much narrower her shoulders were, but it was still claustrophobic. Until they hit a safety wall.

"Okay. It won't open until I get the outer hull sealed again, then it might be quick, so brace yourself."

Maker followed his instructions and maglocked her boots to the walls, holding her legs at an uncomfortable angle. Above her, Rodriguez did the same, but in reverse. His hands remained close enough to the hatch to pull it shut behind them and use his field tablet to lock it into place. Abruptly, the safety wall retracted, her mag boots unlocked, and Maker was falling down a half-meter wide tube with vapor clouding around her and completely covering her faceplate. Her shoulder slammed into an angle in the tube, wrenching it out of socket

"Fuck-" She attempted to stop herself by pressing her palm against opposite sides of the tube. For a minute her descent halted. Then Rodriguez's boots connected with her legs, shoved her into the side of the tube, and sent her hurtling down. She almost got herself stopped a second time, but Rodriguez lost his magnetic lock again and they continued to fall. She crashed through a vent screen and then fell another three meters to the metal floor grates. Directly onto her dislocated shoulder. Rodriguez landed on top of her and knocked the wind out of her.

She wasn't able to suck in any air until the mechanic levered his weight off of her.

"Well. Shit." Rodriguez pulled her into a sitting position, and she cradled her arm to keep it from getting jostled. In front of her were two pairs of standard issue Coalition boots. Maker gripped her own elbow and followed black cargo pants up long legs to field jackets. Despite never having seen either of them before, she was sure she recognized one of their faces.

"Malak." Of course it was him. "Great. As if my day wasn't bad enough."

CHAPTER 15: EXECUTIVE PRIVILEGE

SEMERA Drive. Noun. REDACTED.

Hour 0930
January 8, 2153

President Yardley strode down the sun-dappled arcade in the Coalition's legislative seat with no regard for the politicians that tried to snag his attention or the staffers that scuttled out of his way. His security was keeping up with him admirably, but his assistant had fallen to the rear of his entourage. It was just as well. With the head of steam he had worked up on the train from Paris, it would be best if there were fewer witnesses to the ass-reaming he was about to hand out.

The heavy doors to the Science and Research Annex opened ahead of him, and his footsteps did not slow as he stalked down polished wooden corridors. An office manager, and then a personal assistant, rose from their seats when he entered the largest office suite, but he did not pause.

"Clear the room." He clenched his jaw to prevent anything else from coming out of his mouth.

Helen Maker raised one perfectly manicured brow and gestured to the assorted Ministry staff and legislative aides that had gathered for a meeting. He waited until they had filed out before tossing a tablet onto the sofa cushion next to her.

"What is this?" She picked it up with a slender hand, aged and pale, but still steady.

"You know what it is."

Images flickered to life on the screen, highlighting her polite nod. "I see. Are you looking for an apology or an explanation?"

"You're fired."

She laughed. Yardley clenched his fist to keep from hitting her.

"Excuse me?"

"You will have a letter of resignation on my desk by the end of the week."

"I don't think so." She leaned back against pristine blue cushions and reached for a nearby teacup. "You will want to wait until midterms, at least, to get the most political gain from an open Cabinet position and justify holding off on appointments until after elections are certified. Next year would be better."

"Are you trying to negotiate your firing, Minister Maker? Keep pushing me, and this offer will be rescinded and replaced with a tribunal summons."

"Tribunal? Don't be dramatic, Mr. President. Why don't you calm down and have some tea before-"

"One hundred eight thousand dead," he snarled. "We nearly lost the most valuable piece of intel to become available in years. You risked lives – you wasted them – redirecting one of our best ships – my ship – away from the Alnitak system. If they had arrived sooner instead of wasting time deploying a search party thousands of people might have been saved. Keres Legion was left exposed and could have lost the device because of the unit you directed to have sent to RB14! I allowed you to stay when I came into office because your projects have proved to be effective – but I told you no more interference! You agreed to keep yourself out of military decisions. You've crossed a line, Minister. It ends here."

"Agreed? I am afraid I did nothing of the sort, Mr. President. Still, I have adhered to your request for the most part. In this instance time was of the essence. I had an asset that needed to be on RB14, and so I took action. It will all work out for the best. Trust me."

"Trust you?" Yardley took an involuntary step back. "Madame, I don't trust you anymore than I trust a scorpion in my sock. I'd rather have a Culler at my back in a fight than you. I reviewed the crew casualty and injury lists. That was my crew. Did you think I wouldn't? My god, woman, your own granddaughter was down there unprepared with enough of the enemy to overrun a *Khutura* class! She could have been killed – she nearly was!"

For the first time since he had met her, Helen Maker hesitated. Her teacup stopped inches from her lips. She blinked slowly.

"Everything worked out. For the best, as I said." She cleared her throat and took a sip. "We did get the intel, didn't we? Do you have an update on when the object will be arriving so that my people can begin assessing it?"

"It won't." He cut her off before she could speak again. "It will remain with the Keres Legion. I am directly authorizing new resources to them for evaluation and assessment. Resources not associated with this Ministry."

"SAR will-"

"SAR will not be involved." Yardley's eyes narrowed. Helen's mouth was pinched at the corners, tightening her elegant face. A few drops of tea sloshed over the rim of her cup as she replaced it on her saucer. "Perhaps you are right," he said slowly. "Perhaps after the midterms would be better for your resignation."

"What has changed your mind?"

He ignored her question. "Stay on top of the *Zanbato* project. I want a prototype ready for initial field testing before the end of my first term."

"That is nearly two years ahead of my schedule, Mr.-"

"Not your schedule. Not anymore, Minister." He linked his arms behind his back. His anger had cooled, replaced with the calm calculation that had made him one of the most successful captains in Coalition history. "After the midterms," he reminded her. Yardley paused on the way out of her office, one hand on the door. "And Minister, don't subvert military orders again. I will not tolerate you risking my people."

"Oh?" She raised one brow again, but the expression was brittle. "Is Keres Legion yours now?"

"I am the Commander in Chief, Helen. They are all my people. Including your granddaughter."

CHAPTER 16: SMOKE SCREENING

__R-DETB (Remote Deployed Enemy Tracking Beacon).__ Noun. Subspace transciever capable of being fired at an enemy ship. Upon contact, it deploys a two-part molecular bond to adhere to the hull and siphons electricity from the ship to power its signal. It can be tracked at a distance of up to seven light years, but may be manually removed by cutting away the bonded portion of a hull.

Hour 1800
May 19, 2156

"You do realize we don't actually have a brig?"

Malak refused to acknowledge Smierc. Of course the *Han* didn't have a brig. It didn't need one. They were a covert unit on a covert ship, designed to appear suddenly behind enemy lines, decimate their opponents, and leave. They didn't take prisoners, and Keres Legion did not disobey orders. There was no need for a brig.

Unless I need to lock up an inconvenient lieutenant.

"I found a place for her, of course. I am creative and industrious. You should remember that during my next evaluation. A raise would be nice."

Smierc only grinned at Malak's scowl. He punched the door controls to the supply room where he had stashed the other

Coalition soldier when they had first arrived on the *Han*. The door hissed, opened partway, abruptly stopped, and then whined and jolted apart. Malak looked at the slim male standing next to an open panel, exposed wires in his hands and a grimace on his face.

"This isn't what it looks like."

"It looks like you were trying to escape." Smierc strode first into the room, grabbing the man by his shoulder and casually tossing him back against a shelving unit. He let out a huff of air before sliding to the floor.

"Escape…" He struggled to inhale but finally caught his breath. "Such an inaccurate term. It implies that I have either been captured by the enemy – or that I am under some sort of interrogation hold. Neither can possibly be true here."

Malak could hear the man's pulse thundering and smell the anxiety wafting off of him, but his teeth remained bared in a friendly smile, and his body language was open and relaxed. He was either an idiot or Malak was missing important information about how and why Zulu had come to the *Han*. Smierc continued the interrogation.

"Why is that?"

"Well, you are far too beautiful to be a Culler." He widened his smile at Smierc. "And I am far too uninteresting to be interrogated. You are wasting your time on me. I just follow orders and look good. Oh – is that why I'm here? You noticed how good I look? I am flattered, of course, but I am in a long-standing relationship with my LT. She hasn't acknowledged our destiny yet, but when she does I could let her know that you would be interested in joining our-"

"Enough." Malak didn't move any closer, but the stench of catecolines increased. The even white smile remained. "What are you doing here?"

"Following orders, sir." He gave a sloppy salute. At the slight shake of Smierc's head, his hand fell limply to his lap. Once he started talking his mouth didn't seem to stop running. "Our ship picked up a civilian beacon. We just came off of a rather nasty engagement in the Navi system. We were limping home and in no condition to redirect to check on a ship that wasn't in distress, but the LT was ordered to take the *Dido* and an assessment crew to evaluate. We were having trouble picking up life signs – could be metallic resonance in the dust particles here or could be your ship has a prototy – er, some problem with our sensors probably. Our XO is a real prick. He would give us all shit assignments if he thought we had taken it easy on this one, so we had to come investigate. LT didn't want to crack a docking port and risk depressurization, so I found us a back door. Speaking of-" he smiled up at Smierc, who returned the expression with all of her teeth- "or not," he hastily redirected his attention to Malak. "Bit of a fuck up, if you ask me. But it always is when the SIS gets involved. Say, don't suppose I could see my lieutenant now? I get separation anxiety."

"Talk to me more about this metallic resonance." Smierc was obviously interested in what the soldier had figured out about the *Han*. Malak had more pressing questions.

"How is SIS involved?"

"Oh, uh. I wasn't there, but I guess the Intelligence Officer on our ship, the *Khalid*, had a pissing contest with our XO. He wanted LT to come check out your signal. The XO didn't. Which is kind of strange since this is the sort of shitty job that Commander Soon would love giving to-"

"How did the SIS know about the signal?"

"C&E? They wouldn't have probably picked it up, but LT – I mean-"

Malak turned to walk out. The soldier surged up from the

floor with surprising athleticism, but was still easily caught by Smierc.

"Are you leaving to talk to her? You don't need to. I'm the brains here. Best mechanic in this quadrant," he boasted.

There was a desperation to him that Malak couldn't understand. It was almost as if he was trying to protect his superior officer – the one who had gotten him into his current situation. Malak hadn't seen that kind of loyalty among human soldiers before. He looked over his shoulder and studied the man more carefully. He was a little dirty and rumpled from the trip down the vapor shaft. His belt was loaded with utility tools. His name patch read, *Rodriguez D.*

Of course he is loyal to her. They had been on multiple dangerous missions together.

She had nearly gotten him killed more than once. *She's a reckless fool.*

"Hey! We were following orders. Leave-" The door shut behind Malak and he stood in the corridor for a long moment, considering. Finally he turned toward the bridge and his ready room, sending Smierc a message to meet him there once she had finished with Rodriguez. He didn't have to wait long, just long enough to wonder why Zulu – *Maker* – kept appearing in his path. And what the Sol Intelligence Service had to do with it.

"I will admit that I don't do a lot of interrogations. Actually, none before that I can think of." Smierc strolled into his ready room casually. "But I thought they would be more...challenging. I didn't even have to threaten him. He just spilled everything. I know more about Daniel Rodriguez than I thought there was to know about anyone. Have you ever heard of something called a vintner's reserve? Apparently he once got into-"

"Pertinent information," Malak reminded her gruffly.

"Very well. But it was interesting."

Smierc ran through what she had found out relating to Zulu's assignment. It all seemed to be aboveboard on her part. A case of two officers who disliked each other and also Zulu and were using her to irritate one another. Malak's shoulder had settled into a dull throb, and the new nerves in his back were still twitching. He didn't trust her. She was always exactly where she shouldn't be. Out of the nearly two billion soldiers in the Coalition, he had run across her three times. During decades of service he had never seen an individual human soldier more than once in the field. Except her.

Because you didn't kill her.

Because you saved her.

She saved you.

Ondrea broke into his line of thought through the comm.

"Captain, the Coalition ship is sending out a hail."

"Let me hear it."

"I...can't, sir. It is encrypted."

Smierc answered for him. "Then decrypt it."

There was a brief, quiet discussion between Ondrea and the Falcon serving next to her before she answered. "Our software does not seem to be able to do so."

Zulu.

"Go get her."

"You want me to bring her here?" Smierc's expression was indecipherable, but she was watching him closely.

"Now."

The bridge was silent for a few moments after Smierc left until Hemah leaned back in her chair and cocked her head to the side, studying the visual display of a small *Runa*. "They've got a good pilot. If it was on auto, that little transport would stay exactly the same distance at all times. But she's dipping close enough to get her sensors in range and then back away again before a standard *Cicuta* would be able to get a weapons lock."

Her twin mused, "I wonder what they would do if they knew we have a longer range."

Smierc arrived before they could continue their conversation. Zulu walked in front of her, helmet off and eyes blazing. Her jaw remained locked tightly, but she didn't need to speak for Malak to know what she was thinking. She smelled of sweat and lingering pain and anger.

"Sir," Ondrea's Falcon broke the tension Malak could feel building against the back of his skull. "A second hail, also encrypted."

"Give my people the decryption code," he ordered Zulu.

"Where is my engineer?"

"The Major gave you an order, Lieutenant." Smierc raised a brow, but Zulu did not turn her gaze from Malak. The heat of her emotion might have burned a hole through him if he were human.

"Where is my engineer...*Major*?"

He could feel a growl building in his chest. This reckless idiot that called herself a soldier had risked her life and the lives her the people under her command, time and again. Her actions had interfered with his own missions more than once. Malak was not used to insubordination and his immediate, visceral reaction surprised him. His upper lip curled back from his teeth.

"Secure and unharmed in a holding area," Smierc answered.

Her eyes cut to him with a frown, and Malak swallowed down his emotions to grab Zulu by the neck and shake compliance out of her. Smierc continued, "All Coalition protocols have been followed for the situation. Now you need to follow the orders of a superior officer and decrypt the message your ship is sending out."

Zulu spat a few words in a language Malak did not recognize. "Yes, *sir*." The insincerity translated easily. She stalked over to the sensors station and motioned Ondrea out of the way.

"You can instruct me," Ondrea began, but Zulu interrupted.

"This will be faster, and they are getting impatient."

Ondrea waited for a nod from Malak before stepping aside. He could acknowledge even as he was still seething with irritation and a lingering headache that the sight was comical. The *Han* had been fitted to be more ergonomic for Legionnaires who averaged six inches taller than humans. Zulu was nearly that much shorter than the standard Coalition soldier and gave the impression of a child at play. The speed at which her fingers danced across the screen belied the image. A gruff voice broke over the bridge comm mid-sentence.

"- Coalition transport *Dido*. Zulu, we are no longer picking up the signals from your personal comms. You now have eight minutes to respond before we will summon reinforcements. Come in, Zulu."

"Now what, Major? Do we wait for the *Khalid* to arrive?" Zulu was smiling with lips closed over her teeth. It was more annoying than her sarcasm had been.

"Tell them you are fine and to hold their position until further instruction."

"And then what?"

"Send the communication, Lieutenant," Smierc said before

Malak could reprimand Zulu.

"What are you planning to do with my engineer?"

Malak's eyes narrowed. He could kill them both and destroy the *Dido*. He had the authority and they were liabilities.

She had written encryption his people could not break. She had cut into transmissions that Parshav had assured Malak was impenetrable. *You would have died on Navi without her interference,* an unwanted voice in his head reminded him. He inhaled deeply. She was sweaty, injured, and annoyed. She was also afraid. *My engineer*, she had said. Not *us*. Her fear was for her people, not herself. Was it because he had saved her in the past, or because this human – against everything he knew about their species – treated the lives of those she was responsible for as more important than her own? Everything about her was frustrating.

He owed her his life.

"My ready room." He turned on his heel, knowing Smierc would make certain Zulu followed. He walked to the far end of the table and waited, fists braced on the surface. The stance was intimidating. It also took some pressure off of his back. Zulu stepped inside and when Smierc would have followed Malak shook his head. Her green eyes widened, but she shut the door between them without voicing a question.

She opened her mouth but he spoke first to try to avoid an argument.

"Send the message to the Dido."

"Tell me what you are planning to do with my people."

"I don't know." Malak blinked, but managed to contain any other reaction to his own surprise. He had not planned to reveal his indecision to her.

"Then why should I make it easier for you to pull the blackout card and make this situation disappear?" She folded her arms across her chest. Despite the defiant stance, her scent had mellowed, the fear and aggression dropping substantially.

He swallowed down the instinctual response to explain that there was nothing she could do to make it difficult for him to kill her. Instead he studied the wrinkle between her eyes and the compression around her mouth. Why had she saved him? It had to have been a risk to her career. The after-action reports proved that it had put ships in the battle at risk and cost the lives of human soldiers fighting the Cullers in space. It had saved three times as many civilians and his own teams, but she had been willing to risk sacrificing military assets – her own kind – to do it. Malak could not understand why she was so different than the humans he had come to know. Even Thomas, who had worked with Malak for his entire career, would not have made that call.

If it had been Thomas in Zulu's position on VK-10 or that damned deserted colony, Malak would have left him to die. He had let her live.

"What happened to your back?"

Malak straightened reflexively, then bit down the wince that came with the sudden stretch and bunch of fresh skin and healing muscle.

"Nothing." He needed to get her on target and falling in line. Questioning her motives or his own was not improving the situation. "Explain to me how your arrival on my ship is a coincidence." He glanced at the time readout on the wall. "You have five minutes before you will send the comm to your ship."

Her story mirrored what Rodriguez had said – with considerably less colorful language or verbal abuse of her superiors. It was a coincidence. The idea defied belief. *Unless it isn't. Unless the SIS sent her here to get inside Legion security.* He dismissed the thought. As strange as it was to admit, Maker knew Zulu. She was reckless and loyal to her people and brilliant and weak and had shockingly poor aim, but she was no tool of the Intelligence Service. She had kept her knowledge of the Legion to herself until his own life depended on breaking her silence. She was tired, irritated, and worried – but not conniving.

I know her like one of my own. Like pack, but that was impossible.

"How did you come to be this close to the Navi retreat route and dead in the water?"

"Prototype, working out the kinks." He clamped his jaw closed. He should not have answered her, but his mouth had gone ahead without thinking.

"You can't just blow up the *Dido*, not until you get this ship fixed," she reasoned out loud. "It would draw attention to your location if our beacon suddenly disappeared. You can't kill my engineer and me without the *Dido* alerting the *Khalid* – and then you are still facing more attention than you want from the rank and file. You can't send us back to the *Dido* because we've seen your prototype and presumably now know too much sensitive information. You've no doubt already talked to Rodriguez and come to the conclusion he couldn't keep his mouth shut if his life depended on it."

She wasn't wrong. Rodriguez was potentially the biggest risk to the Legion's secrecy they had ever come across.

"That isn't true," she argued with his unspoken thoughts. "He's gone this long without saying anything, and he's a good soldier. He will not betray a trust."

She shifted, wincing as if her back was bothering her.

"There is one man on the *Dido* who is an unknown, but everyone else on my team I would trust with my life. I would trust them with yours. I have – whether you knew it or not."

Malak was not certain if that was a problem. It was disconcerting to know that a small band of humans he had never met had been protecting his mission even it was only by staying silent. He didn't like it. That he was certain about.

"Let Rodriguez take a look at your technical issue. He can at least help get it fixed faster."

Malak grudgingly admitted the sense in that. The engineer had already displayed remarkable aptitude. With a Falcon watching over him the risk of having him work on ship systems was small enough to be acceptable. He sent a short message to Smierc.

"You have to let us go," she concluded, somewhat smugly. That, too, was annoying. "I can report nothing out of the ordinary – just a civilian ship with a wicked computer virus and a technician too incompetent to make repairs. Rodriguez will back me up and the others don't actually know anything except that we ran into a retrofitted *Cicuta*. We'll get the SIS off of your scent – if that was Giradot's intention in sending us out here and not just to piss off Soon. You are welcome, by the way-" she smiled, showing off her uselessly small, straight teeth and pushing her cheeks up into soft-looking pink circles- "for saving you again."

Malak bared his own teeth, an expression that was less friendly.

"Major," Ondrea's voice cut over the ready room comm. "We're being hailed by a second contact."

Malak bit off an expletive and stalked over to open the door and to stare at the Legionnaire who had interrupted their argument. *Her argument.* The Major had yet to say anything in his own defense. He had an inkling of fear that if he opened his mouth he would tell her more things she didn't need to know.

"Standard message," he rasped from deep in his chest. On the visual display a small speck was growing closer, thirty degrees away from the location of the *Dido*. A Falcon technician arrived with Rodriguez, and they shuffled to the side while waiting instruction. Malak did not miss the man's relief at seeing Zulu.

"I already sent it once," Ondrea assured him, "but they-"

Zulu slipped past him and headed to the comms station. "What's the frequency?" She grabbed the spare headset from the console.

"Lieutenant-" He began, but she cut him off as if she were the ranking officer

"Shhh, I'm busy. Why is everything so damned tall around here?" She pulled up the encryption data and spoke to the Falcon comms officer. "This one is already in your database," she said as she started running analysis on the newcomer's systems. Another comm came in while she worked, this one from the *Dido*. She opened the line and dropped any protocol. "What is it, Bretavic?"

"There's a transport vessel out here hailing me. They're running a low level sensor sweep too. You want me to respond? Order them to back off? Also, nice to hear your voice."

"You too. No contact with them for now. Hold on."

"Zulu," Malak said tightly, gripping her shoulder to get her attention. He didn't particularly want to reprimand her in front of his crew, but it was his ship and he needed her out of the way so he could deal with the situation. Smierc stood up from the command chair, tensed and ready to move. "Step down. We have-"

She interrupted. "You are on a blackout op. Let me get rid of these newcomers before you have another problem to deal with." Her hands paused for a moment and she looked up at him. "This is something I do better than you."

He trusted her. He didn't like her. He didn't like that he trusted her against his better judgment and with no conscious decision on his part, but he did.

"Hn." He released his hold on her. "You have the conn Lieutenant Maker."

"Thank you, *sir*." She turned back to the console. She wasn't smirking, but he knew in his bones that she wanted to. "If we run into anything that wants to kill us – I'll gladly let you take the lead."

He watched silently while she worked. From her low conversation with Ondrea and the Falcon he could guess that she was pulling apart the newcomer's frequency signature and the computer's analysis. He gathered that without her decryption program, the *Han's* systems would have not have picked up on the problem until it was too late. She swore creatively.

"Are they one of yours? The *Dolcezza?*"

"Er, no." Ondrea's eyes cut to Malak. "But we've run across it before."

"Ensign," Zulu snapped her fingers once at the Falcon. "Show me the last log from this ship." Zulu repressed a sigh and began pulling it up herself while the Falcon who had been manning the comm station stared at her. Malak chuffed at his sensor officer and she hurried to assist Zulu.

"Lieutenant, uh.."

"Maker," he supplied for Ondrea as he signaled to Af to be prepared to target the new ship.

"Oh," Zulu interjected as she scanned the logs, "so you know who I am when the SIS is trailing you, but not when I'm saving your skin at Navi."

"What do you mean, SIS?" Malak stepped up beside her, crowding Ondrea over. The Falcon wisely melted away. Smierc regained her seat and pulled up sensors.

"How can you tell?" the redhead asked.

"Signature masking," Zulu huffed. Her elbow glanced his ribs but he ignored it to look over her head at the control screen. "They're covering with fake static – made to look like a nonlethal radiation leak. Sloppy, but it would pass cursory inspection. It hides a couple of subspace lines they are transferring data packets on. Too much information for nonmilitary use. Could be corporate espionage, but we're too far off the shipping lanes for that. Do. You. Mind?" She glared at him over her shoulder. "A little space?"

He ignored her.

"Af," he ordered, "get me a weapons lock." She nodded, but paused when Zulu interjected.

"Don't! Are you out of your mind? Aren't you supposed to be clandestine?"

"I think LT is trying to say that we were under the impression the Legion is on Blackout status." Rodriguez smiled winningly. The Falcon next to him shook his head in a warning to stay silent. Malak would have been shocked if the man listened to good advice.

"If we were this Legion," Smierc said casually as she continued to review data, "then that would mean we should kill you *and* the crew of the *Dolcezza*. Right?"

"Probably we were wrong," Rodriguez muttered. Smierc grinned down at her console.

Another insistent comm request from the *Dolcezza* pinged under Zulu's fingertips. Malak reached around her to flick open the readout. The pilot on the *Dido* was still talking.

"If these sensor sweeps get any more invasive, they're going to owe me a drink. Kerry's over here arming up, ready to do a free walk and bring the heavy gun to you. What's the call, Maker?"

Malak zoomed the bridge display to focus on the approaching *Dolcezza*. Tactical had already painted it red with a firing solution.

"Af-" Malak began, but Maker cut him off. Again. His lip curled in a snarl.

"Right. We can fix this." She slipped under Malak's arm, holding her headset in place, and took quick stock of the people crowded onto the bridge. "Hold on, Bretavic, give me a second." She pulled the headset to dangle around her neck. "Rodriguez, can you downgrade this ship's bridge camera? Whatever they've got, I want it grainy and looking like rats have been chewing on the cables. And can you cut the frame to crop out tactical and helm? Just the captain's chair?"

"No problem on the resolution. If you don't mind, sir?" He carefully removed his arm from the forceful grip of the Falcon next to him. When they didn't immediately seize him again, he snagged the toolkit from their other hand and jogged to the front of the bridge, pulling off a panel to the side of the display screen. "Cropping is going to be harder; they're still gonna see comms, maybe part of helm."

"Zulu."

She ignored him. Again. It was starting to irritate Malak.

"Can you blur the background, keep a tight focus on me?"

The engineer shrugged even as he stuck his head and shoulders inside an access hatch. "Sure," his voice echoed back. "What are you thinking?"

Malak had the same question, but also the desire to follow it up with throwing Zulu back on VK-10 with the hope that the lightning might take her off of his hands. Instead, he grabbed her bicep, holding tightly and lifting her up enough so that their faces were close. Her adrenaline flooded his nose.

"I said. Stand. Down."

"And I said that I can fix this for you without killing a bunch of the people who are supposed to be on our side." She cocked her head. Her warm breath puffed against his chin. "They may be assholes, but they aren't the enemy."

"That remains to be seen."

A swift smile crossed her face before disappearing again. "Let me return the favor. This is what I am good at," she insisted again.

He let her down. The moment her boots touched the floor she was striding to the center of the lower bridge, keeping the command chair behind her by a good meter and a half. Malak ordered anyone not fully human to clear the bridge. Only he and Smierc stayed behind, taking over at helm and tactical. Zulu double-checked their outbound video feed, making certain that the angle was tight enough that the Legionnaires were not on camera. The Falcon at the sensor station gave an update.

"Another hail. Much more aggressive." He put it on the bridge comm.

"Unmarked ship, this is *Dolcezza*. Respond immediately."

Zulu zipped up her flight suit and took up a wide stance, arms behind her back. "Put them through." She took a deep breath and twisted her face into a bored expression at odds with her elevated heart rate and tension-filled scent. The transmission from the *Dolcezza* flickered to life on the display. Malak recognized the man although it had been years since he and his ship had accosted the *Lead Belly*. The captain's persistence had been unfortunate at the time, but not suspicious. Malak should have known better. The SIS had been closer to the Legion than he had ever suspected. Parshav had spent years perfecting techniques to be certain that no Legion ship could be used to identify another. The *Dolcezza* could have only picked up on the *Han* if they knew what they were looking for – which was only possible with classified information.

"Unmarked ship, this is the *Dolcezza.* We picked up your distress-" A smile remained on the man's face, but his expression stiffened as Zulu interrupted him.

"*Dolcezza* this is Lieutenant Maker of the *Khalid.* Are you aware that approaching a Class II Electronic Contagion without Coalition authorization is a felony offense?"

"I..." He stumbled for words. Zulu didn't give him much of an opportunity to respond.

"You will return to your previously charted course of-" She snapped her fingers without looking away from the display. After only a second of hesitation the Falcon at sensors repeated the navigation markers for her. "That. Return to your previously charted course and I will consider a verbal warning adequate. If you waste any more of my time, I won't have any difficulty locating the forms necessary to report this."

"Lieutenant, I did not mean to violate any Coalition protocol-"

"Laws, *Dolcezza.* Not protocol. This is a law you have broken."

"-but we aren't within CSNS. Coalition law-"

"Applies on any ship, in any sector, that is captained by a Coalition officer." She pointed to the stripe on her shoulder. "It applies here. You have one minute to comply, *Dolcezza.* Do you need an escort? The *Dido* is available to make *certain* you get back on course – even all the way to your destination." Her smile was small and tight and more vicious than it had any right to be. "When we get there I can file a Docking Restriction Request for your ship."

The covert SIS captain grit his teeth but managed to continue with his deception. "That...civilian craft...is unmarked. Please give me the designation so that I can avoid it in the future."

"Dolcezza." Zulu rocked forward onto her toes and narrowed her eyes. "If you want to know my designation, you can file a request with the SIS. Mark it for Commander Giradot. I am sure you will receive a prompt response. You have thirty seconds to return to your course.

The captain of the *Dolcezza* was silent for a long time. Malak began counting down, ready to reposition them if Smeirc needed to open fire.

"Ma'am," The SIS captain said tightly. The transmission ended abruptly.

"They are moving away," the Falcon reported. "Returning to their previous course."

She glanced at Rodriguez. "Dan?"

"Transmission ended. We're clean with no comm riders or anything uploaded to our system."

Zulu relaxed her stance. Her smell fluctuated wildly with adrenaline and hormones."Hell. Let's not do that again."

The bridge door hissed open, and the crew began to filter back in. Grudging respect warred with anger. She'd taunted the SIS. They would have been better served to simply destroy the *Dolcezza.* Zulu rolled her head on her neck.

"There. Problem solved. You're welcome."

Anger won.

"Smeirc-" his gravelly voice snapped out commands, bringing the tension on the bridge back up to uncomfortable levels- "take these two into custody and secure them."

"What?!" Zulu snapped to attention, only to find an unyielding hand gripping each of her arms. The *Dido's* shouted questions were cut off as Ondrea took over comms. Smeirc pushed Zulu toward the door while Af moved to get Rodriguez. "Malak – I just saved your ass. Again!"

He only glared at her until the bridge doors closed between them.

CHAPTER 17: INVERSE SURVEILLANCE

Andrae-Scott-Zurek Wormhole. Proper Noun. Discovered in 2029, the ASZ wormhole was the first such phenomena found to be traversable. Although it was too small for human travel, multiple probes were dispatched and sent conclusive data of unknown star systems, potentially in another galaxy, before it collapsed.

Hour 1000
April 21, 2155

"Mr. President." Helen Maker smiled warmly and held out her hand for the cameras flashing along the roped perimeter at the construction station.

"Minister." Yardley gripped her palm for the requisite two pumps and then turned his back to their audience, gesturing to the behemoth hull clamped in the space dock outside the plastisteel window. The area, as well as every reporter on site, had been scanned for bugs and listening devices, but he still lowered his voice. "You are ten months behind schedule."

"Fourteen months ahead by my calculations, Mr. President. But why quibble over an unimportant distinction in the face of such a precipitous moment."

Not so unimportant, Yardley thought, *since it backed me into a corner and pushed your resignation off again.*

He said, "How are the...engine...tests looking?"

"Right on target. We'll be ready to install next week, after all of the reporters and safety inspectors have completed their tours." She pointed to something on the hull as if explaining one feature or another to him. Yardley had studied the plans hundreds of times. He could have walked the corridors blindfolded after the hours he had put in to make certain Helen wasn't hiding more secrets in the newest Coalition ship. She continued, "I have drawn up a few crew statistics and suggestions to ensure that we have the right people in place to manage the technology and the mission."

"Send it to my assistant." Yardley's staff would have to put in overtime to determine who on her list was actually a plant more loyal to the woman than the government. He had already discovered a handful of her people in his own office. He began strolling down the corridor toward the podium area where the press conference would take place. A handful of politicians, engineers, and private corporate representatives milled around admiring the ship being built.

"I do need to ask a personal favor, Mr. President."

Yardley barely managed not to snort. He would sooner shove a pen straight into his ear than grant any favor to Helen Maker, and they both knew it.

"Go ahead."

"My granddaughter has been reassigned to the *Khalid*. That ship has a rather long tour ahead of it, and I was hoping that she might have the opportunity to teach at the Academy. They are eager to have her in the Communications Department."

"I'm not surprised. Lieutenant Maker has an excellent ear if I recall." He had listened to the recordings of her speaking Culler nearly as many times as he had gone over the ship blueprints. Helen had never used her position to elevate the younger woman as far as Yardley could tell. It might have just been political savvy – not wanting to have anything less than aboveboard in the promotions to invite scrutiny from the press or opponents. It felt like something more. Especially that she was asking for favoritism now. From him. "I will take your wishes into consideration, but the lieutenant is in high demand. Captain Jones personally requested her for the *Khalid*, and I would find it difficult to intervene just to give her a position off of the front line. It could be viewed as nepotism." Yardley hadn't suggested the posting to his former XO, but he had asked Jones to keep an eye on the Lieutenant. Why Helen, who had so frequently intervened to push her granddaughter into dangerous situations would now want to protect her was another puzzle he would have to solve.

"Of course, Mr. President. How obtuse of me."

Yardley paused. He looked over Helen's face. Her expression, as always, was serene. He felt like he was on the field of battle again. He was being flanked. He was sure of it.

She continued, "Have you considered any of the potential names suggested by the Public Relations office? Several of them had quite a bit of gravitas."

He glanced from the Minister of Science and Research to the greatest ship humanity had ever dreamed of. One would bring their enemy to its knees. The other had the potential to do better than that.

"The first of the new *Zanbato* class." He could not resist a jab. "I was thinking of *Omaha*."

Helen smiled, an uncharacteristic tightness at the corners of her mouth. "Flattering, but perhaps you might find a more universally inspiring name, Mr. President."

He nodded and returned the expression. "Perhaps you are right.

I will think about it." He had already decided on the *Zanbato's* christening. *Eirene* would be humanity's best chance of a future. "I believe there is a seat reserved for you on the dais, Minister."

She frowned when she caught sight of the discrete name tag. "I requested to be off to the side. It is far more appropriate for our private partners and the Chief of Engineering on the project to be center stage."

"Oh, no, Minister." Yardley offered her a genuine smile. "I asked that you be seated right next to me. Where I can keep an eye on you."

CHAPTER 18: SINGLE ENVELOPMENT

Epigenetics. Noun. The study of heritable phenotype changes that do not involve alterations in the DNA sequence.

Ex. Dave contracted such a violent strain of H1N3 that his immune response genes were turned off, which is why he died before he could receive treatment.

Hour 1730
May 20, 2156

"How are repairs coming?"

Rodriguez had bags under his eyes and a slump in his posture, but he replied promptly, "Nearly done."

"What was the issue?" Malak asked more to see if Rodriguez would start running his mouth as he had when he first came on board than because he needed an answer. The man maintained the clipped, professional tone he had used since Smierc had informed him that Zulu was locked up and would remain that way until the job was done, and that if the *Dido* called for assistance or moved away from the sublight flight path that Hemah had established the *Runa* would be destroyed.

"Poor design. The wiring for the secondary venting controls were crossing the transformers for your stealth system – overheating everything and triggering a safety auto-shutdown of your ISG drive. I showed your techs how to deal with it if this crops up on any other systems."

Malak should have been satisfied. His ship would be working again soon, and he had an excellent reason to request additional technical training resources for the Falcons. Instead, there was a tightness along his spine that had nothing to do with his injury. He tried to tell himself that almost thirty hours without sleep was to blame. If Smierc hadn't locked Zulu up in his own bunk, he might have been forced to consider other reasons.

"Would you have-"

Smierc opened the door to his ready room and interrupted him. "Major, two minutes until check-in with the *Dido*. Shall I have the prisoner brought up?"

Malak scowled. Smierc smiled, knowing he disliked that she was referring to Zulu as a captive. She did it because it irritated him and would do it joyfully if he asked her to stop.

"Fine." He turned his attention back to the engineer. "Report back when you are finished."

"Yes, sir." He saluted. Malak tried to see any mockery in the motion, but there was nothing in the man's expression or scent that hinted at deception or sarcasm. Once the human had left he stepped out onto the bridge. "Status?"

All stations reported nominal except for sensors. Ondrea frowned at her console.

"Sir, I think we are picking up an ISG exit."

"Think?" Smierc raised her brows and returned to the command chair. Malak positioned himself behind her with a grip on the railing separating the upper and lower bridge.

"Lieutenant Maker adjusted some of the algorithms the computer uses to calculate anomalies. I'm picking up what looks like a gravity well disturbance, but at a distance much farther than expected from our sensor range."

Malak shared a look with Smierc. They both knew the reported field positions of every nonclassified Coalition ship in the sector and most of the classified ones. Nothing should have been anywhere near them. If it was the SIS back again, they would have to be dealt with directly. They would not fall for Zulu's misdirection a second time.

"Adjust heading to intercept. Silent running. Notify the *Dido* of the course change. Keep them close."

"Yes, sir. Fifteen minutes until precise sensor range."

Malak reviewed the reports from engineering while he waited for Zulu to arrive for her scheduled check-in with the *Dido*. When she did appear, she was in mid-conversation with the Legionnaire escorting her. Her hair was wet and she smelled better. Less like sweat and high emotions and more like...soap. He scowled and wondered how she had talked one of his people into letting her use the showers. Unwelcome guests – she wasn't a prisoner – should not be allowed free run of the *Han*.

"I have the *Dido* for you, Lieutenant." Ondrea opened the channel at Malak's nod.

"*Dido*, this is Zulu-actual. Over."

He was surprised she maintained any form of comm protocol, but even though her manner was professional, her tone and expression were relaxed. Water dripped out of the twist of her hair and seeped into the open collar of her flightsuit.

"Zulu, this is *Dido*. Everything on schedule and friendly? Over." Bretavic had identified himself by name after the exchange with the SIS and Malak had looked up his file. He was the same pilot that had disobeyed orders and rescued Zulu on RB-14. Hemah's observation had been correct. He was excellent at his job although he sounded angry with his superior officer. Malak considered that a point in his favor. He was glad he did not have to deal on a regular basis with her recklessness and penchant for finding trouble she was not equipped for.

"*Dido*, this is Zulu." She spouted something in that other language again, and Malak narrowed his eyes, wishing he had turned on the James for her conversation.

Bretavic laughed. "Zulu, this is – hold."

Zulu tensed and Malak did as well. Ondrea spoke up before Bretavic could come back on the line.

"We have a sensor lock, sir. The ISG disturbance is-"

"Zulu, this is *Dido*. You have a *Red* Class coming out of ISG! Heading-"

"-a Culler ship. *Red* Class. I have another on sensors following it, possibly *Citrine*. Sir, they have exited ISG and are using-"

"-on top of you in a few minutes. They're pushing sublight to the max! What are your orders? Over."

"*Dido*, this is Zulu. Transfer of command to Major Malak of the *Han* for the purpose of combat engagement. Security code Nine-six-bravo-zed. Over." Then she hit the control to flip the comm to Ondrea's headset and slid into the secondary sensors station.

Malak didn't have time to acknowledge her decision. "Ondrea, get the *Dido* on our aft rear. Keep the *Han* between them and the line of fire. Is the stealth up?"

"Yes, sir. ISG is still down, but we are camouflaged." Malak hoped that the *Runa* would benefit from that as well. If the *Dido* was visible, it was possible a Culler ship as big as a *Red* would not bother to stop and destroy such a small Coalition vessel. Possible. Not likely.

"Tell me the moment they take an interest in us or the *Runa*."

"Sir." Ondrea sent out a silent alarm to the entire *Han* to alert them of enemy presence while she gave orders to the *Dido*. "They started scanning wide-band as soon as they exited ISG. I have no way of knowing if they have seen us unless they change course or lock weapons."

"I'm on it." Zulu had one hand on the console and the other pressing one side of her headset to her ear. "I have their bridge chatter now." Ondrea turned to stare at the small human. Smierc did the same. Malak was aware she understood Culler, but as he watched her lips move silently he wondered exactly how good she was. "Nothing yet. They are hitting a resupply on the exoplanet in this cloud. Short stop on their way…Nothing about their mission yet. I'll tap the *Citrine* as well."

Af's eyes were wide, her mouth open slightly.

"Tactical," Malak barked to get her attention. "I want a constant lock on both targets."

"Yes, sir!"

"Silent running," he told Smierc, who sent the order via comm bracer to each person on board. She gestured for him to take the chair, but he shook his head no.

Where are you going, he wondered, following the small shape of a massive enemy ship on the display. He wished Parshav were there to tell him what the chances were that Zulu, the SIS, and two enemy ships all arriving at his location within hours of each other was a coincidence. He doubted they were good. The bridge was tense as the *Red* approached, then passed their position.

"Tactical." He watched the display while Af replied.

"No target locks from the enemy ships."

"Zulu, report."

"Chatter remains nonaggressive. If they've seen us or *Dido*, they aren't talking about it."

From the corner of his eye he caught her frown.

"What is it?"

"They..." Her eyes closed and her lips moved soundlessly while she listened. Her hair was beginning to dry; short, fluffy bits softened the sharp angles of her face. "They're looking for something. 'It must be near' they're saying or," she frowned again. "The two ships' crew aren't having the same conversation. The *Red* is searching for a damaged ship – one from the battle at Navi, possibly. The *Citrine*...they have a special unit on board. They're looking for something else. It's..." She made a frustrated noise and opened blue eyes to stare at the display. "I'm not sure. They don't have a lot of adjectives in their language. Whatever it is, they have a VIP with them to get it and haul it back to their staging area."

"What kind of special unit?" Malak was thinking about the devices. If they had one with them, then the ship would also have information about its intended use.

"A weapon?" Af asked without looking up from her controls.

"No," Zulu shook her head. "A military unit. Special forces or...they have a higher rank or caste than typical Culler soldiers, but I don't know their purpose."

A low throb was building at the back of Malak's skull. With an effort of will he ignored it, and found that the pain almost disappeared entirely, as if he wasn't feeling it, but only hearing it described. He ignored that too.

"Are sensors still clear?"

"Yes, sir. No indication that they have noticed us or the *Dido*."

"Follow them, keep us at the edge of range. Tactical, maintain target locks. Zulu-" he pinned her with his gaze, wanting to impress upon her the imperative to follow his orders and not take any initiative- "the *Dido* stays in our shadow. Tell them. And keep your ears on those ships."

"Mm." She typed a message to send out, but she didn't look at him. Instead she rubbed her free hand against her neck. He waited for an acknowledgment, but when no 'yes, sir' left her mouth he clenched his jaw and turned back to the display. The irritated move caused pain to flare in the back of his skull again.

An hour of tense sublight travel brought them within visual range of the exoplanet. It had a high albedo, the surface sharply reflective in places that made it nearly as bright as a planet bound to a star even without such a direct source of light. In contrast, huge swaths of the planet were so dark as to appear nearly black. The Culler ships slowed and took up an orbit.

"Geological significance?"

Zulu raised a brow at the question, but Ondrea answered quickly. She had no doubt been expecting it.

"Nothing with significant magneto-resonance. Low iron and lead levels."

So it was not a site for the Culler wormhole weapons. Malak watched the *Citrine* hang back while the *Red* launched several *Urchins* and a cargo hauler. Whatever they intended to get from the surface, it was not as large as a wormhole device.

Unless it was in pieces.

"We will wait until they spool up ISG. Hemah, once the *Red* goes through I want the *Han* in motion. Af, target the *Citrine's* drive, then weapons. I want-"

"Malak-" Zulu began quietly.

"Major," Smierc corrected as she entered commands at her console, notifying the crew they would be entering combat.

"There's something…" She pressed the heel of her hand to her brow. Malak became aware of a sharp increase in the ghost of pain in his own head. "They know we're here."

Ondrea was already shaking her head. "No indications on sensors. No change in course or threat levels."

Malak took one step, then another closer to Zulu. Her light colored skin had taken on a gray tone. Sweat beaded along her hairline in the cool air of the bridge.

"Tactical?" Smierc took over questioning the crew.

"No change, Lieutenant." Af answered smoothly.

Zulu's eyes opened wide. She looked straight at him, but she was not seeing him. "They hear us!"

"Sir, I don't-" Ondrea began. Af interrupted.

"Weapons hot!"

"Got it," Ondrea tapped at her controls. "Additional *Urchins* launching. The *Red* is turning. Sir, it looks like they are developing a grid pattern."

"Two locks on the *Dido*, sir," Af answered as Hemah held the *Han* steady, waiting for his order to reposition them.

He was close enough to grab Zulu's arm, close enough to hear her whispered translation.

"It is close. Tell them to wound the small one. Use it to flush It into the open."

Malak bit off a growl. If the Cullers thought they could outflank him, they were inescapably wrong. "Helm – defensive maneuvers."

The *Han* proved to be an excellent addition to the Legion. The *Red* Class positioned itself for an assault, methodically firing laser cannon shots in a grid pattern in an effort to locate the ever-moving stealth ship. Six Urchins were reduced to spinning debris before a single shot got near the new ship, and then only because Hemah was restricted by trying not to lose the *Dido*.

Smierc quickly and calmly contacted engineering, "Damage report."

"Cosmetic." It was Rodriguez who answered instead of the Falcon in charge. "You're visible for now, but we'll have stealth back on in fifteen minutes. Hull integrity at one hundred percent.

"Sir, the *Dido*-" Ondrea flipped on the bridge comm.

"-through to Helm, dammit!"

"*Dido*, this is *Han*. You have bridge-actual. Go ahead."

"Stop pussyfooting around and get the hell out of the way of these shots!" Bretavic followed up with more of his native language. Malak recognized the intent, if not the actual words. It wasn't complimentary.

Af called out, "Targeting solution for *Red* starboard cannon number two. Taking the shot now."

Hemah grit out a response, "Orders are to give you cover, *Dido*."

"I'll find my own cover! Stop getting shot for fuck's sake!"

Bretavic was a talented pilot. He would be able to keep up with Hemah. Or he wouldn't, and Malak would have three fewer problems to deal with once the battle was over. The thought tugged at his conscience, but he had more pressing matters.

"Helm, get Tactical into position. Maneuver at will."

"Sir, yes, sir!" Hemah's grin was feral. The Han swooped so suddenly it took the artificial gravity a moment to adjust, leaving Malak's stomach flipping over. He checked sensors himself. The *Dido* was keeping up.

"Incoming!" Ondrea yelled. "It's a tracker. The *Citrine* is spooling up ISG."

"Reinforcements," Zulu muttered, then spoke louder. "They intend to bring reinforcements and follow us if we retreat. It-it's here…there…"

"Follow them." Malak returned to his position behind the command chair and gripped the railing. "Tactical, shoot them down in ISG if necessary, but neither ship makes their destination."

"Yes, Major!"

"ISG coming online," Hemah said flatly as she dodged another laser cannon shot.

"Tracker drone still inbound," Ondrea warned. "If that attaches to our hull we are dead in the water until it is manually removed."

"Tactical-"

"Too erratic," Af interrupted him even as she obliterated another of the *Red's* four cannons. "I can't hit anything that small and agile at this range, not until I can use the repeater turrets."

"That's too close. It will be inside of deployment then and lock onto our electronic signature." Ondrea flipped to another channel and began a heated conversation with the *Dido*.

"*Ictus? Emici?*" Zulu asked.

"Trial run," Smierc answered for Malak. "No fighter complement yet."

"The *Citrine* is -"

"Deploy our own tracking beacon." He gripped the railing. The beacon would only be good for as long as it took the Cullers to pry it off their own hull. It would be a race to see which crew could free themselves first.

"-an order, *Dido!*" Ondrea yelled into her headset, but it was too late. With a nimbleness he had never seen before in a *Runa*, Bretavic skimmed around the *Han*. He cut the movement so close that it blocked all the cameras for the forward display and the proximity warnings went off.

"Impact in five!"

The Culler tracking drone hit the *Dido*. It had been sized and speed adjusted for the larger *Han*, so it ripped into the smaller *Runa's* hull. The force knocked the *Dido* off course and propelled it back into the Han, activating the impacoral layer of the hull.

"Four more *Urchins* incoming!"

Hemah surged around the debilitated *Dido* and Af was prepared. Two of the spiny Culler fighter ships were destroyed the moment the *Han* was clear of the *Dido*. Another had to jerk away at the last moment to avoid slamming into the larger ship.

"Our beacon is on target and attached. *Citrine* entering ISG."

"*Dido* is caught in the gravity well of the planet. Sir, they are being pulled down."

Another *Urchin* was hit by the *Han's* rail gun as Malak watched the scarred shell of the *Dido* spin slowly as it was pulled away. The surface of the exoplanet loomed, alternately dark and bright. Orange atmospheric friction flared to life around the *Dido*. Bretavic did not fire his sublight engines and the *Runa* gained speed, hurtling toward the surface. Another *Urchin* emerged from the *Red* and targeted the *Han* with enough speed to ram and puncture the hull. Zulu left her station to approach him.

"You have to take us down."

Malak ignored Zulu, although the insistent press of her anxiety against his mind and nose made it difficult. The closest *Urchin* was picking up more speed. Hemah dodged and Af fired.

"Sensors."

"The *Red* is preparing for ISG. Shall we pursue, sir?"

"Major! The *Dido*!" Zulu was short enough that he could easily look over her angry face to the Tactical station. Af was scowling at her targeting screen.

"Near miss," she reported, grinding her back teeth. "Nonstructural hit. That one is out of the fight but ambulatory. Two *Urchins* are still pursuing the *Dido*."

He needed to go after that *Red* class.

"Major!"

He did not want Zulu on board while he entered a major confrontation to seize a classified weapon with a Culler warship in his own untried prototype.

"The *Dido* is making an emergency landing. *Urchins* still in pursuit."

"Malak!" She shoved ineffectually at his arm, trying to get his attention.

The pain in his head was blooming, licking fire along the base of his skull. He did not want Zulu on board at all.

"Helm, take us into the atmosphere. Weapons, target those *Urchins*." He made eye contact with Ondrea, "Don't lose the *Red*."

A chorus rang out on the bridge.

"Yes, sir."

Zulu's voice was noticeably absent.

CHAPTER 19: WHAT THE EYE CAN'T SEE

Systematic desensitization. Noun. Colloquially referred to as 'exposure therapy, it was developed by psychiatrist Joseph Wolpe as treatment for phobias in which the patient is exposed to progressively more anxiety-provoking situations to reduce response intensity.

Ex. I used to feel nauseated at the thought of eating dummy bars, but after a few years in the Coalition I kind of like the taste.

Hour 0300
May 21, 2156

"He scuttled us."

Gonzales cursed fluently in two language. Bretavic snorted and replied to Rodriguez.

"Are you surprised?"

Maker ignored the group behind her and continued to stare out the open rear hatch at the desolate planet around them. Swamp. Small patches of open, shallow water. Scraggly short grass. A fetid sort of peat bog. A distant ocean or lake that washed the shore in orange tinted liquid before slipping away on a strong tide. Highly reflective mountains of what might have been mica or metallic crystal that amplified the light of the surrounding nebula and created enough heat to sustain life. If there weren't so many alien insects swarming the air, it might have been a relaxing view. Although the knowledge that she and her crew now had no way off of the planet marred any tranquility.

"Maker, get in here and take a look at the comms!"

She kept her helmet on, not because the air was unbreatheable, but because it stank. Badly. Sulfur and something else that was less rotten egg and more old, wet potatoes permeated the air. Even through the filtration system in her suit, the steam from muddy, bubbling waters was noticeable and stomach-churning. That, and the bugs.

"Hey, Maker! You deaf?"

The contrail from Malak's ship was long faded, but she still glanced up at the place where she had last seen him. *The prick.*

"Lay off, Taav."

From the corner of her helmet she watched Gonzales help Kerry and Rodriguez pack up the mechanic's gear. Of course they were packing it up. Because of course there was no way to repair the ship. Malak had wanted them to stay put, so he had made certain they would stay put. No engines, no comms to call the Coalition for assistance. Enough power to keep them warm, the recyclers running, and the ground sensors active. Enough rations to last them a few days – weeks if they were careful - and that said something about how long Malak expected them to be stranded. *Says something really shitty,* she thought with a sour twist of her lips.

"Suck my dick, Gonzales. I'm talkin' to C & E, not you."

"You're talking to your commanding officer," Kerry insisted. "And it's going to earn you a busted lip."

"Who's gonna do that, tuber? You?" Taav sneered.

Maker sighed. Malak had scuttled her ship. Her people. And now she had to deal with Taav. Next time she saw the Legion she was going to shoot Malak in the leg. Or maybe a kidney. Whichever would hurt more and take longer to heal. *Probably livers are a bitch to grow back, maybe I should hit him there.* She shook her head and focused on the problems she could address in the moment.

"Kerry." He was at her side before she could turn around. "How is the inventory coming?"

"Almost done."

"Rodriguez, report."

"We're fucked."

Maker turned in time to see Gonzales clip the back of the mechanic's helmet with a toolkit. Hard. His gloved hand went automatically to rub at the spot.

"That is to say, technically, we are fucked. Ma'am." He pointed out the access hatch that Malak's people had opened and the loose wires that hung out. "They removed the flight stabilization control processor. Even if we had enough fuel to get out of the atmosphere – which we don't thanks to that Culler beacon tearing us a new asshole – we'd crash hard before we could reach escape altitude. Bretavic is good, but no pilot is going more than a hundred yards without that processor."

"Bretavic?"

The pilot eased into a sitting position against the exterior of the ship. "Ground maneuvers – maybe. I'd need to stay close enough to kiss dirt to keep us from tipping or catching thermals." He paused. "And my HUD is alerting me I have a head injury."

Maker noted the long scrape and dent on one side of his helmet. Anything that had hit him hard enough to do that had likely caused brain damage. He continued although his voice was rough.

"I shot up on painkillers and stims, but when they wear off my hands are going to be shaking – assuming I don't pass out. Even if one of you had the training to take over, the *Dido* was not intended to be flown on complete manual – especially not in atmo."

"Fuck that," Taav growled. "Get the fucking comms up and we'll have the *Khalid* here in twenty-four hours. Then that fucking *Cicuta* motherfucker can have the whole fucking Coalition on his ass. Or better – get him back here and I swear on my left nut that I will make him cough up our parts or he can cough up-"

"Yeah, that would work great." Rodriguez stood and stretched his back. The crack was loud. "I'd love to see you teach Ma-Maker's new pal a lesson. I'm sure you would come out the winner in that fight." Taav was hunching his shoulders and clenching his fists, but with Kerry standing next to Rodriguez he managed to hold on to his temper. "Actually – maybe I *should* take another look at comms. Hold on Taav, let me pull out my magic wand and create spare parts from nothing so you can commit suicide by friendly fire. If I haven't got it done by nightfall – just keep waiting out here. Sensors said the local animals weren't any more than eighty or ninety kilograms. Big, smart soldier like you should be fine."

"But what if he's not fine?" Gonzales asked in a bored tone.

"Hm, well, that would be unfortunate. I guess you would get seconds at dinner from now on?"

Their pilot added in an irritated, sour tone, "Do we have any salisbury steak? I'll throw him into a mud pit for salisbury steak."

Why Bretavic felt the need to join in on irritating Taav, Maker had no idea. She could usually depend on Bretavic to be the adult in the group – or at least the scowling, silent member.

"You know-" Rodriguez cupped his helmet with his hand as if thinking hard- "I think we might have-"

"Enough." She turned and hopped onto the ledge outside the airlock, kicking her boots to get off as much stinking mud as possible.

"L.T.," Rodriguez whined.

"We're going to be here a while. Get comfortable. Keep yourselves busy."

"So what's Taav supposed to do after he's done jerking off? There's another twenty-three hours and fifty-six minutes left in every-"

"That's *it* you stupid little-"

Taav's charge was abruptly stopped by Kerry, who dropped the other soldier like a sack of wet manure. Maker waited only long enough for her HUD to verify he was still breathing before heading into the ship. If she had to endure a month being responsible for keeping Taav from killing Rodriguez and everyone else from killing Taav she was going to do more than shoot Malak. She was going to gut him.

* * *

Two days later.

"I got another sensor flare up, L.T."

Gutting is too good for him, she fumed in her head as she rolled out of her bunk and made for the cockpit. *Salt. Salt the wound.* She slipped in a fresh smear of mud on the floor and nearly ran into the doorway. They had all tried to keep the dirt out of the ship – but it seemed to stick to every crevice, and they didn't even have enough resources to wash it out. She didn't even notice the stench anymore. *Salt it, and sew it shut.*

"Where?" she asked Rodriguez once she had righted herself and navigated to the copilot's seat. He gestured on the display to an area a few kilometers away.

"Looks like atmo entry, but it was quick and done before sensors got a good lock. I'd say it was more meteors like what we saw yesterday, but then I'd have to worry we might be in for another storm ourselves, and I'm trying not to invite bad energy into my aura right now."

Maker stared at him. Without his helmet on the exhaustion on his face was obvious. His usually rich, glowing skin had a gray undertone and greasy, untrimmed hair fell over the crease in his forehead. They hadn't been able to spare extra water rations for showers. *Too bad Malak didn't think to inspect the planet or the surrounding space for potential hazards before he left us here.* She tried to shake off her anger and focus on what the engineer was saying.

"You have to put out into the universe what you want to get back," Rodriguez clarified. Then he shrugged. "I've been reading to try and stay awake. I only have one book I can access. My sister sent it to me for Christmas last year. *Subspace Wave Healing: the Magical Energy of Self-Actualization and You.* It gets better after the fourth time through."

"I'll take your word for it. How many objects did you clock?"

"Just two, but they were pretty big. With the margin of error, the computer thinks as large as an *Ictus*. Or on the low end, about the size of a donkey," he finished dryly.

"Not terribly helpful. We'd be either a smoking crater or just on fire. Can we relocate?"

"You tell me. Has Pilar or John commed in yet?"

Maker shook her head. After the meteor shower she had decided they needed to scout out a more protected location to move the *Dido*. Given that Bretavic would have to fly low and slow, and they didn't have any fuel to waste, she had sent out two teams to check out the most likely locations. Gonzales had gone with Taav to keep him on task and because she was the least likely to go rooting around for his spleen with her service knife. Kerry had been sent in the opposite direction to the farthest target since he was stronger and faster than the rest of them.

"You're sure it is another meteor shower?"

"The sensors are still glitching out, even after we rewired them. It's on the other side of the mica ridge. With this cloud cover I couldn't make visual confirmation unless I was standing on top of it."

Maker blew out a breath. If they moved the ship without having a sheltered landing spot in mind, they would be burning precious fuel and were just as likely to fly into a meteor storm as away from one.

Sew his gut shut, and then toss him in a vat of lemon juice. With ants.

"Okay. We'll start a watch rotation outside. Best case scenario, the sensors go off again and nothing hits down and we'll know it is a phantom ping. Worst case, one of us gets permanently relieved of the duty assignment from hell."

"Sounds like a win-win, LT. You want to rock-paper-scissors for first shift, or are you feeling extra bossy today and want to make it an order?"

She snorted. "You think I'm sending you out there? You're half-asleep as it is. I'd be lucky if you spent any time watching anything other than the backs of your eyelids." Neither of them brought up Bretavic. His concussion seemed to be getting better, but the more rest he could get the more likely he would be to not fly them into the side of a mountain when the time came to move. "Put an alarm on the sensors and take a nap, Fuzz."

"Ma'am, yes, ma'am." Rodriguez was already slouching down and kicking his muddy boots up on her seat before she was through the doorway.

Maker dragged a cargo container a few meters away from the ship and used it to stretch and try and work out some of the kinks in her spine while she watched the skies. Their transport was fine for short missions – it even had a shower, not that they had enough water to make use of it – but the mattresses on each narrow bunk left a lot to be desired. She scanned the area with the equipment in her suit to help pass the time.

Mucky grass. Soft, oozing soil. Mud. Rock formations. Chemical compositions of water. More mud. She felt like she would go crazy if she had to stare at it any longer. *At least Taav isn't here to cause problems.* Maker felt a twinge of guilt over having inflicted the man on Gonzales – but not bad enough to have seriously considered trading places with her. After an hour, Maker started to get drowsy. She opened a comm to the ship, keeping it on text mode so she wouldn't wake Rodriguez.

Headed up to the ridge to check out the meteor site.

There weren't many obstacles in her path. Most of the open water was just large enough to require her to watch her step. Between that and the increasing cloud cover there wasn't much to see, but it did keep her alert. She was nearly halfway up the ridge when Rodriguez contacted her.

"Hey, L.T. We got another contact incoming. Same location as the last. Where are you?"

"About three minutes from the top. Can't you see me on the display?" Her boot came down wrong on some loose gravel, and she slid backward a few steps before she could catch herself.

"A lot of condensation on the cameras but I- there you are. Not that I don't like admiring your ass in uniform, but you should head back double time. This reading is looking bigger than the others, and if sensors are off even a little, it could come down on top of you."

"Remind me again what the downside of that would be?"

Rodriguez laughed and Maker grinned for the first time in days as she finally got a glove on the top of the ridge and pulled herself up and over to lie on her belly. Her HUD was giving her mixed signals and huge margins of error for the size of the incoming meteor. She was panting from exertion and had to wipe the drops of fog from her faceplate before she could look up at the low clouds. They were churning, rolling under themselves as if a storm was brewing, but no rain fell. She frowned.

"Fuzz, you sure about that ping? I thought a meteor would have moved fast enough to touch down by now."

"They do – I mean. It should have. Let me...Now I know this isn't right. Computer says it is slowing down."

"That can't be right. Now I know we have a sensor glit-" Maker did a quick sweep of the valley floor, and her words got stuck in her throat. Parked at either end of a wide stone clearing was an *Urchin*. The spiny hulls of the Culler fighter ships blended in with the dull yellow-gray of the grass and mud of the planet. As far as she could tell, the ships were in standby mode, engines powered down. She held her breath, as if that would keep her from being seen, and switched her display to thermal view. She scanned the area, then did it again slower. If the pilots weren't inside those *Urchins*, they weren't anywhere in her sensor range either. She carefully looked over each ship, but the residual heat from their entry through atmosphere made it impossible to tell if there was anyone inside. The Cullers could be anywhere. They might have seen the *Dido* on entry. She tried to remember how fast they could run. The *Runa* was on auxiliary power, but it wasn't exactly hidden. She double-checked her map. Gonzales and Taav were still a few clicks out from their target location. Kerry was three-quarters of the way to his, and all of them were distant enough that the Cullers would not have noticed them.

All of the soldiers were far enough away that they would not be able to help.

A sick deja vu fell over her. The best she could hope for was to make certain there was a record left to find when Malak returned for her crew. That, and to keep as many of her people alive as possible.

There was no reason for the Cullers to be on this planet. Unless there was a reason.

"*Dido, Dido*, this is Zulu. Come in."

Her mouth was dry. A phantom ache started in her shoulder while she waited for Rodriguez to respond. The clouds rotated overhead. The *Urchins* remained still and silent.

"Di-" She had to pause to swallow. "*Dido, Dido*, this is-"

"Got it. Got it, Maker. Damn, I fell asleep again. What's-"

"*Dido*, this is Zulu. Sending you image data now. Over." She had to send it directly to his in-suit communication system, since the ship's comms were inoperable, and it took a few long seconds for the large files to transmit.

"Fu...Uh, Zulu, this is *Dido*. Please confirm situation. Over." His voice was thready, his breath audible over the line. Maker sympathized. The ship hadn't been equipped with enough firepower to combat two *Urchins* before a Culler beacon had ripped through the hull. It wouldn't have been able to outrun them even if Malak's people hadn't crippled the controls.

In short, terse words she described the scene and finished with, "Unusual atmospheric activity overhead. Can you confirm last sensor readings? Over."

"Zulu, this is *Dido*. Readings confirmed. Unknown object approaching your location." He gave a size range and approximate speed. It was too big to be an *Urchin* and too small for a *Citrine*, but whatever it was was preparing to land. Heat gathered and pressed at the backs of her optic nerves. "What are your orders? Over."

There was a fire of pain out there. She was separated from it only by a simple door, and she knew if she even touched the knob she would get burned.

You have to find out what they want.

You have to run like hell and hope they don't chase you down, another, more realistic part of her argued.

"Zulu? Zulu? I repeat, what are your orders, over."

Everybody goes home.

You won't know until you ask.

Maker swallowed.

"*Dido-*" her voice broke but she kept going- "this is Zulu. Take your pilot and emergency supplies and bug out to location -" she checked her map and pinged Kerry's target- "to location provided. I repeat, bug out to scouting target Bravo immediately. Over."

"Zulu...Hell, Maker," he was panting into his comm, hopefully moving to follow orders. She tried to estimate how long it would take him to grab the emergency medical kit, his pack and Bretavic's, and get the pilot moving. "We've got almost half a klick of open ground to cover and you have twice that. That incoming object is going to land before you make it."

She abandoned communication protocol. What was the Coalition going to do? Give her a demerit? She would be lucky to live long enough for that to happen.

"I'm going to leave this channel open. Mute your end, but keep recording."

"Clara…" There was shuffling on Rodriguez's end, muffled conversation and movement that carried across the proximity comm. "What are you going to do?"

She ignored the question. "Ping me when you reach cover. Move, Ensign. Double time. That is a direct order. Over." There was no sound other than breathing on Rodriguez's end for a long minute.

"Zulu, this is *Dido*. Wilco. Out."

She followed the glowing green dots that represented Rodriguez and Bretavic on her map. Her heart was beating so hard it hurt. Her tongue was thick in her mouth, her cheeks cottony. Above her, the green-gray of Culler technology broke through the cloud cover. Her stomach flipped. It was bigger than a *Runa*, but of a design she had never seen before. Mounted on either side of the hull was a laser cannon – powerful enough to sheer straight through the Coalition transport across the flat expanse of the planet, and cut down two small green dots long before they made the jagged foothills and any sort of cover. The bow was sharply angled and venting steam as it touched down. Rocks crunched and broke under the weight of the ship. The hiss and grate of hydraulics was painfully loud through her helmet's audio sensors.

Like a horrifying, parasitic flower, the front of the Culler vessel split into three fleshy petals, each parting and widening until a corridor large enough for two of the aliens to walk abreast had formed to make a ramp from the ground into the ship. It looked like a throat. It looked like a pit straight to hell.

One long talon clicked delicately out of the darkness. It was followed by a slender, hard-shelled leg and reverse joint. The rest of the body slid into view, and Maker was seized with a cold, shivering fear. It was smaller than other Cullers she had come up against – about the same height as Malak – but instead of naked chitin or clammy rags, it wore wrappings. Overlapping bands of shifting, silvery fabric or flexible armor covered it from knee to elbow and over the top of its head. The only place on its body left exposed was a narrow, slitted cross-mark on the torso.

Just large enough for a mouth and beak.

Come here, it called out, grating sharp language making her spine stiffen involuntarily. Fear darkened the edges of her vision for a moment, thinking that this...thing...this strange and frightening new enemy was calling to her.

Another Culler, built along the lines of every other she had seen in the flesh, followed out of the ship. The relief Maker felt upon seeing a familiar figure, the same size and shape and deadly clawed monstrosity that had nearly killed her many times was so misplaced it was almost funny. Why the smaller creature with its *clothing* made her eyes water and her lungs seize, while the one more similar to all those that had actually punctured her body and killed her fellow soldiers was inexplicable, but her fear was real and almost paralyzing.

This one obeys. The taller of the two made a graceful bowing motion, bending back its claws and exposing the delicate tactile nodules at the elbow.

It is here. Take the others and find It.

There are humans here.

Maker had to swallow down bile. Of course their sensors had picked up heat signatures and movement. Of course they had noticed the Coalition ship on the surface. She checked the map again. Bretavic and Rodriguez were nearly to the screen of mica rocks that would shelter them.

Kill them as long as you find It, the leader stated in a shrill, piercing tone. *Only It is important. Bring It back alive.*

The tall Culler clicked loudly back into the ship and another alien began moving forward. There wasn't enough time. If they cleared the ridge they would see her people and then there would be no escape.

They'll see you too.

Stall, her mind suggested, followed immediately by, *How?*

Communicate. That's your job.

Her lungs weren't taking in enough air. Her heart was hard and sluggish in her chest. Her shoulder ached. Her head throbbed. Two blue dots glowed on her map. Maker stood up.

You shouldn't be here, she screeched in their language.

The taller Cullers reacted wildly, swinging their talons around in search of an enemy and screaming surprised nonsense noises. The leader did not jump into a defense position, but tipped its head, turning large black eyes on Maker. It hurt. It hurt more than hours of translation or a talon through her joint or the memory of another soldier in a mining station alley long ago, broken and torn – a harbinger of her own future. Those black eyes on hers, unerringly finding her gaze through her opaque helmet, *hurt.*

It made a noise of inquisition that stabbed right through her ear and into her brain.

AH. SMALLER THAN I THOUGHT.

Blue dots cleared the edge of the mountain foothills and began winding through narrow canyons and tunnels. They were as safe as they were going to get. She wasn't safe though. She was never going to be safe again. That she knew in the same deep, dark place inside herself that had been scarred by silvery eyes and screeching thoughts.

Why have you come?

One of the larger Cullers slid a talon forward with its shock stick gripped in its tubules.

No, the leader clicked at it. *Wait.* It tipped its head the opposite direction and spoke to Maker. *I have come to find It.*

Her skull was too tight. Her stomach threatened to revolt with every second it looked at her.

What is It?

The end. Upper talons folded back to reveal not two long, flexible finger tubes, but three. They massaged at the air between Maker and the leader as if tasting it, tasting and testing the distance. And maybe more than that.

The end of what?

All that would end us. It leaned forward. The mouth on its torso parted slightly, letting pink inner flesh stand out starkly against the dark clothing. *All that would displease Them.*

Who... Maker had to pause to swallow, to ease the burn in her throat and the bile rising up. *Who are They?*

They... The leader clicked forward but stopped short of leaving the tunnel for the planet's surface. *Are not here. But you...you are here. Talons flashed. Go. Get It. Get the one.*

The taller Cullers surged forward, talons raking across the flaky mica. Maker desperately called out. *What are the machines for? What are you doing with the-*

A shock stick collided with her side. Electricity coursed across her muscles; her teeth snapped closed on her tongue.. Her knees gave out and her feet slipped from under her. Her faceplate smacked into a rock when she hit the ground. Cracks spider-webbed across her vision.

Strong, thin fingers wrapped around her shaking limbs, lifting her, carrying her. Her service weapon was pulled from her belt and discarded, but she was having trouble focusing on struggling, on fighting back. Her muscles were contracting sporadically. The aliens holding her were not speaking, but she could hear them. Their grating, shrill speech was in her head.

THIS ONE DOES NOT WANT TO TOUCH IT.

THAT ONE ORDERS, THESE ONES OBEY.

WILL THE HUMANS HERE DIE SOON?

DO NOT THIRST FOR IT. THE PILOTS WILL BURN THEIR HUSKS.

Urchins were powering up. Maker could feel the vibration of their engines, knew the satisfaction of the ones dragging her forward, the eagerness of the pilots to hunt down and kill her friends.

You do not have time. Her speech was slurred. She spit out a chunk of her tongue, leaving blood spattered on the inside of her cracked helmet. The two holding her hesitated but did not stop. Maker focused on the leader, now only a meter away. *He is coming.* She thought about Malak. Remembered seeing him cut down one alien after another, lit by purple lightning while he pried their carapaces apart. The leader recoiled, eyes burning with a pinprick of silver in the center. Maker stared there, stared into the light.

LEGION, it whispered. The word trembled through her mind, carried by fear.

Yes. She tried desperately not to think of the others, not to picture Kerry and Gonzales, exhausted Rodriguez and concussed Bretavic. *Legion is coming for you.* She opened her mouth, speaking, but also forcing the thought into the other's eyes, stabbing out with it like a weapon. *Flee, before He eats you.*

The Cullers holding her flinched, nearly dropping her. The chaos of their words, their thoughts reverberated around her. The leader leaned close, not touching her, but hovering over her with those slender finger-nodules.

IT IS DIFFERENT. THE ONE. GOOD ENOUGH TO EAT.

Sweat prickled her scalp. Blood dripped down her chin inside her suit. Her spine clenched.

Come, the leader screeched to the others. *Bring It.*

Finally, she could force her muscles to struggle in earnest as they dragged her up the ramp and the tunnel began to close around them, blocking out the sulfurous mud, the cloudy sky, and the hot rain beginning to fall. Sticky mucus trailed across her faceplate in the wake of convex finger tubules. Black eyes leaned closer to her in the dim lighting. They widened, silver pupils swallowing up the inky surface, swallowing her up. Darkening her own vision.

I WILL CUT IT OUT.

CHAPTER 20: UNARY CODING

Today, we are the best of all that has come before. United. Resolved. Adamant. We will have retribution and we will have peace. Together, humanity will find security in justice.

- 2084, Presidential Inaugural Speech at the formation of the Sol Coalition.

Hour 0430
May 24, 2156

It had been a short run from the destroyed Runa, following the day-old tracks in the soft peat, but Malak had surged ahead of the rest of the ground team. The footprints were filling in with water, some dragged out, none small enough to be Zulu's. His sprint ate up the kilometers while he clenched his jaw and tried not to think about the remains of the *Dido*. Only laser fire from a Culler weapon could have cut metal so cleanly and burned so hot. He had left the Coalition soldiers on the surface of the exoplanet to keep them out of his battle, only for them to find one of their own.

It is Zulu, he snarled to himself. *Of course she found trouble.*

But who was here to get her out of it?

He pushed himself harder, bounding up the slick, flaking mica rock formations to a heat signature on a high ledge. He gripped the edge with one hand and kicked his legs to the side, flinging his body up and over to land in a crouch. He nearly crushed the soldier standing in the mouth of a shallow cave. A heavy gun swung at Malak's head. He ducked, unable to completely avoid the hit but suffered only a glancing blow to his helmet. He spun with one leg out, but his opponent jumped over it with surprising reflexes. The heavy gun pulled wide, but it was a feint for a large fist aimed at Malak's head. He saw it for what it was, caught the fist and threw his own weight the same direction, pulling the soldier to the ground and twisting his arm until he was subdued.

"Wait, wait!" A slimmer soldier jumped up from the huddle of bedrolls in the back. His helmet was transparent. The dirty, exhausted face of Dan Rodriguez peered out. "Malak?"

Malak gave a short nod.

"Finally." The engineer nearly crumpled with relief. "Kerry, it's fine. This is him. Maker's friend."

The man on the ground growled something that might have been 'fucking die'. Malak released him quickly and stepped away to put his back to the wall. He kept the slowly standing soldier in his peripheral vision as he examined the cave. Five bedrolls were angled around an emergency heater. One was occupied by a broad-chested soldier who breathed shallowly. No one else was inside.

"Where is she?"

"She's-" Rodriguez was cut off.

"What the fuck do you care?" the big soldier growled. The mud caking his flight suit nearly covered his name badge, Kerry J. "You left us here without any means of defense. Just send a signal to the Coalition and get the hell out."

"Where is she?" Malak repeated.

Kerry took a menacing step forward. "We'll take care of our own."

Gunnar and Hanako flipped over the ledge and positioned themselves between Kerry and Malak.

"Easy," Gunnar ordered, palms out. Hanako let her hand rest on her Klim. Malak turned to Rodriguez.

"I have the recording. You can listen to it after we get Bretavic on your ship. His head is messed up, and he hasn't been conscious since we left the *Dido*. Pilar and Taav went to search for potable water. They are out of personal comm range, but your ship can let them know where to meet us."

"Where. Is. She?"

Malak tried to find that light pressure at the back of his skull, the tingle of awareness he had felt when he blacked out on Navi and again when he grabbed her shoulder on the *Han*. There was nothing there. No one was inside his head but him.

"They took her. She...Clara was alive when they took her.

Glossary

Andrae-Scott-Zurek Wormhole. Proper Noun. Discovered in 2029, the ASZ wormhole was the first such phenomena found to be traversable. Although it was too small for human travel, multiple probes were dispatched and sent conclusive data of unknown star systems, potentially in another galaxy, before it collapsed.

Basebot. Noun. A mobile 3D printer used by the Sol Coalition to build initial fortifications and temporary housing. Local source material such as sand or dirt can be extruded into nearly any shape including building blocks, interlocking pavers for temporary roads, even simple equipment such as helmets.
Ex. The basebots don't build attractive barracks – but it sure as hell beats a tent.

Black. Adjective. As used by the government, specifically military, to describe operations, budgets, and files that have the highest top secret classification. Only those individuals directly involved (writing the budget, carrying out the operation, etc.) and a single superior officer are aware of the situation. Those involved may be disavowed at any time.

Blackout. Adjective. A level above black for classified information. Individuals who gain any knowledge about the situation may be terminated by those authorized to have knowledge. Those involved do not exist.

Burner. Noun. Slang. Individual who flees the Sol System to avoid mandatory military service.
Ex. When the Home Guard caught the burner, he was sentenced to ten years of hard labor in a corporate mining colony.

Calque. *(KAL-kuh)* Verb. Slang. Calculated the risk and determined it to be acceptable.
Ex. See Dick sit down. See Jane buckle up. See Spot hide. See Jane calque coordinates. See Dick engage sublight engines. See

Spot immolated as hull stress causes localized system failures and hydrogen leaks onto the bridge. See Dick snap his femur as gravity kickback smashes him against the console. Jane did not calque well. Dick will buckle up next time.

Catecholamine. Noun. A group of organic compounds used as neurotransmitters including tyrosine. Release of catecholamines is part of the fight-or-flight response, and high levels of tyrosine have been linked to extreme anger, aggression, and violent defensive action.
Ex. Stims are one thing, but if you really want to keep your edge in a fight, a catecholamine enhancer will do the trick. Or give you a heart attack – but we're all going to die eventually, right?

Cicuta. Noun. A classification of medium-sized military vessels with a crew complement of twenty-five, space for one hundred ground troops and twelve combat pilots in single-manned ships. Although the *Cicuta* was taken out of production in 2146, older ships are still routinely retrofitted due to their speed and durability. The *Pale Horse* was modified to carry two *Runa* class, including the *Scythe*, and a deep-attack small vessel, such as the *Viper*, with a combination of combat fighters.
Ex. "If you don't open those maintenance bay doors, I will fly this Cicuta *straight up your ass, Titan Station!"*

CSNS. (Close Space Near Sol). Noun. An area of the local arm of the Milky Way, centering on Sol and seventy-five light years in diameter. In 2119 Culler forces were driven out of CSNS in a prolonged military action later named the Expulsion. The borders of CSNS are constantly patrolled by a special division of the Coalition, monitored by millions of probes and satellites, and maintained by a rigorous defense grid of space stations and military outposts.
Ex. The soldiers can't wait to get back to CSNS and for regular mail and R&R.

Dark. As in, **The Dark.** Noun. Space between solar systems where the effects of the gravitational pull of objects (e.g., stars) has no discernible effect on ISG drives, providing the widest margin of error for safe departure and reentry into sublight space travel. Note: also allows interstellar travel that leaves no commonly monitored trail.

Ex. See Spot run. See Jane chase Spot. See them run down the hall in the family ship. See the blue giant star shining through the window. See Dick engage the ISG drive. See Jane slam against the bulkhead as local star gravity pulls the ship backward. See Spot be sucked into a microfissure as the hull is damaged by conflicting gravity wells. See Dick disengage the ISG drive. See Jane undergo emergency cranial surgery. See Spot be mopped off of the floor. Dick may not pilot the ship again.

DARS. Noun. Docking and Restocking. Refers to putting a ship in at a station or base to resupply and make crew changes. It is generally accompanied by a crew leave rotation.

Ex. It has been so long since we had a DARS scheduled, the galley is serving soylent for dinner.

Dove. Noun. Pejorative. Person who supports a non-violent end to the Culler war, i.e., diplomacy.

Ex. The Smiths are all doves, they would hand over their own children if it kept them from having to carry a gun.

Dummy Bar. Alt. **DME Bar**. Noun. Daily Meal Enhancement. Dense nutrient supplement designed to provide one soldier with necessary calories for 24 hours of active duty along with essential vitamins, minerals, and immune system boosters. Nicknamed after the soldiers who willingly consume the Coalition's version of hardtack.

Emici. Noun. A classification of fighter-sized military vessels with a maximum crew of one. Designed for close combat, the ships are highly maneuverable and require intense, specialized training to pilot.

Ex. "Congratulations, soldier. You have qualified to be an Emici pilot."

"But that means another twelve months until I see the front lines, ma'am."

"Yep. You're guaranteed to live longer than twenty percent of rookies. Assuming you don't kill yourself during training. Try not to. Those are expensive ships."

Ennead. Proper Noun. Alien race encountered by humans in 2082. After initial disastrous first diplomatic meeting, where translation software malfunction resulted in the death of the diplomat, the Sol Confederation negotiated a trade alliance with the Ennead. They utilize a different, slower form of interstellar travel than humans, Cullers, or Nick, and are extremely long-lived. They consider themselves a pacifist race.

Epigenetics. Noun. The study of heritable phenotype changes that do not involve alterations in the DNA sequence.
Ex. Dave contracted such a violent strain of H1N3 that his immune response genes were turned off, which is why he died before he could receive treatment.

Eugenics. Noun. A social philosophy and the actions to carry it out which aim to design the human race through selective breeding which had a resurgence of popularity in the United States and United Kingdom in the early 20th century and was later a key component of Nazi regime policies. Embryonic gene therapy was criticized through the early 21st century as a tool of eugenics. Most detractors were silenced in 2047 with the approval of a select list of health-related and minor aesthetic changes covered by insurance and ensuring equal access.

Fronterra Colony Massacre. Noun. Attack by the Cullers in 2104 on a Coalition colony at the edge of Sol-controlled space. Twenty-seven thousand eight hundred sixty-three human colonists and border patrol soldiers were killed. There were nine survivors.
Ex. The survivors of the Fronterra Colony Massacre were treated as

heroes; only five of them committed suicide.

Gravitron Apple. Noun. **<u>CLASSIFICATION: TS</u>**. An artificial gravity field projection unit that can be used to fool sensors into believing that surrounding space is warped around a high mass object. Resulting sensor readings would make ISG travel highly inadvisable. Note: The unit does not actually create a large gravity field.
Ex. The black ops base was mined with gravitron apples to keep civilians from accidentally discovering it.

Homogeneity. Noun. The quality or state of being all the same or all of the same kind.
Ex. In 2031, terrorists attacked the western grain supply by releasing a biological weapon on United States cornfields. Due to the relative homogeneity of seed supply, crop production was devestated. World cereal markets and related livestock markets crashed. Starvation rates in developing nations skyrocketed as exports dwindled. Although seed manufacturers developed resistant strains, the engineered crop disease spread to Africa, decimating more than 50% of grain produced and consumed on that continent. An estimated 400-650 million deaths are attributed to the attack.

Holocene Extinction Event Apex. Noun. The sixth mass extinction on Earth which began with the extinction of mammoths. It reached its peak in the mid-twenty-first century and had an overall rate of species loss estimated to be seven hundred sixty-two percent higher than natural extinction rates.
Ex. During the last century of the Holocene Extinction Event, commonly referred to as the Apex, a quarter of all species of flora and fauna on Earth died out.

Ictus. Noun. A classification of fighter-sized military vessels with a maximum crew complement of two. They lack the maneuverability of the Emeci, but are equipped with superior firepower.
Ex. The Ictus *seeded the entire hull with explosives that disabled the*

Cullers' engines.

Impacoral. Noun. Proprietary plasma compound designed to absorb kinetic energy. The compound remains in a liquid state until sufficient kinetic force collides with it. Upon collision, the compound hardens, absorbing the energy, and then reliquefies. It is commonly found in vehicle safety restraints, personal and structural armor systems, and medical immobilization devices. The Sol Coalition utilizes a generic substitute for enlisted personnel combat suits.

Interstellar Gravity Drive. (ISG) Noun. Propulsion device reverse engineered from Culler ships which crashed on Earth during the Repulsion. Speed varies based on ship design and quality of dark matter fuel but exceeds the speed of light. Within star systems and near large gravity wells, such as black holes, ISG is prohibited without authorization.
Ex. The new ISG got the ship from Sol to Polaris in four weeks.

James. (i.e., ***a james***) Noun. Derogatory term for a late twenty-first century real-time language translation program. So called after the Sol Coalition implemented use of the first models during negotiations with another species. Misuse of a common alien phrase resulted in the imprisonment and later execution of the political liaison in charge of discussions, Randolph James. Resistance among troops to use the infamous device resulted in a preference for human interpreters.
Ex. "Should we ask them to put away their weapons?" "Our unit has a james, not a translator." "Oh, might as well start shooting then."

Judicial Equity. Proper Noun. Refers to a series of bills passed from 2088-2092 allowing criminals accused of avoiding mandatory military service or violent crimes, and later some nonviolent crimes, to serve a reduced sentence through labor. Although the Confederation and some member nations still operate prisons and worksites, most individuals found guilty of felonies or repeat misdemeanors are ordered to one of the many contracted labor sites run off-world by corporations.

Khutura. Noun. A military carrier vessel with a crew complement of seven hundred, an infantry complement of up to three thousand, and fifteen hundred fighters with their pilots. *Khutura* are the largest ships in the Sol Coalition complement and are the workhorses that move soldiers and ships across Sol-controlled space and into the outer reaches of our arm of the Milky Way galaxy.
Ex. The Defense budget included a new Khutura-class, which is to be christened when it is completed in three years.

Kill Box. Noun. 1) A three-dimensional target area, defined to facilitate the integration of coordinated joint weapons fire. 2) Any position which can be fired upon from more than one combatant and generally having limited, or no, points of egress.

Klimovsk Service Pistol. a.k.a. ***Klim.*** Noun. Standard issue semi-automatic pistol issued to Sol Coalition forces which is capable of holding up to five types of ammunition. The Klim integrates into the personal tech of each soldier, allowing for ammunition selection, assisted targeting, and safety measures for crowd control. Although the variety of ammunition available is nearly limitless, new soldiers are equipped with standard projectiles, armor piercing rounds, incendiary rounds, and slag rounds. The last of these shred upon impact, releasing a liquid core of metal and corrosive chemicals.

Lightfoot. Noun. A person born in space, rather than on a planet or planetary satellite. Designated thus because most spaceships and stations are set with gravity slightly lower than Earth standard.
Ex. John is a real lightfoot; he knows all the trade routes like the back of his hand.

Lost Ninth. Proper Noun. In 2061 a Culler attack on the Pluto surveillance outpost destroyed three Earth military vessels, leaving nineteen thousand soldiers dead. Damage to the dwarf planet is so severe, its orbit destabilized within the year. Pluto gradually broke apart over the next four decades. The devastation to human life and the Sol system was memorialized in the Coalition seal, featuring a nine-pointed star – one point for each of the original planets in the solar system.

Lynas Laws. Noun. Series of bills passed in 2078 that restricted the rights of Genetically Modified Humans. The legislation defined GMH as incorporating nonhuman DNA and legally demoted such individuals to have less than human rights.
Ex. The notices for job openings clearly stated that GMH applicants would be denied, in accordance with the Lynas Laws.

Ministry of Defense. Proper Noun. In 2084, with the ratification of the Sol Confederation, the authority and responsibility of Earth's defense was removed from the then defunct United Nations to the new Sol Confederation. Undeniably the most powerful voice within the Presidential Cabinet, the Ministry of Defense directly oversees the Sol Coalition, which is led by the General of the Army and the Fleet Admiral, with assistance from the Sol Intelligence Service.

Navi. Proper Noun. A binary star in the Cassiopeia system. Navi (I & II) has unusually high x-ray emissions in a variable and unpredictable pattern. Comprised of two blue supergiants, its luminosity exceeds others of its type. The combined effects allow for a habitable zone far distant from the star. Three rocky planets orbit Navi.

Nick. Noun. Slang. Species originating in the Nu Lupi system. Bipedal, endothermic amniotes distinguished by short, pervasive body hair, reverse jointed knees, and long upper limbs. Culture is heavily influenced by the concepts of barter and cunning. The second alien species known to humanity.
Ex. Watch out for that trader; he's such a cheat you'd think he was a Nick.

Oort Siege. Proper Noun. A series of Culler attacks against the

Sol Coalition in 2090-2091. Culminated in the successful test of the Oort Defense Station System (ODSS). Nine weaponized space stations at the far edge of the Sol System were activated and utilized along with the Coalition Fleet to destroy six hundred twelve Culler ships. 1.6 billion human lives were lost. It is considered the second greatest success in the War, after the Expulsion.

Peppermint. Noun. Slang, Offensive. An individual who did not receive standard embryonic genetic therapy to remove nondesirable aesthetic or minor health concerns. Such an individual may have had medically threatening genetic material removed, such as markers for Tay Sachs or Cystic Fibrosis. Often shortened to 'mint', or 'minty'.
Ex. He's handsome for a peppermint.

RAIRAC. Noun. Acronym for Reasonably Appropriate Individual Rights and Conveniences. An oft-referenced list of standards of living and quality of life for soldiers in the field and on base, notably in square footage allotted per person, access to hygiene facilities, nutrient consumption, personal relationships, and exposure to vegetative life.
Ex. See Jane revise Dick's RAIRAC; when in hostile territory, he does not have the expectation of a bedtime story, but he may receive up to three different nutritional flavor supplements.

R-DETB (Remote Deployed Enemy Tracking Beacon). Noun. Subspace transceiver capable of being fired at an enemy ship. Upon contact, it deploys a two-part molecular bond to adhere to the hull and siphons electricity from the ship to power its signal. It can be tracked at a distance of up to seven light years, but may be manually removed by cutting away the bonded portion of a hull.

ResQFoam^TM. Noun. An expanding medical foam designed to stabilize wounds and allow continued activity after trauma-induced hemorrhage. Generic versions issued to Coalition troops are often pejoratively called WuSS Foam, i.e., Wound Stabilization System.

Runa. Noun. A classification of small-size military vessels with a minimum crew complement of four. Recommended carrying capacity is twelve to fifteen infantry and limited support staff. Generally they are used for short-range missions.
Ex. We were already in the Runa when our carrier ship was blown to hell, so we had time to watch our crew die before we escaped.

SEMERA Drive. Noun. **<u>REDACTED.</u>**

Ship Classification. Noun. Sol Coalition forces identify Culler ships based on a color-coded system. The largest are *Red Class*, followed, in decreasing size, by *Titian, Amber,* and *Citrine.* Combat fighters were originally classified as *Violet*, but the name *Urchin* - based on their appearance - is used almost exclusively.

Sica. Noun. A classification of small-sized military vessels with a minimum crew complement of four. Recommended carrying capacity is thirty-six infantry and limited support staff. Generally they are used for deep attack missions and can carry ground transports.
Ex. The Sica *redesign was faster, far more covert, and had enough heavy weapons to take out a Culler outpost.*

Sidus. Noun. A battleship military vessel which carries the bulk of the Coalition's ground forces with capacity for more than forty-five hundred soldiers. Compared to the *Khutura*-class, it requires a smaller crew of only five hundred, and has only one third of the fighters.
Ex. The Hannibal was the first Sidus *class to complete five tours; prior to that, all* Sidus *had been destroyed before meeting that service anniversary.*

Societal Collapse. Noun. The end or diminishing of a society, culture, or civilization most commonly resulting from economic, environmental, or cultural change. Forces contributing to such a collapse include sub-replacement fertility, prolonged armed conflicts (internal or external), and natural disasters.

Ex. The fall of the Roman Empire was predicated with internal political struggles, a series of expensive military expansions and overextended borders, and low birth rate among the ruling class.

Souriau Particles. Noun. Exotic matter named after French mathematician Jean-Marie Souriau and the fuel for faster than light travel. Although the existence of such matter was theorized prior to the Invasion, it was only through the reverse engineering of Culler technology that the nature of Souriau particles was understood.

Ex. Try not to touch the Souriau Particles. Your hand will cease to exist, and the resulting explosion will destroy the entire ship.

Struo. Noun. Cargo ships used by the Coalition for resupply and medical transports, *Struos* like the *Huangfu* carry minimal defensive fighters but multiple modified shuttles for ship to ship-and-ship to surface transports.

Ex. The Struo *class may be slow, but they have enough armor that they can take laser cannon fire without so much as waking the patients.*

Systematic desensitization. Noun. Colloquially referred to as exposure therapy, it was developed by psychiatrist Joseph Wolpe as treatment for phobias in which the patient is exposed to progressively more anxiety-provoking situations to reduce response intensity.

Ex. I used to feel nauseated at the thought of eating dummy bars, but after a few years in the Coalition I kind of like the taste.

TABI (Technological and Biological Interface) Device. Noun. Also commonly referred to by the generic term, implants. TABI comprise a wide range of software and hardware components that can be integrated into the human body, surgically or by injection, to regulate, stabilize, or increase performance in physical or cognitive areas as well as provide increased interaction with technology outside the subject body. Common examples include communications implants, neural sensors for prosthesis, and microscopic visual enhancements for fine motor skills.

Troisi Doctrine. Noun. Also known as the ***Prosperity Curtain.*** A decision made in 2024 by the former European Union to close borders to all refugees, including those seeking political asylum. An estimated 350,000 died of starvation and disease in temporary camps outside of military checkpoints during the fourteen months the policy was in effect.

Tuber. Noun. Slang, Offensive. An individual who received non-human DNA during embryonic gene therapy. Banned by the Sol Confederation in 2097.
Ex. This bar has really gone downhill; they even let tubers in.

TUNA. Noun. Acronym for Tactical Unit Nautical Assault. Culler aquatic vehicle used in the invasion of Earth in 2056. TUNA were jettisoned from low orbit to Earth's oceans carrying twenty-five Cullers and then used to ambush ships and port cities.
Ex. There isn't much left of old Miami except a few shelled-out hotel towers and the armada of wrecked TUNA in the shoals.

Unobjectionable Forfeit. Euphemism. The intentional loss, harm, damage to friendly targets in pursuit of a larger goal which is determined to be more important.
Ex. See Jane use Dick as a living shield. See Jane maneuver and destroy the enemy. See Dick exsanguinate. Dick was an unobjectionable forfeit.

Vindloo Factor. Noun. Score, between 1 and 100, on a standardized test evaluating the subject's ability to cope with stressful situations and decisions which may harm others or the subject. Lower scores indicate aptitude for compartmentalization and suitability for frontline or high-tension assignments. Higher scores indicate a tendency towards emotionally charged responses to stress and development of post-traumatic stress disorder.

Ex. Jane has a high Vindloo Factor. She pilots her ship into a Culler destroyer, killing all aliens and two thousand Coalition soldiers. Good job Jane. Dick has a low Vindloo Factor. Dick works in the engine room and keeps the ship in top shape. Good job Dick.

Wormhole. Noun. A connection between two positions that crosses both space and time, e.g., Einstein-Rosen Bridge, Ellis Wormhole. The first traversable wormhole was discovered by Andrae-Scott-Zurek in 2029. It was too small for human use, but numerous probes studied the phenomena and its destination in another galaxy before its practical collapse in 2036.

Ex. See Jane enter a wormhole. See Dick travel through normal space. Dick waits for many years, but Jane does not arrive. Jane has traveled through time and space, arriving centuries after Dick's death. Whoops.

Yemen Mass Suicide. Proper Noun. In reaction to the revelation that aliens exist, 512 men, women, and children gathered in an open field to commit homicide/suicide. Similar, smaller movements by religious cults claimed more than 5,000 lives across the globe in the year 2056.

BOOKS IN THIS SERIES
HELLHOUND

Follow Malak and Clara Maker as the Sol Coalition battles the alien Cullers! Read more about the series and the Coalition universe at suzannebrodine.com, or follow the author @suzannebrodine .

Hellhound 1: Siege Engine

Hellhound 2: Killing Field

Hellhound 3: False Flag